WESTERN

THE NIGHTHAWK TRAIL

Also available in Large Print
by Max Brand:

Max Brand's Best
    Western Stories, Volume I
The Fastest Draw
Singing Guns
One Man Posse
Lost Wolf
The Black Signal

Brand

THAWK
TRAIL

G.K.HALL &CO.
Boston, Massachusetts
1990

The Nighthawk Trail is comprised of "Nighthawk Trail,"
first published in Western Story Magazine in 1932; "Outlaws
from Afar," first published in Western Story Magazine in
1932; and "Speedy's Desert Dance," first published in
Western Story Magazine in 1933.

Published in Large Print by arrangement with
Dodd, Mead and Company, Inc.

British Commonwealth Rights Courtesy of
A. M. Heath & Co. Ltd.

G.K. Hall Large Print Book Series.

Set in 18 pt. Plantin.

Library of Congress Cataloging in Publication Data
Brand, Max, 1892–1944.
    The nighthawk trail / Max Brand.
        p.   cm.——(G.K. Hall large print book series)
    ISBN 0-8161-4626-8 (lg. print)
    1. Large type books.   I. Title.
[PS3511.A87N5   1990]
813'.52—dc20

AL DUPRAY took the old river road with a feeling of shame and guilt. He knew that many others in the town had visited the crystal gazer in the gypsy camp, but he was not the sort of man whom the world would expect to give way to superstitions of this kind.

People had accepted him, ever since Tom Older's killing and the establishment of his own innocence, as an extraordinary fellow. After that he preferred to live on in the town of Clausen, because there, at least, they seemed to take it for granted that he was free from the stain of bad blood; and the town's newspaper was always singing his praises, both for his charities and public gifts to the place. For, from the beginning, he had donated to Clausen the whole of Tom Older's half in the mine! That made a tide of money that was more than enough to buy the favorable opinions of the people of Clausen.

But would it buy the favorable opinion of

Sue Crane? Her opinion, just now, meant more to him than all the rest of the world.

At a turn of the road he looked back across the hills, and there he saw the trees divide and the front of the Crane house gleam out against the west, its windows turning to rose and golden fire in the light of a brilliant sunset.

Terrible old Joshua Crane was up there in front of the house at this time of the day, seated in his wheelchair, with a blanket wrapped around his paralyzed legs and a rifle lying across his knees. He never was without that rifle, day or night, and it was said that he never knew when he would need it, he had so many enemies from the old days when he rode this range and started to win his fortune and his way with an iron hand. He had never weakened then. He did not weaken now that years and his malady made him a cripple. For five years he had not been able to take a step, but in those five years he had stretched forth the power of his mind farther than ever across the range. Men knew him and feared him more than ever.

And this was the man whose daughter's hand Al Dupray intended to ask—he, the nephew of Charley Dupray, long-hunted bandit, robber, and killer extraordinary!

Doubt in himself overwhelmed Dupray, and he shook his head as he hurried his mustang down the road. There was not far to go, and presently he came to the camp. The gypsies had put up their tents and built their wretched lean-tos inside an elbow turn of the river, where the ground was level. There was a good growth of pines and brush, and in a number of little clearings where the grass grew thick they had found pasture for their horses, mules, and burros.

By this time, though, the heads of the mountains were still gleaming, and under the dark pines it seemed as though night had already come. The fires gleamed yellow; lanterns hung from a number of the yellow boughs.

They were going about the ordinary camp work now. Later on people would wander down from Clausen to see the jugglers, and knife throwers. Men would come to trade horses with these keen strangers, who knew horseflesh with a strange, intuitive knowledge. They would visit the tents of the fortune-tellers, also. Above all, they would consult the crystal gazer, who was said to lay bare the past, present, and future at a glance.

One could test the truth of his predictions by his wonderful knowledge of the past, that strange old bearded man with the young and steady voice. Well, there was enough in Al Dupray's past that was hidden. If the old man could tell him about that, Al would willingly trust his predictions about the future.

He gave hardly a glance to right or left as he made for the tent of the crystal gazer, which was distinguished by the flag above it with the yellow star and crescent on the crimson field. Al Dupray noticed many little things, as a man will do when his heart is ill at ease. The tent was altogether bigger and more comfortable than the rest; and it was plain that the owner was the kingpin of the tribe.

When Dupray came to the entrance flap he found it open, and a small fire burning on the ground with a pot steaming over it. Behind the fire, leaning against an Indian backrest, was the crystal gazer. He sat with legs crossed upon the ground, smoking a long-stemmed pipe. A turban was wound about his head; a long white beard streamed down over his breast. It seemed to Al Dupray that under their dark and shaggy brows the eyes of the seer were keener and more glowing than the coals of the fire. There was no other light in the tent.

"Am I after hours?" asked Dupray.

"Enter, my son," said a soft voice.

He had heard that voice described before, but none of the descriptions had done it justice. There was a caress to it, and there was a menace, as well; furthermore, it was oddly though vaguely familiar, as though he might have heard it before, but never from one with such a face.

"Have you come in need or in folly?" said the crystal gazer.

Al Dupray frowned. "I kind of thought that you'd be able to answer that question yourself, old-timer," said he.

"When I look in the crystal, yes," said the other. "Be seated. Cross my hand with silver. Tell me what you would know."

He spoke gravely. He had repose of manner. And Al Dupray sat down on the very low stool before the man of mystery.

"You can start back somewhere in the past with me," said Dupray. "Suppose that you lay in and tell me the worst minute that I ever had in my life?"

He crossed the extended, slender palm with a whole silver dollar, which the old rascal examined, turned this way and that, and then dropped it into a capacious pocket, where it jingled against other coins.

5

The seer now produced a crystal ball, which he placed upon the raised point of the index finger of his left hand. With a twist of the fingers of his right hand, he started the ball rapidly whirling. It seemed to Al Dupray a miracle of cleverness that the man could support the ball in such perfect equilibrium.

In the meantime, he saw the reflection from the fire in the crystal like a little flickering sword blade of golden light.

The voice of the gazer murmured, "I see you manacled against a wall. The pale gleaming of steel bars is about you. On the floor lies a man, dead or senseless. Before you kneels a man who handles the locks of your chains."

Al Dupray almost rose from the stool on which he was seated. "By thunder!" he muttered.

He relaxed, and as he blinked again he saw that the crystal ball had disappeared. The old man had picked up his long-stemmed pipe once more.

"By the almighty tearing thunder, you've hit on it!" said Al Dupray. "If you can see that, then see what's gonna happen to me tonight."

The other held forth a slender hand again.

"You get silver every shot out of the box?" asked Dupray.

"It is for the eye of the spirit," said the other.

"The eye of the—" began Dupray, and stopped short. "It's worth it," he muttered, and handed over another dollar to the seer.

Once more the crystal ball appeared, was balanced with the same dexterity upon a fingertip, and once more the ball went spinning.

The soft, menacing voice began again:

"This picture I see—a woman's face smiling on you."

"Smiling?" cried Al Dupray, starting joyously.

"Smiling sadly," said the old man, "as she bids you farewell!"

Dupray groaned. "She says farewell," he repeated. "You mean for good and all?"

The crystal ball had disappeared again.

"As for the future," said the gazer, "that would need another crossing of silver. I have shown you the past and the present, one flash at each. For the spirit can see only one picture at a time."

Al Dupray gripped his hands hard. "I don't know but what I'm being a fool," said he. "And if that's what's gonna happen to-

7

night, it'd be no good to me to know it, anyway." He added grimly, "Things that go wrong have gotta be made to go right!"

The old man picked up his long pipe and puffed at it, the smallest white cloud of fragrant smoke issuing from his lips. His eyes looked steadily past the young fellow and toward the outer night.

Al Dupray stood up.

"She gives me a smile and says good-bye. Is that it?" he asked. "It's gotta be different."

He pulled his hat lower down on his head and thrust out his jaw. People who found a great likeness to the terrible and celebrated uncle in his face would have had their opinion reinforced by a glance at the young fellow. He turned toward the door, with a wave of his hand to the crystal gazer. As he reached the entrance flap of the tent he heard quite a different voice speak behind him.

"Come back here, Al."

He spun about, bewildered.

There he saw a man sitting in the robes of the crystal gazer, with the turban still about his head, but the beard and the shaggy eyebrows were gone; the lines that had seamed and roughened the face had disappeared also, as if by magic. Now he was looking at a dark-eyed young fellow, not very much older than himself, a sensitive and handsome face that would have been too feminine except for the glint of wholly masculine humor about the eyes.

"Speedy!" cried Al Dupray.

_____ 2

IN ACCORDANCE with Speedy's request, Dupray closed the tent flap. Then he came striding hastily to grip the hand of his friend.

"You rapscallion," said Dupray, "you're the crystal gazer, are you? Gimme back that money!"

"Not a bean of it," answered Speedy. "I earned that coin, because you've broken every bone in my hand."

With that he began to smooth and massage the right hand with the fingers of the left. Still he continued to smile at Al Dupray.

"I thought you were a thousand miles away from here. I thought that you—" began Al Dupray.

Then his voice stopped suddenly, as though he had bumped against an impassable obstacle.

Speedy continued for him: "You thought

that I was on the trail of your uncle, Al. Was that it? Thought that I was drifting along behind Uncle Charley, looking for trouble?"

"Well," sighed the young man, "that's what I imagined."

"Not I," said Speedy. "I'd leave him alone, but he can't forget me. Every now and then something happens that reminds him of the time that John Wilson and I snaked him out of his camp and landed him in jail, with a mighty good chance of having his neck stretched before he got out of it. Whenever he thinks of that, why, he's irritated, Al, and wants my scalp. I'm not trailing him just now, but he's trailing me so close that I thought I'd give him some elbowroom in the hope that he'd settle down. That's why I slipped into this gypsy tribe. Most of 'em, by the way, are no more gypsy than I am. I've heard Mexican, Spanish, and Canadian French around here, but no lingo that sounds Romany to me. What's the trouble about the girl, Al?"

Dupray waved a hand that dismissed that subject.

"About Uncle Charley," he said. "I know he's a devil, Speedy. I know that as well as anybody. But he's been mighty kind to me."

"I know he has," said Speedy. "There's a

good side to him about as big as the bad side, I suppose. I've seen something of it, too."

"You haven't seen all of it, Speedy," said the young fellow. "You haven't heard the way he talks about me leading a straight life, and what he'll do to keep me straight. Sometimes I think that he'd put up every penny he has in the world to keep me happy and contented and going right—and you know how he loves his money more than he loves his own blood!"

"I know all of that," agreed Speedy, nodding.

"He has a lot of respect, and even liking, for you, Speedy," continued Al. "He knows that I'd have hanged for the killing of Tom Older if you hadn't showed that my hands were clean in that deal. He knows that, and he never forgets it.

"But there's the old grudge, Speedy. I think it comes over him with a sweep now and then. When he remembers how you mastered him in his own camp, it makes him feel foolish and helpless. Then, of course, the rest of his men never have forgotten, either. They all want to get back at you, and they keep your memory fresh in his mind. That's the reason he still takes to your trail now and then, and tries to run you down. I think he'd kill you in cold blood. Afterward he'd wish you back on earth."

"I think so, too," said Speedy. "Because it's been a long game between us. I'm just a trick ahead of him now, but half of the time he has me crowded against the wall, and if he ever gets the upper hand, I'm a dead man."

"I know," said Al Dupray. "That's like you, Speedy. You'd keep at it for the sake of the risk."

"Al," said the other, changing the subject abruptly, "you're paying a lot more attention to your grammar than you used to, it seems to me."

"You mean I've fixed up the lingo I talk?" said Al Dupray. "I had to do that. Mostly I roll along just the same as ever, but I try to watch my step a little more. Well, Speedy, it's good to have you back."

Speedy smiled. "The same girl, eh?" he said. "You fixed up your lingo for her sake, Al. Is that it?"

The young fellow flushed.

"Well, Speedy," he said, "I can't help wondering where you got the idea that I was to see a girl tonight!"

"I suppose it seems queer to you that I

should guess that," acknowledged Speedy. "But it's no more mysterious than most magic. You never were much for clothes, Al, and when I saw you all dressed up tonight I took it for granted that you were going to see a lady. Since you were so serious about it, I also took it for granted that you were even going so far as to ask her to marry you. Fellows who are simply vaguely interested in a girl don't waste their time going to see fortune-tellers. They don't do it even in the pinch, unless they're pretty uneasy."

"But what made you think that I would have bad luck?" asked the young fellow.

"Oh, that's the crystal," said Speedy seriously, and yet with a faint smile of deception.

"You mean that you believe in that crystal?" asked the other quickly, and with a frown.

The smile of Speedy persisted.

"What sort of a magician would I be, Al," he asked, "if I didn't believe in my own magic?"

Al Dupray stood back, frowning.

"You get me sort of nervous, Speedy," said he.

"I'm sorry about that," answered the

13

other. "Forget about me, and the fool crystal, too."

Dupray shook his head. "There's always something behind you," he mourned. "You never are shooting quite in the dark, like other fellows. Out with it, Speedy; tell me how you could guess that I'd hear the girl say good-bye to me tonight?"

But Speedy resolutely shook his head. "I've talked a lot too much," said he.

"I don't say that," argued the young fellow.

"But I do," persisted Speedy.

"You know," said Al Dupray, "in spite of the fact that I know you don't even know her name, I feel like asking your advice about what to do."

"Don't!" said Speedy quickly. "Ask my advice about everything else, if you want to, but not about that. Nobody ever follows advice about a woman, anyhow. Don't ask me what to do."

"I'll ask you one thing," said Al Dupray. "D'you think that people around Clausen, here, have sort of forgotten and forgiven me for having Dupray blood in my body?"

"Are you ashamed of that blood?" snapped Speedy as he had snapped at Dupray once before in the past.

"No, not ashamed," said the young fellow slowly. "But you know the poem where they hang the dead albatross around the neck of the man who shot it. It seems to me sometimes that that name of Dupray is hung around my neck the same way."

"Well," said Speedy, "the Duprays have a pretty purple record. And some of the stain will rub off on you. Then, you were accused of murder."

"I was cleared of that, clean as a whistle," said the young man. "You cleared me yourself, Speedy!"

"That isn't what matters. After a little while, all people will remember is that you were once accused of murder, not that you were cleared of it. Presently they begin to say: 'Where's there's smoke there's fire! There's bound to be.' "

"For every two dollars that I've made out of the mine," replied Dupray, "I've given one to charity, here in Clausen, in the name of Tom Older."

"People will say that you're trying to ease a bad conscience," said Speedy.

"Damn it, Speedy," cried Dupray, "you don't mean that!"

"I do," insisted Speedy. "For everything a man does, he's partly envied and partly hated,

15

so long as the action has any strength in it. Not for things that are simply foolish and cowardly, but for everything that's outstanding. If you kill a man—well, half the people will envy your courage in doing it, the other half will want to help hang you. If you don't murder, but are a hero and save a life at the risk of your own, then envy is aroused again. Men shrug their shoulders and smile and sneer, as if to say that they know certain things about you, if they only chose to speak 'em out. We're made that way, all of us."

"Not you, Speedy!" cried the young fellow.

"Stuff," said Speedy. "We're all cut out of the same sort of flesh and blood. I have a good digestion; that's all."

Dupray paused uncertainly. And then Speedy said, "Sooner or later you'll talk to her. Go tonight and have it over with, Al. Then come back here and tell me what's happened."

Dupray sighed. "I'll do it," he said. "She's expecting me after dinner."

He held out his hand, and Speedy extended his.

"I won't take your left hand, Speedy," said the young fellow.

"You've broken my right hand once already, Al," replied the other man. "Get out and try your luck. When you come back, I'll be waiting for you here, with somebody probably crossing my hand with silver."

So Dupray went out, found his horse, and rode again up the river road, his head lifted at intervals to glance toward the hill where the lights of the Crane house were gleaming in the darkness.

_____ 3

OLD MAN CRANE sat on the veranda of his house. The night was chilly and the wind blew the cold straight to the bone now and then, but he hated to go inside the front door.

As long as he remained on the veranda before his house, even through the darkness his eyes envisaged the prospect of his fields and hills. The darker shadows of his woodlands were dear to his eye, also. At a time, thirty years before, when many improvident people were clearing their lands, taking down trees big and small with their reckless axes, he had worked with care, selecting only sufficient trees to clear the ground. Now his forests would go on and on under this sort of handling, growing bigger all the time. He had even extended them, planting new trees in districts. Perhaps they would not yield a penny to him, but they would be a sure source of revenue to his daughter.

He never thought of her without a spasm of pain. She should have been a boy. An excellent boy she would have made.

He had reached this point in his reflections when a horseman came up the road, tethered his horse at the hitching rack in front of the house, and came up the steps.

"Mr. Crane?" said Al Dupray.

"Yeah, that's me," said Crane. "Come and set down. Here's a chair, if it ain't too cold for you out here."

Dupray sat down, and he and the old man had a few minutes' talk. At length Dupray said, "There's something I've been wanting to say to you, sir."

"Well, fire it into my face, then," said the rancher. "I ain't ever been one to waste time, at that!"

"I want to marry Sue," replied the young fellow.

"You wanta marry Sue," said the harsh voice of Crane. "That ain't surprising. There's a lot of boys on the range that wanta marry Sue. What of it?"

"Well—" began Dupray.

The old man broke in, more savagely than ever. "You wanta marry Sue. Does she wanta marry you?"

"I haven't asked her."

"Then go and ask her now," replied the other. "There ain't any use of me having my say till she's had hers."

"I'll go, then," said the young fellow with a faint sigh of relief.

"Wait a minute," said Crane. "She might as well step out here. Hey, Sue!"

A voice came, far away, in answer. Footfalls hurried. "Always running," said the father, as harshly as ever. "Always runnin', when I pipe for her. She ain't no modern woman. Not one of these damn newfangled, high-headed, worthless mustangs. She's made proper, is what I mean to say!"

The screen door opened; the girl came hurrying out. The light from the hall gleamed in her hair; then the darkness enveloped her.

"Yes, father?" she asked.

"Here's Al Dupray wanting you," said the father.

"Hello, Al," the girl called out.

He was only able to mutter words of no sense in reply.

"Here's Al," said Crane, raising his voice

as though he were addressing an entire crowd. "He's come over here, wanting to marry you."

"Ah?" said the girl.

It seemed to Al Dupray that all his heart's blood leaped, for when she cried out and moved it was a little toward him, not away. Only a trifle, a mere gesture, a mere leaning, but he had seen it, and he felt that he understood it.

"He's come here to marry you," said Crane. "Whatcha say about it, Sue?"

She went behind the wheel chair and laid her hands on his shoulders.

"You're to say for me, father."

"You like him all right?" asked Crane.

"Yes, I like Al," said she.

The music of the spheres hummed in the ears of Al Dupray.

"She likes you, Al Dupray," commenced the father. "Now, Sue, you say that I'm gonna have the disposing of you?"

"Yes," said the girl.

"Tell him why," went on Crane.

"Because," said the girl, "I'm all that father has to leave the place to. I'm only a girl. He wanted a son. He prayed for a son. But he only had a daughter, so he wants to pick the right man for me. The sort who'll carry on with the place."

The heart of the young man sank.

"D'you understand that, Al Dupray?" asked the father.

"Yes, I hear what she says."

The old man swept an arm before him.

"This here is my work. I made it," he said. "I growed most of them trees. I bred the cows that eat that grass. It's my place. It's all mine. It's gotta go down into the hands of a reliable fellow that'll handle it right."

"I understand," said Al Dupray.

His strength and confidence were ebbing fast. He prayed inwardly that the girl might speak again, but she was silent.

"Whatcha know about cows, Al?" asked Crane.

"I can ride a herd. I can handle a rope, cut, and brand—all that."

"I don't ask if you can daub a rope. I don't ask you are you a cowhand," said the old rancher. "Any fool can throw a rope. But d'you know cows?"

"In what way?"

"Know how to foller the Eastern markets, so's to pick the right time for selling? Know how to keep your barns full of hay against a bad winter? Know when to keep your whole herd over maybe three years, till bad times turn into good times? Do you know any of those things, I'd like to know?"

"I'm not much of a businessman, I suppose," said Dupray faintly.

"Ain't you?"

"No, I'm not."

"Well, whatcha got to say for yourself? I'm listening to whatcha got to say. I ain't gonna be in no rush about making up my mind. Sue, she likes you, all right."

"I don't know what to say," said the young fellow. "I suppose you know that I'm pretty well fixed with money. I've over a hundred thousand out of the mine; and it's still producing."

"Damn money!" said Crane. "Damn your hundred thousand and all mines, anyway. They never do nothing but rot the hearts and the souls out of the folks that dig the money out of the rock. Easy come and easy go. Cows is the business for this country. Cows and timber. That's what I got, ain't it?"

"Yes, it's what you have," said Dupray, turning to ice.

"And it's the right thing to have," said the terrible Crane. "Cows and timber is the thing to have. And no fool is gonna marry my girl. Not if I'm living, and she's true to her word to me. Listen to me, Sue. Am I livin'?"

"Of course," said she.

"And are you true to your word?"

"Yes," said the girl faintly.

"Then, by thunder," said Joshua Crane, "I ain't gonna throw you away on Dupray! Do you hear me, Dupray?"

"I hear you," said the young fellow.

"You're a Dupray, ain't you?"

"Yes."

"And your uncle is Charley Murderer Dupray, ain't he?"

"Charles Dupray is my uncle," groaned Al.

"Then," cried Joshua Crane, "I wouldn't have you married to Sue. By thunder, I'd rise right out of the grave and haunt you both!"

"Father!" moaned the girl.

"Are you cryin' out for him?" asked Joshua Crane in a terrible voice.

"No, father," said she.

"You cried out for him, but you didn't cry big," said Joshua Crane. "Al Dupray, you've heard most of what I've got to say."

"I've heard a good deal," said the young fellow bitterly.

"But mind you, it ain't nothing to what I could lay onto you if my girl wasn't here, and her liking you, all right. I'm holding off. I'm holding back, I can tell you."

Al Dupray said nothing. He turned his head and strained his eyes toward Sue Crane. It seemed impossible, if she "liked him all right," she would let him leave her as hopelessly and with such a cruel dismissal as this.

Joshua Crane broke in. "Sue!"

"Yes, father."

"He don't seem to know that he ain't tied with a rope. You go and set him free and let him gallop. We don't want no more of him around here. We don't want no Duprays!"

She stepped across to Dupray, and, in so doing, a shaft of light fell on her face. It was sad, with a faint, wistful smile upon it. She held out her hand.

"Good-bye, Al," said she.

He did not touch the hand, but another ghostly hand closed over his heart. He stepped suddenly back from her, gasping out, "Speedy! It's what Speedy said!"

That was his odd good-bye to her. Running down the steps, he mounted his horse and rode like mad down the steep pitch of the roadway and away into the darkness. The iron clanging of the hoofs against the stones came back to them in fainter and fainter rhythm.

"Look here, Sue," said Crane.

"Yes, father," said she.

"Are you all right? You ain't grieving?"

"No, I'm not grieving."

"I thought I heard you sort of moan, like you'd stifled a sob or something."

"It's only the wind rising," said the girl. "It makes mournful sounds, you know."

"It does," said he. "And if the wind's rising, it's time for me to be getting back inside the house."

4

DUPRAY'S MUSTANG sprinted all the way back to the gypsy camp, while the stars flew above the trees as he stormed down the way.

He could not enter the tent, however. Young Ed Walker and Tommy Legrange were in there. He could hear their foolish, brawling voices that grated savagely on his ear. The long moments dragged on, while the voices of Legrange and Walker grew less and less boisterous; finally there was nothing but the pause and murmur of the crystal gazer.

At last the pair came out. As they were passing close by the place where Dupray stood in the dark, he heard Walker muttering, "Dog-gone me, he seen right through us. D'you think that he really knows anything about it?"

What ever that guilty secret might be, which Speedy had unraveled, or nearly so, Dupray cared nothing for it. The load on his own heart was too great for him to bear, and he hurried in at once before the seer.

Speedy raised a warning hand.

"It's all right," murmured Dupray. "I know it's business hours with you, Speedy."

He sat down on the stool and said in a rapid whisper, "Speedy, tell me, did you know that Sue would refuse me?"

"I didn't know that her name was Sue," replied Speedy.

"You saw the whole picture just as it turned out, her hand out to me, and her face sad, saying good-bye. How did you know that?" said Al Dupray.

"I didn't know it, really," said Speedy. "Or, rather, the crystal knew, not I."

"That doesn't go with me," said Dupray. "I know that the crystal is only your own uncanny guessing, Speedy."

"D'you think so?" muttered Speedy. "I

used to think that myself. Sometimes now I'm not so sure. I don't know where the guesses come from half the time."

"Tell me if you can, where they came from this evening about what was going to happen to me," said the young fellow.

"I don't want to step on your toes, Al."

"Never mind my toes. I'm burning up, Speedy. She refused me. Not the girl, really, but that demon of a father; he forced her to!"

He added, "How did you know anything about her saying good-bye to me?"

"It's like this," replied Speedy slowly. "You were worked up about a girl. That was easily guessed, as I told you before. And it was plain that you were about to bring the thing to a head. Well, then, from all of your excitement I gathered that the girl might be somebody important. And—well, partner, everybody in the West knows that you're the nephew of Charley Dupray, and Charley's record is a pretty long and black one. On the strength of that record I imagined that she would refuse you. If she was the right sort of a girl, though, she'd be sorry for the refusal in a way, and sorry for you, too."

Dupray closed his eyes and groaned. "Speedy," he said. "She likes me a lot, and

I'll swear it. It was only the old man who did me in, damn him. Old Joshua Crane, wrapped up in his blanket, grinning like an Indian, he did me in!"

He dropped his face in his trembling hands.

"A girl that's worth her salt would never let her father give you the run, partner. Ever think of that?" asked Speedy.

"Yes, I've thought of that," said the young fellow. "But she's not like other girls. He's raised her in a special way. He's raised her to have a lot of respect for her parents, and all that. He's done the job brown, Speedy. Then, you see, she's the sole heir to his ranch, and he loves that ranch more than he loves life. He's worked all his days at it. The girl has known for years that her husband must be a fellow who can handle the ranch in the right way. Don't you see what that means?"

"I know. Businessman. Keen head, iron hand, and all that sort of thing," replied Speedy.

"That's it. Old Joshua wanted a son, but when his wife died a little after their marriage and left the girl, he wouldn't marry again."

"He's brought the girl up according to his own ideas, has he?" asked Speedy.

"She thinks that his word is a law from heaven," replied the young fellow.

Speedy nodded. "I've seen one woman in the world before this," said he, "that was the same way."

"So what she says when her father commands her doesn't mean much. You'll agree to that?"

Speedy nodded again.

"But the point is," said Al Dupray, "that I don't see how I can do anything about it. Nobody could think of what to do except you, partner!"

He made a brief gesture. There was a world of appeal in his face and his eyes.

"You're pretty fond of her?" asked Speedy.

"I can't live without her," answered the young fellow.

Speedy frowned. "That's caused more trouble than anything else in the world," he declared. "I mean, that attitude that people of our age get sometimes—that they can't live without a certain girl."

"It's true," said Al Dupray.

"It's not true," Speedy contradicted. "Suppose that Sue Crane didn't exist, d'you think that you'd never run into another girl that you'd want to marry?"

"Speedy, you might as well tell a tree after lightning has split it to pieces, that it's lucky—that there's stronger thunder than that in the sky!" said Al.

Speedy smiled faintly.

"If you take it that way, I guess I've got to help you, Al."

Dupray leaned back with a sigh, and then smiled.

"I sort of knew that you'd come through for me in a pinch."

"You act," said Speedy, "as though the thing were done this instant just because I take a hand!"

"It is as good as done," said Al Dupray, his eyes shining with confidence. "You've never failed in anything you tackled before, and you won't fail at this job, either. It may take time, but you always win!"

"You think so?" asked Speedy.

He looked wistfully at the young fellow. Suddenly his expression was that of an old, old man who, down the great perspective of the years, peers at the face of modern youth and finds it very strange.

"Well," he went on, "whether I can do

anything about it or not, I don't know. Have you any ideas of your own?"

"Me?" said Al, as though greatly surprised. "Why, Speedy, when you step into the picture I don't expect to use my own head. I'm just a hired man, now. I do what you tell me to do, and jump when you tell me to jump."

"Even when there's a cliff ahead of you?"

"Yes, even when there's a cliff."

"All right," murmured Speedy almost wearily. "All right. I'll try it. But you ought to have some idea of how we can go about it."

"I could kidnap her," said Al. "Once I had her, I know that I could make her happy, some way or other."

He sat up, hopeful with this suggestion.

Speedy lifted a hand.

"That's no good," he declared. "It isn't the girl that we have to work on."

"You mean we have to tackle the father?"

"That's it."

"You can't manage that," said Al Dupray. "I don't pretend to do your thinking for you, Speedy, but I tell you that nothing will change the old man. He's as hard as rock."

"Are you sure?"

"Yes, I'm dead sure. I'm surer of that

31

than I ever was of anything in my entire life."

"Just the same," said Speedy, "I've an idea that he may be changed. Anything that's human can be changed."

"He ain't human," broke out the young fellow. "He's an Egyptian mummy. The blood dried up in him five thousand years ago."

"He's pretty cold," agreed Speedy, "but I think that he can be handled one way or another." Then he shrugged his shoulders. "What will your uncle think about this?" he asked.

"What difference does that make?" asked the young man in his turn.

"He'll be on my shoulders all the faster, that's all," said Speedy.

"If he ever tries to harm you—" began Dupray, his face contracting with a great passion at the very thought.

"Oh, that's all right," interrupted Speedy. "It would make the game all the better. But Charley Dupray on one side, and friend Joshua Crane on the other—well, we'll have to try juggling. That's all. Tomorrow I'll tell you what we're to do about it. Tomorrow, at noon, I'll meet you at your house. Is that all right?"

"Anything that you say is all right," said Al Dupray, rising to his feet. "Anything goes, as long as you're in the game on my side."

He sighed contentedly and stretched himself.

"I'm going to go and get some supper, Speedy," said he. "The fact is, ten minutes ago I didn't care whether I lived or died. But now I know that I want to live, and that life is going to be a song!"

_____ 5

OLD JOSHUA CRANE, once he was in his wheelchair, would propel himself considerable distances from the house. Though his legs were powerless, his strength seemed to have retreated entirely to his leathery arms, and their might was redoubled. Working the two-handed crank, he used to dash down slopes at a terrific speed in order to force his way up the next hill.

More than once he had upset himself in this manner. Also, as he went careening and dodging through the trees of his woodlands, he was likely to tip over. After falling, he could not manage to get himself back into the chair, and once he had lain in a heavy rain for five hours until the searching parties found him, in the dark of the evening.

On this mid-morning he sat two hills removed from his house, on a fine summit that commanded a wide view of the grazing lands that were his own. Now and then he shifted his look toward adjoining pieces of property. There had been times when he could not look on them without desire and envy, but that feeling had passed away from him by degrees, and he was coming to a pleasant, tranquil state of mind in which he regarded his estate as perfect.

He closed his eyes presently to enjoy the heat of the sun and his own contented thoughts; when he opened them he saw a strange figure coming up the slope not twenty steps from him, a form in a long red coat of silk, with red slippers on the feet and a black skullcap with a red tassel on the head. His step was light and long, but he wore a beard, and his face appeared to be seamed with age.

"Gypsy!" said Joshua Crane to himself. And his heart hardened.

The stranger paused before him, lifted a hand to his forehead, and bowed long.

"Don't begin your lingo. Get out!" said Joshua Crane.

He handled the Winchester that lay across his knees.

"Brother—" began the stranger.

"Brother to what? To you, you smoky-faced son of trouble?" broke in the rancher. "I told you to get out! Now budge, will you?"

The other stood up straight and, folding his arms, his hands disappeared into the opposite sleeves.

"Grief is come to you, Joshua Crane," said he, "and yet you give yourself to vain passions!"

"Grief?" said Crane. "I never felt better in my life. Whatcha mean by grief, you?"

The white beard wagged slowly from side to side. "Oh brother," said he, "it is a vain thing to attempt to penetrate the future except with help."

"You get inside the future, do you?" said Crane.

"Brother, I do."

"I understand," said Crane, "you're the crystal gazer that works down there by the river. Ain't that so?"

"I look in the crystal," said the gypsy. "And I see in it a flood of light!"

The ball of crystal appeared in his hands as he spoke, and the sun turned it into an intolerable blaze of white fire. Joshua Crane blinked.

"I've heard tell something about you," said he. "Somebody was telling my girl—some fool was telling her. But you ain't had your palm crossed with silver by me. There ain't nothing that you can tell about my future."

He grinned as he conceived this retort, and thrust out his lean chin.

"The silver is not needed," said the man of the red robe. "That is the wretched device to which I am driven by need. I am not rich. I am only the slave of the crystal, and it drives me. But by cheap and foolish tricks I try to earn my daily food."

He sighed and shook his head. At this the rancher thrust himself still farther forward in the chair, and stared earnestly into the eyes of the other. He could generally boast that by such a glance he was able to draw up something from the shadowy deeps of the soul.

But now he was baffled. Eyes as keen and as steady as his own looked back at him. They seemed to be young eyes, in spite of the face, and they were dark and brilliant.

Joshua Crane leaned back again in his chair with an ill-natured grunt.

"You say that you're half a fraud. I say that you're all a fraud," said he.

"Brother," said the stranger, "you say many things that are not the truth!"

"Are you callin' me a liar?" demanded Crane fiercely.

"I am not a deceiver," said the man in the red robe. "And that you know, and that you fear."

"Hold on! I'm afraid of you, am I?"

"You are a little afraid," said the other. "Every moment your fear increases and your anger grows less."

"That's a lie as broad as it's long," said Crane, "and it's a mile long, the way I see it."

The other waved his hand and shrugged his shoulders.

He caused the blazing crystal to disappear.

"Well, I'll tell you what I'll do," said Joshua Crane. "I've heard that you can tell the future. Any fool can do that. I can do it. You bet I can. Put a white hoss and a black rider under a thin moon, with a wind blowing—pile up a lot of folderol like that and folks are pretty sure to believe in you, eh?"

"Of course they are," said the gypsy.

Joshua Crane blinked again.

"You admit that you tell lies to folks that come to you?"

"If I did not tell lies," said the stranger, "they would soon stop coming. The pleasant lies are what most men wish to hear. I tell them so much that is pleasant that very soon they are crossing and recrossing my hand with silver. In that way I live, although I am only the slave of the crystal. But there is little that is pleasant in the truth as the crystal tells it."

"Doggone me," said Joshua Crane, "but you kind of interest me. I dunno that I ever heard nobody yarn like this before, and I'd like to know what you're driving at. You say that the crystal don't tell you much that's good about people?"

"How can it?" said the seer. "If I look through it into the mind of a young man I see folly that shivers the glass, and if I look into the mind of an old man I see death; at least, the darkness of a shadow that is soon coming. If I look into the mind of a bride, she is less happy than she is vain. If I examine the mind of a rich and great man, he sees in the whole world nothing but himself."

"Well," said Joshua Crane, "I'm old, and I'm gonna die soon, certain. But what's brought you up here to spin yarns with me?"

38

"I have not come for money," said the other.

"What has fetched you, then?"

"The crystal," said the other, "for I am its slave!"

He produced it again and raised it. Looking up at the crystal, its fiery point of light, gathered from the sun, seemed to glance into the eyes of the man in the red robe as if it were burning out the very nerves of vision, but he merely smiled as he looked up toward his treasure.

Old Joshua Crane exclaimed, "That's a lot of bunk. You can't talk to me like that, stranger. But doggone me, you could fool a lot of people on the stage, you do it so good. You oughtn't to be wasting your time with a mangy lot of wandering gypsies. You oughta be doing your turn on the stage with the lingo that you've got. I've heard lots that were worse!"

He nodded as he said this, and smiled upon the stranger with a good deal of self-satisfaction.

"You ain't told me yet," he said, "why the crystal fetched you here to me. Lemme hear your lingo about that."

The gypsy frowned and then sighed again. "There is only one thing that I did not see clearly," said the man of the red robe, "and it makes me sorry that I have come. I saw that you were about to die, but I did not see—"

"You seen that I was about to die, and any fool that knows what this here kind of paralysis is would know that," said the rancher, unmoved. "But what did the doggone crystal tell you that was worth while, I'd like to know?"

"It did not tell me, for one thing, or else I was unable to look clearly into it, that you were so old. I thought that I was coming to see a young man. Tell me, brother, if you have not a son, exactly like you in the face, but very young?"

"I've got a girl," said the rancher. "I ain't got a boy."

"Then," said the crystal gazer, "it is true that I did not look closely enough; I saw the face clearly, so that I knew you at sight, but I did not see you closely enough to realize that you are not young."

"You mean that you looked into your crystal ball and all at once you seen me?"

"That is what I mean, and what I saw made me come in haste."

"Now looka here," warned the rancher, "I don't mind yarning with you for a minute, but you ain't gonna get a single penny out of me."

The man of the crystal ball drew himself up with a great deal of dignity. "Brother," he said, "do you think that all men who have dark skins are dogs, to be kicked from your path?"

Joshua Crane twisted his mouth and bit his lip.

"Well," he said, "I dunno that I've been talking none too smooth to you, stranger, but I don't like cheats, and I don't like intruders. This here is my land, and all that I've knowed about gypsies is that they're scoundrels and thieves, hoss thieves most of all. I've always thought that it might be one of your folks that stole the Nighthawk from me!"

His face darkened savagely as he mentioned the name.

"One of your sneakin' gangs!" he repeated. "Seven thousand dollars' worth of hossflesh, cheap at that price, too, and he was stole from me!"

"To lose a horse," said the man of the crystal, "is a sorrow like the loss of a child."

"He was worth about ten ordinary kids," said the rancher. "Seven thousand dollars of him. He was worth that in the stud, without never having raced. Just his strain was worth that. And some one of you damn gypsies or greaser hoss rustlers, you got that stallion after I'd cured him up for running."

He flushed and sweated with his passion.

Then he broke out: "Stranger, I guess I don't wanta talk to you no more. I'm tired of talk. At my age, lookin' is better than talkin'. Just settin' and lookin' and thinkin'!"

He shook his head and settled back in his chair, half closing his eyes. When he looked up again he found the stranger still before him.

"Vamose!" said Crane angrily. "Or," he went on, letting his head fall back once more, "you don't need to bother none about the future or the past. You just tell me what I'm thinkin' about this very minute, will you?"

He looked at the horizon as he spoke, and the man of the red robe instantly produced the crystal, raised it, and spun it so that it whirled rapidly on the top of one finger. Yet so steadily was it balanced that the image of the blazing sun in the ball trembled, but did not waver from side to side.

Presently the voice of the gazer said, "I see the face of a woman. She is young. Her eyes are like my eyes."

A great, stifled cry broke from the rancher;

the gazer caused the crystal to disappear once more.

6

OLD JOSHUA CRANE had gripped his withered throat with both hands, but presently he drew them away and passed them across his staring eyes. Then, bracing himself forward in the chair, he demanded, "What devil told you that, stranger?"

"The crystal ball," said the man of the red robe.

Old Crane groaned aloud. "Can there be something in it?" he muttered. "Ain't it one more trick? Ain't it one more trick, I say?"

"How could it be a trick, brother?" replied the crystal gazer.

"You've gone and pried into the story of my house!" cried Joshua Crane. "That's what you've done. You gone spying on my past. You've got hold of a picture of my poor dead girl, and you dare, you sneakin', greasy-faced hound, to stand out here in the open day and speak about her."

He paused, choking with emotion.

"Brother, no matter what I may have spied out about you, what am I to gain from it?"

asked the gypsy. "And what am I to do? And how could I spy on your own mind and see her face, except that the crystal showed it to me?"

The rancher, his eyes closed tight, breathed hard.

"Look here," said Crane, "you came here for something. What is it?"

"Brother," said the man of the crystal, "I came here to give you warning."

"You come up here to warn me that I was gonna die, eh? That's pretty smart, all right, seein' the age that I am."

"There was something else," said the stranger, "something worse than that—the image of a girl and a man, and you beside them, seated, and the girl holding out her hand with a sad face. She was saying farewell."

"To me?" snarled the rancher.

"No, to the young man."

"This is getting doggone strange," muttered Crane. "You seen sorrow in her face? How could you see that when there wasn't no light, hardly?"

"I did not see. The crystal saw. It can look, dimly, through the darkest night, brother."

"Is that all there was to it?" asked Crane, actual fear beginning to show in his eyes.

"That was not all," said the stranger slowly and impressively.

"What else?" muttered Crane.

"The picture had come suddenly before my eyes," said the man of the crystal. "Therefore I looked very earnestly and long at it, and I prayed that the crystal might continue to spin for a long time. Then I was sorry that I had gazed so long, for the dark curtain fell." He was silent.

"What's the dark curtain?" asked Crane.

"Death!"

"Death?" said Crane. "I'm ready for that."

"You need have no fear. There are years before you; but not for the other. There are only weeks and months, perhaps. Over that face the dark curtain fell first with a sudden rush."

"Dupray's face?" said Crane. "I wouldn't be surprised none if he was bumped off almost any time. He's got bad blood in him, and bad blood is gonna lead to gun plays, and gun plays are sure death. I ain't surprised. It kind of shows me that you are able to see something."

"It was not the face of a man," said the seer.

45

"What?"

"It was not the face of a man."

"D'you mean that it was my girl, Sue?" breathed Crane.

The man of the red robe bowed his head.

"Ah, brother," said he, "is she your daughter?" He spoke gently.

Strange stories swarmed through the mind of Crane. Was there not the instance of the old woman who, seated at her door in midafternoon, saw the street darken and the image of a sinking ship, when, at that very moment, a thousand miles away, the ship which carried her son was going down in a storm? The strength went out of his iron heart as he said, "There wouldn't be nobody or nothing in the world that would touch Sue. She's plumb gentle."

"Ah, no, brother," said the stranger. "That which I saw in her face as the curtain fell was neither violence nor pain, but grief."

"What's that?" cried Crane.

The old man remained for a long time with his head bowed, considering.

At last he said, "It might be. There's a romance, kind of, hangin' around the necks of scoundrels and scapegraces. Folks talked about him a lot. Folks have pitied him because of the name that weighs him down.

Dupray! I'd rather that he was called the devil!"

"Ah, brother," said the other, "I know nothing of names!"

"Then get out with you!" said the rancher.

"I go in sorrow," said the crystal gazer.

"I'll make your sorrow a mite less, anyway. It's likely all a lie, but, by thunder, the like of it I never heard. Here's ten dollars in gold for you, you rascal."

The crystal gazer made a sweeping gesture of refusal.

"Do you think that I have come this long distance and endured many cruel words for the sake of winning a little gold? No, I came because grief makes us all brethren, and I, too, have known grief. Brother, farewell!"

He turned as he said this, and hurried down the hill with the same strangely light, long stride which the rancher had noticed before. Crane watched him go. Evidently the refusal of the money had removed any final doubts. The old man was fearful of the future.

7

THE MAN of the red robe stepped over the hill, and, passing through a small grove, came out on the farther side minus white beard, manufactured wrinkles, shaggy eyebrows, and all; the robe, the red slippers, the skullcap were gone, as well. He called out softly as he approached a nest of rocks where Al Dupray was waiting.

"What's the luck, Speedy?" asked Dupray anxiously. "There has been luck; I can tell that, right enough."

His eyes began to shine as he hurried toward the other, leading his horse.

"Jump into the saddle," said Speedy. "Ride like the devil for the Crane house, and get hold of Sue if you can. Old Crane will be back there before long, full of excitement and beginning to think that he's just seen an evil spirit or a prophet on earth. He won't be sure which!"

He smiled faintly as he said this.

Dupray was already in the saddle, but he lingered to ask, "What did you do, Speedy?"

Speedy gave a full account of the meeting. Then he added, "He has an idea that perhaps he's breaking Sue's heart by driving you away. Ten chances to one he'll go back to his house to make sure. When he gets there, he must find you already on the spot. He'll curse you, I suppose, and tell you to get out, but if you put a little pressure on him, then he's very apt to change his mind. Hurry up, partner. I'll be waiting here."

"Not at the camp?" said the other.

"No," replied Speedy. "I think that I'll leave them my empty tent; and they'll be glad to have that. The crystal tells me, Al, that there's likely to be a job for both of us before long."

Dupray did not wait to thank his friend, but drove his mustang with arrowy speed straight across the hills and toward the house of Joshua Crane.

The old man and the wheel chair he did not see as he approached, so he flung himself to the ground, threw the reins of his horse, and rapped at the door.

The old woman who cooked for the house appeared at the door and wiped her hands on her apron, while she looked thoughtfully at the young man. She did not know whether she knew that Sue was at home or not, but she would go to see. So she went back, with a waddling step through the dim hallway; and presently Sue Crane came and stood before him on the veranda. It was plain that she was frightened, and that she was gathering courage to face him.

"Look here, Sue," said he, "I haven't any right to come back here, have I?"

"Not till father permits you to come," answered the girl.

"Well, there's one thing that gives me a right," he went on. "I've never asked you yourself how you feel about me."

"I can't talk about that unless—" she began.

He struck right in fiercely. He would not have dared to adopt such a tone, but he was fresh from Speedy, and he was inspired.

"You're able to send me away spinning," said he. "You're able to say that your father doesn't want me around. Then why aren't you able to tell me whether you want me around yourself?"

"What I want doesn't count," said she, shaking her head.

Her lip began to tremble.

"Don't cry, Sue," he entreated.

"I'm not going to," she answered. "But if you care about me, I must not give you any reason to hope. Father will never change his mind."

"What do I care about his mind?" demanded the young fellow. "There's only one important affair, and that's between you and me. Ever since I first knew you, you've known that I was crazy about you, haven't you?"

She was silent, and flushed.

"Look at me, Sue, and say 'yes' or 'no,'" he commanded.

"I've thought you liked me pretty well," said she.

"Now," said Dupray, "I'm thrown off the place. Well, there are reasons. They're all summed up in my name. I'm a Dupray. That's poison. Your father can't stand that, and so he throws me off the place. But what I want to know now is, was I making myself a fool from the very start?"

"No, no, Al," said the girl anxiously.

"You didn't think, then, that I was just a poison snake?"

"No, no!"

"You think it now, but you didn't think it then?"

"I don't think it now. I never thought it," said she, her voice growing uncertain.

"Then," said he, "you thought I was fair enough in the old days?"

She was silent, appealing to him with her eyes.

"I'm not asking what you think now," he pointed out. "I'm just asking about the beginning. I'm asking about the old days. You could have liked me then?"

"I did like you a lot, Al," said the girl.

"When I came to see you, you didn't mind that?"

"No, I didn't mind that," said she. "I liked it. I liked seeing you, Al. Only—"

"Then I wasn't making a fool of myself?"

"No, you weren't."

"If your father had said to you one of these days, 'Sue, Dupray is the sort of man I want for your husband. I command you to marry him.' Suppose that he had said that. Would you have broken your heart about it, Sue?"

She half turned to escape, then she covered her face with her hands. At that moment a hard, high-pitched nasal voice yelled out of the near distance, "Dupray!"

He turned and saw old Joshua Crane sweeping toward them, turning the double-handled crank of his wheelchair with all his strength. The girl caught the arm of Dupray.

"Al, nothing will happen?" she pleaded.

"Nothing'll happen," he assured her.

"Sue, get inside that house!" shouted the father.

She fled at once, while Dupray hurried down the steps and faced the tyrant.

"You damn puppy!" cried out the old man.

Al Dupray stood silent. He was not very angry, for he felt that in some manner Speedy had turned this affair into a game in which he, through Speedy's clever machinations, was sure to win.

"You came back anyway, did you?" said Crane.

"I saw her once more," said the young fellow. "I wanted to say good-bye to her."

"You did, did you?"

"Yes, I did."

"Are you through with it now?"

"No," said Al Dupray boldly. "You sent her back into the house before we'd finished talking."

"You—you—" stammered old Joshua Crane. "You had her crying. Oh, I know the kind you are, Al Dupray." He brought out the name like an oath.

"Maybe I'm bad," said Dupray. "Maybe my blood's bad. But I never could be unkind to her."

"I'd oughta up with the rifle and shoot you through the head," declared Crane. "If I catch you around here again, I'm gonna do it. And I'll pass the word along to my cowpunchers, that when they see you, they're to make you hop! Understand?"

Dupray said nothing.

"Get out!" yelled Crane.

"What a mean old hound you are!" said the young fellow.

"I'm a what?"

"A mean old hound! You've got an idea that I want Sue because of this ranch you've got together. I don't give a damn about the ranch or about you. She's all I want. But you're never going to let go of her until you've passed her along to somebody that don't care a rap about anything but pasture lands and cows. A sweet life she'll have of it!"

"She'll have the sort of life that I want for her!" shouted Crane.

"You look," said Al Dupray, "like the kind that could pick out the right sort of a life for a girl like Sue. You're a bully first.

But second, you're a fool. And there's more fool than bully in you."

Crane grew suddenly cold sober. "If I was twenty years younger—" he muttered, and then he was still, watching the young fellow with bright, hostile eyes.

"You'd get up and kick me off the place, eh?" said Al Dupray. "Maybe you'd try that trick. But I don't think that you've ever been a real man. You've talked your life away. You've never done anything real except to raise beef and sell it!"

Joshua Crane drew in a great breath, as though he needed cooling. Then he made a sweeping gesture with his hand.

"You're a man, are you?"

"You mean am I the right sort of foreman for your ranch. No, maybe I'm not," said the young man.

"What you ever done in your life, then?" demanded the rancher.

Al Dupray stiffened a little.

"What ought a fellow do to prove that he's worthy of Sue?" he demanded.

"If you'd ever done one real, decent thing in your life, I might take another think about you and Sue," said Joshua Crane. "I might give you a chance at her, Dupray or no Dupray."

"Give me a job, then, and make it man-sized," said the young fellow. "As long as it doesn't turn into hay and beef, I could try my hand at it. Give me a chance to earn Sue, will you?"

"Earn Sue? Earn my girl. You?" said the other angrily.

Then he changed suddenly, as though he felt a stroke of keenest physical pain. "Well," he said at last, "I dunno. Even supposing that I was wrong—"

His voice died out, then he began again: "Why, what do I care what you do, so long as it proves that you got the right stuff in you? Do something that takes brains and patience and courage. Well, do anything. Go and find the Nighthawk for me."

He smote his hands together. "The Nighthawk," he repeated. "That's the trick. Go out and find him, and bring him back here safe and sound. When I see him out in front of the house, I'll know that a real man has rode up to our front door!"

_____ 8

IN THE town of El Rey, far south of the Rio Grande, nested high among the mountains, there was an inn, and in the inn there was a large room overlooking the patio. In this room sat Al Dupray, giving orders to a slender, brown-skinned youth who stood on the threshold of the open door, bowing and cringing. His clothes were in tatters. His bare shanks showed from the knees to the sandals he wore. His coat was a mere rag; a rag of a torn red shirt showed beneath it.

"You have been gone three days," said Dupray, speaking a fair sample of Mexican. "The servants of this cursed *fonda* have had to look after my horses while you were away. How much moldy hay they've given 'em in the meantime, I can only guess. I never had much use for you, and I've less than none now, you son of a rat! Close the door!"

The door was closed. Young Al Dupray stood up and began to beat the floor with his quirt, while the brown-skinned youth skipped and wailed and howled for mercy.

At length, panting, Dupray laid the quirt aside. Subdued laughter could be heard as Dupray said, "Well, sit down, Speedy. As a matter of fact, I thought you'd never get here. Two days is a devilish time to be sitting here waiting."

Speedy rolled a cigarette, lighted it, and threw himself flat on his back on the bed, his eyes closed with pleasure as he inhaled the smoke with great breaths.

"Anything turned up?" asked Dupray.

There was no answer, and Dupray went on querulously, "We've followed a wrong trail for a long time, I think. The trouble is that it's not so easy to describe the Nighthawk. Plenty of horses are dark brown with black points. Plenty of horses are sixteen one. That's tall, but there are plenty more just as tall. He's no beauty, either, to fill your eye. It needs a horseman to read his points, as I understand it."

"It needs a horseman," said Speedy, yawning and puffing forth a great cloud of smoke.

Dupray glared at him.

"Here I've been sitting like a fool these two days," said he, "telling lies to the greasers, Speedy, while you wander around and have the fun. What the devil have you been doing all this while?"

"Finding the Nighthawk," answered Speedy.

Dupray bounded to his feet. "Speedy," he said, "this isn't one of your infernal jokes, is it?"

Speedy yawned and puffed forth more smoke.

"I'm tired," he said. "I haven't slept for a

couple of days. Let me alone for an hour or so, Al."

Dupray, burning up with curiosity, nevertheless realized that he had better remain silent. If he importuned Speedy too much, the latter might defend himself with a still longer silence.

Dupray waited two restless hours. Then that silent figure on the bed stirred and instantly sat up. There was one yawn. After that the magic fingers made a cigarette with what seemed no more than a gesture.

Still Al Dupray dared not ask a question, for he could guess that his headlong manner of questioning had offended the other.

Through a cloud of smoke, Speedy said, "It was a long trail, Al. I would have talked to you a lot more and argued out my plans with you, but most of the time I was going on instinct."

"What sort of an instinct, Speedy?"

"Well, that nobody but a Mexican could have done the job. Nobody but a Mexican would have picked out that one horse and gone off with it. There were twenty more in the field, and a good American rustler would have made a clean sweep of the lot. That is, that was my guess. But there was another chance."

Dupray waited, and Speedy went on slowly, "It might have been some old jockey gone to the bad and on the road, someone who knew the breeding of the Nighthawk, and wanted to race the stallion. He's of a famous line, you know."

"I know," murmured Dupray. "Seven thousand dollars is a lot, but even at that price, I understand old Crane couldn't have got him except that he'd broken down in training."

"He broke down, but two years on the range fixed him. He's hard as iron now, I believe, and if he were taken to the big Eastern tracks he'd make a lot of money."

Dupray nodded.

"It might have been that he was stolen like that," said Speedy. "There was a good chance of it. But there are more Mexicans than jockeys in that part of the range, so I put my bet on the Mexican idea. That's why we headed straight south. We were nearly to the Rio Grande before I hit another clue. That was only a hint—Vicente Bardillo, of the town of El Rey, who can't be caught in the open because he rides a brown stallion as fast as the wind."

"I do remember," said the young fellow. "That didn't mean much to me at the time, though. Vicente Bardillo would never leave his town long enough to ride as far north as the Crane place to steal a horse."

"That's true. On the other hand, any Mexican horse thief with half a brain would realize that no man south of the Rio Grande would pay as much for a perfect horse as Bardillo would. I worked on that chance. This morning I saw the horse."

Al Dupray turned white.

"You saw the Nighthawk?"

"I saw him."

"There are lots of brown stallions in the world," said the young fellow doubtfully.

"Of course there are," said Speedy. "I know that, but not so many just about sixteen hands high in this part of the world, with ugly heads, perfect legs, hip bones that stick out a good bit, and quarters that look too stringy and thin to be strong. At first glance this fellow seems all overbalanced, but when you look closer you can see that he's simply a running machine. He's an ugly devil, but he's hammered iron from head to foot. It's the Nighthawk, and no mistake about that!"

Dupray said through clenched teeth, "If you've found him, then I'll get him, Speedy. You've done the miracle for me."

He was walking up and down the floor in a tremor of exultation. He was not a handsome fellow, but in the fierceness of his determination he looked capable of great deeds.

Speedy regarded him with an approving eye.

Presently he said, "You'd better find out where he is, Al."

"You'll tell me that," said the young fellow.

"Well, he's kept by the men of Bardillo, of course."

"Yes, I could guess that, naturally. Where do they pasture him?"

"They don't pasture him," said Speedy.

"What!" exclaimed Dupray.

"They take the Nighthawk out on a lead, and two men go out with him," said Speedy. "One is on a horse, holding the tether. The other is walking. And they're both armed to the teeth. They let the big fellow graze a while, and then they take him back into the barn. You can't very well call that pasturing him, can you? At least, he doesn't run loose."

Al Dupray groaned.

"You mean that they guard him like a baby?"

"Like a king's baby; like the heir to the

throne. He's always under guard," said Speedy.

"In the stable? too?" asked Dupray.

"You see how it is, Al," Speedy answered. "There isn't a chance in a thousand that any thief would dare to come up here to El Rey, right into Bardillo's hometown, and then still try to get at the horse. But the Nighthawk means so much to Bardillo that he takes no chances. When he rides out, the Nighthawk goes on a lead. He's kept for the pinches. He's the horse that's to save the crook when his life's in danger. Looked at that way, the Nighthawk means more than twenty good men to Bardillo. Besides, I think it pleases Bardillo to treat the horse like some great thing. It flatters him. You see the idea? When such care is taken of the horse, imagine the greatness of the master!"

"He's guarded day and night?"

"Day and night," said Speedy. "But we'll have to find the right key to the problem. I'm going up there this afternoon."

9
_____

It was not long after this that a clamor broke out in the upper hall of the inn, outside the room of the American guest, Al Dupray. Suddenly the door was thrown open, and that slender, brown-legged peon, Pedro, leaped out and dashed down the hallway, howling and yelling for help, while the blows of the whip cracked loudly about him.

Down the stairs he bounded, and leaped into the middle of the patio, where he stood dancing up and down, as though in pain, and rubbing his shoulders where the blows had evidently fallen.

Two *mozos* stood near, watching him and laughing at his plight.

"Now you see, Pedro," said one of them, "what it means to work for a gringo."

And the second servant added, "It's a lucky thing for you that you're not in the gringo land north of the Rio Grande. If you were, that master of yours would cut your heart out. Young fool!"

"The devil take him. And roast him ten thousand years," said Pedro, shaking his brown fist furiously toward the window of the room of Al Dupray. "I leave him now, and I am going to take service with another man and a greater man."

"What other and greater man?" asked one of the *mozos*.

"With the great Señor Bardillo."

The two *mozos* broke out into hearty laughter.

"You are going to the *casa grande* to ask for work?" said one of them.

"Yes. Why not?" asked Speedy.

"Because," said one of the *mozos,* "you don't know what happens to people who ask for work at the gate of that house!"

"What happens to them?" asked Speedy.

"Why—" began the first one.

But the second snapped, "Let him go! He is one of those wise young ones that has to learn."

Speedy shrugged his shoulders. "Well," he said, "if you are friends, you'll tell me what they do to people who ask for work at the house of Señor Bardillo."

"A hundred men before you have tried," said one of the *mozos.* "And they've all—" He broke off, laughing.

"You mean," said Speedy, "that nobody can get a place working in the *casa grande,* as you call it?"

"Go ahead and try it yourself," the *mozo* said after a while. "Then you'll know."

They both began to laugh again, and although Speedy tried a few more questions, he got nothing out of them and stepped out into the street. Above and beyond its winding he saw the high wall of the big house that had once been the castle of a great man, and was still the open stronghold of a famous brigand. Law did not choose to ride so far as that nest of robbers in the mountains. Justice would cost too much bloodshed.

Bardillo, furthermore, knew certain palms that needed to be crossed with silver. When that was done, all was well, and he could be sure of another year of peace, at the least.

Speedy, looking up at that big, rough wall, shook his head and sighed a little. He was armed with a single slender-bladed knife with a weighted handle. Otherwise he had no weapon. He had only his bare hands, and yet he must open the door of that *casa grande*, enter it, and survive whatever grueling test was given to strangers. After that he would have to do the impossible—manage the liberation of the famous stallion.

He settled the ragged straw hat on his head, smiled, and started trudging up the street. Behind him, raucous laughter broke out, and, turning, he saw the faces of the two *mozos* of the inn. He waved a hand to them and continued on his way, wondering what the mystery might be.

He passed the last of the houses in this part of the little town and came into an irregularly shaped plaza before the walls of the great castle. Before him there was a single postern door with a strong arch above it, opening into the wall of the great house. Before the door sat a powerfully built fellow with wide mustachios, waxed, and turning up at the points like the horns of a steer. The sun shone on those mustachios. He was magnificently dressed for his type, with silver conchas down the side of his trousers, and a jacket covered with metal braid. It was plain that he was a grandee among his own particular order of men.

When he saw the young fellow coming toward him he raised a hand.

"What errand?" he asked.

"To ring the bell outside the door, señor," said Speedy, bowing humbly.

The big man suddenly grinned and stood up.

"You want to ring the bell?" he asked.

"Yes," said Speedy.

"You are a beggar, then? You want help?"

"I am not a beggar, señor," said Speedy, bowing almost to the ground. "I look for honest work to do."

"You look for work?" said the other.

"Is that a fault?" asked Speedy humbly.

"Not a fault, but a folly," said the other.

"Only men are wanted in this *casa grande*. Now, then, go and ring the bell if you think that you are a man."

He smirked as he said it. But Speedy, making a wide, interrogatory gesture with both hands, stepped to the bell pull beside the postern door and gave it a tug. A deep-voiced bell answered, muffled by the thickness of the wall. Instantly the door opened.

Before Speedy stood a caballero even more gaudy than the man outside the postern. "What in the name of the devil is this?" he asked, looking once at Speedy, and then at the outer guard.

"Another fool," said the first man.

"Eh?" asked the second.

"Yes, another fool, who thinks that he's man enough to serve in the *casa grande*. He wants the test!"

He laughed suddenly on the last word.

"This young donkey," said the keeper of the door, "won't have the test. He'll only have the beating. Take him and tie his hands, Juan."

"Willingly," said Juan. "Come here, young rooster."

He drew a cord from his pocket and came with a savage grin. Speedy did not move.

"What have I done, señor, that I should be beaten?" he asked.

"You'll find that out later on," said Juan.

"Yes," said the second man. "You'll find out, all right."

"Hold out your hands," commanded Juan, taking hold of Speedy's shoulder.

"Ah, señor," said Speedy, "I trust there will be no cruel injustice."

As he held out his hands, Juan shifted his grip from the shoulder to the wrist of the smaller man.

"No injustice," he said. "But we'll take all the skin off your back that a quirt can remove. That's all."

He began to laugh. With the first note of his laughter, one hand of Speedy rose and flicked down, striking with the hardened edge of the palm across the wrist of the other.

The Mexican leaped back with an exclamation of rage.

"By the devil," he cried, "the little rat has broken my wrist! Oh, you'll pay for this!"

He rushed in with a poised fist to beat up Speedy. The latter made no apparent effort to avoid him. Only, at the very moment that the blow was shooting toward his face, he swerved suddenly, stooped, caught upward

69

with one lightning hand, and Juan hurtled over his bowed back and landed half a dozen feet away.

He lay stunned upon the stones, merely gasping, "Clemente! Break the neck of the trickster! Clemente!"

But Clemente was already rushing to perform that task unbidden. He reached for Speedy's throat with one hand; in the other he held a clubbed Colt to rap his victim over the head. But the first hand closed on thin air, and on the wrist of the second came that same lightning stroke with the edge of the palm, as with a cleaver.

The gun fell from the numbed fingers; Speedy picked it up.

As Juan rose, staggering, and Clemente turned with a gasp of incredulous rage, to find himself disarmed, the youthful stranger was gently saying, "You have rough games here in the *casa grande*, my friends. But I was raised where men are rough, also. You see that I am not very strong, but a game is a game, nevertheless. Now, will you let someone in authority know that a poor fellow is standing here at the door, asking for work?"

IT WOULD have been hard to say what answers might have been returned by Clemente and the other, but at this time a stern voice called down to them, brawling, "Juan! Clemente!"

"Mother of Heaven," muttered Clemente, "It is that devil of a Diego Marañon. I might have known that he'd be near enough to see us. You've done this, Juan, you thick-witted blunderer, by allowing that fellow to ring the bell. You should have run him off the place."

The voice of Diego Marañon now approached closer, and he appeared at a window just above the gate. He was a man of middle age, with a much wrinkled forehead, the face decorated with long seams that extended beside the corners of the mouth. He wore a very short mustache, and a pointed black beard that curled a little. In his youth he had undoubtedly been a handsome fellow; now he simply looked debauched and worn out.

There was a sardonic cast in his eye as he said to Clemente, "What's the matter, Clemente, with you and Juan? Two heroes, the pair of you, and both thrown about by a young fellow like that? Come along, Clemente! Come along, Juan! This will please Bardillo!"

He paused. They endured his sneer in gloomy silence.

Then he changed his manner and commanded sharply, "He's won the right to have the test, has he not?"

The pair stared at one another and said nothing.

"Answer me!" shouted Marañon in a sudden fury. "Has he won the right or has he not?"

"He has won the right, Señor Marañon," said Clemente finally. But he looked down upon the ground as though he wished that it would open and receive him.

"Very well," said Diego Marañon. "Prepare the test for him. I'll have the bell rung so the people can come and look at the show. I'll fetch Vicente Bardillo, also, so that he can see the sort of people who are now admitted to the test by his guards! Prepare yourselves, my friends. Be ready for anything that may happen, for the temper of

72

Don Vicente is a little on the short side these days!"

He disappeared from the window, the glint of his evil smile being the last that was seen of him.

Clemente turned on Juan as he said, "Afterward I call you to an accounting. Now I go to prepare the test. Stay here and watch him. Shoot him if he tries to escape!"

With that he strode on through the open postern as Juan, the sentinel, muttered to Speedy, "You see what you've done? You've raised hell. That's what you've done. You'll wish you hadn't, too, before Marañon gets through with you."

"He seemed to me like a great señor," said Speedy innocently.

"He is a great señor. He is a fiend, too," declared the other. "And you'll have time to find all of these things out about him. Dolt!"

Speedy merely shrugged his shoulders, as though bewildered. "What am I to do, Don Juan?" said he. "I do only what comes to my mind and to my hand. I'm sorry that I hurt you. But you seemed excited. You and Don Clemente, also. I was afraid. I only tried to protect myself."

The other grinned sourly. "You'll need to

protect yourself a little later," said he. "Wait—there it begins!"

A bell began to ring in the tower that stood up at the right of the *casa grande*. It had a broad, flat, unresonant stroke, as though the body of the bell were of a base metal.

As it rang, voices answered from the town below the *casa grande*—children's voices, first of all, then the murmur of a crowd that began to pour from the end of the main street, thronging the plaza.

Presently there were others appearing on the wall of the *casa grande*, or thronging out through the postern and it was plain to Speedy that their glances were upon him entirely.

They expected from him some very dramatic conclusion of this incident, it was clear!

The bell of the great house still was beating, like a frantic, irregular heartbeat, when Clemente returned, carrying a fluttering bird upon his hand. Everyone shouted with redoubled violence at the sight of this.

"The pigeon! The pigeon!" they yelled.

On the heels of their shouting, a great uproar of laughter began. Speedy saw women and children, and even some old men, bent double, while they wailed and yelled their delight.

His own blood grew a little cold, perhaps, for he gaped about him in bewilderment. "Don Juan," said he, "they are not laughing at me, are they?"

"Why not?" asked Juan, snarling.

"So many people have never noticed me before; not even to laugh at me," said Speedy.

"Oh, they've only just begun to notice you, my fine fellow!" said Juan.

After this a *mozo*—he seemed no more—who walked beside Clemente, took the pigeon from him and held it by the cord that allowed it to flutter perhaps two or three feet just over his head.

There was a fresh yell of delight, and the general cry: "The pigeon! The blood of the pigeon! Justice, Bardillo!"

Here, into the opening of the postern, stepped a man of magnificent presence, very tall, with immensely broad shoulders that sloped away to narrow hips, ideal for a horseman. He wore a cloak that flowed back from his shoulders and gave to his gestures an imperial air of command.

His left hand was gloved, carrying the glove of the right hand, and with this he made his gestures.

That was Bardillo, as Speedy could have guessed. He did not need the sudden silence of all other spectators to understand. As the man issued from the postern, a stream of riders came out behind him, eight of them, carrying long whips.

"Does this fellow understand the test?" asked Bardillo of Juan.

"He wouldn't wait to find out what the test might be," declared Juan.

Bardillo smiled a little, and the people, who saw the smile of the master, gave one ringing whoop of cruel joy, and then were again silent.

"Well, Marañon," said the chief to his first lieutenant. "You may as well explain everything to the young beggar. Experience is apt to be a cruel teacher, and her lessons are not quickly forgotten, eh?"

"No, not quickly," said Marañon with a smile far more cruel than his master's. "They will be remembered, if I'm any judge of men and whips."

As he spoke he looked toward the eight mounted men, then from Speedy to Juan and Clemente.

Speedy cleared his throat, though he was not preparing to speak. His heart and brain grew a little giddy.

"Tell him, Marañon," repeated the chief.

Diego Marañon stepped forward and gathered a solemn frown upon his forehead, although there was still a smile upon his lips.

"Do you hear me?" he asked.

"Ah, yes, señor, I do hear you," replied Speedy.

"You are about to learn the test that is to be given to you."

"I wait humbly; I wait with patience, as your servant, señor," said Speedy, bowing again.

"The fellow has manners," interrupted the great Bardillo, looking calmly down at the scene.

"What is your name?" continued Marañon.

"My name is Pedro, if you are pleased with that name, señor," said Speedy.

"And if it doesn't please me?" said Marañon, "will I be able to change it?"

"Ah, señor," said Speedy, "I would change my skin to win your favor, and what a simple thing it is to turn a skin inside out!"

Brief laughter followed this, like a single shout with several echoes.

"Well," said Marañon, "perhaps you'll want to turn your skin inside out before long, unless there are too many holes worn through it."

"Alas, señor, I tremble," said Speedy.

"Well," went on Marañon, "you are to understand, young fellow, in the old days, the first days of the greatness and the fame of Señor Bardillo, many men came to ask for service with him. Some were cowards, many were fools, a very few were traitors. Now everyone who wishes to join him must pass a test. You understand?"

"I understand," said Speedy. "I tremble, but I understand."

"Well, then," said Marañon, "the test is a very simple one."

He pointed.

"You see the pigeon, señor?"

"I see the pigeon, señor."

"Well, then, presently, at a word from Don Vicente, that pigeon will be set free, with no more than the bit of string dangling down from its legs. All that you need to do, in order to pass the test, is to strike it with bullets from a revolver or a rifle as it rises through the air."

11

PERFECT LAUGHTER is never possible except to the hardhearted. But at the sight of the dismay which opened the mouth and made the jaw of young Speedy droop down, every spectator broke out into noisy mirth, and the great Don Vicente as much as humbler people.

"And Señor Marañon, if I fail?"

"If you fail," said Marañon, his cruel eye flashing fire, "then you will be very sorry for the failure later on, amigo. For you will have to run from this place and hurry down through the long, winding central street of the town. And as you hurry along, these caballeros will follow with their horses, if they are able to keep up with you, and they will urge you to go faster. You see, Pedro, that they carry whips to spur you on and make your steps longer?"

Speedy looked at the long, sinister lashes of those whips, and he knew that the supple, long-seasoned rawhide thongs could be made to bite through the tough hide of a mule at every stroke. How much the more so would they slash his coat and shirt to pieces and cut his body to the bone?

His eyes narrowed a little. They might curl a lash about his feet and trip him up as he fled. Once he had fallen he would be beaten to death, like a dog.

There was no doubt that the riders would go as far as possible with him in order to avenge the insult to two of their men.

He looked back at the pigeon, which was fluttering eagerly at the end of the string, buoyant as a supercharged balloon, tugging to be off and into the heart of the sky.

"You have a gun already, Pedro," said Marañon. "Señor Bardillo, when you are ready, Pedro is ready to hear the word, I presume."

"I have a borrowed gun," said Speedy. "I don't want it. And here it is for the owner. Don Clemente, I thank you for the loan."

He offered the weapon butt first to Clemente, and the big guard snatched it with an oath, blood rushing up into his face at the suggestion of an insult.

"What sort of a gun do you wish, then?" asked the great Bardillo. "If you want a rifle, my son, you may have that, also. I warn you, however, you must exercise extreme care. Put him ten steps from the bird, Marañon."

"He is standing there now," said Marañon.

"Are you taking a rifle, Pedro?" asked Bardillo, not unkindly.

"No, señor. I am prepared with a weapon of my own," said the young fellow.

"You are prepared? What sort of a weapon?"

"A weapon that fits my hand, señor," said Speedy.

"He is a proud young fool," said Marañon in such a voice that Speedy heard him perfectly. "Let the whips give him advice, not your tongue, señor!"

"You're right, Marañon," said Bardillo. "I am always too far from these people to understand them well. You are closer, Marañon. You understand them far better!"

Marañon gave his chief one half-veiled but very sinister glance; the chief disregarded it, still maintaining a slight smile. Perhaps he failed to see it.

Then, turning his long, aristocratic ugly face toward the holder of the bird, he said, "Are you ready?"

"I am ready," said the *mozo*.

"Are you ready?" asked the chief, turning this time to Speedy.

"I am ready, señor."

"I raise my hand," said the robber. "When I let it fall, loose the bird; throw it into the air. Do you hear?"

"I hear," said the *mozo*.

His chest was swelling a little since he was, for a moment, the cynosure of all eyes.

So, for an instant, Bardillo stood, his gloved hand raised; suddenly it fell, and the *mozo* flung the pigeon high into the air.

There it hung for a moment, staggering, regaining its balance after being loosed so roughly. A second later it dipped away at full speed.

Now, as it rose into the air, flung up, it appeared, less by the hand of the *mozo* than by the shout of the mob, Speedy drew from his coat the knife which was his sole weapon and slid it into the palm of his hand with a gesture so rapid that very few people were able to observe exactly what he was doing. As the pigeon fluttered in midair, he took a swift stride forward. As the bird darted to the side he flung the glittering knife.

It dissolved in the air to a glint of light, while utter silence blanketed the amazed people on the plaza. The knife flew on in a broad, flat arc, and the bird shot away, apparently toward freedom.

A new yell of wonder and of savage triumph arose from the crowd, but Speedy sprang forward, and his fingers touched a broad-faced paving stone. He straightened again, and the tips of his fingers were red.

"He has missed! The whips! The whips!" shouted many voices.

Several of the riders spurred their horses and swung the lashes high, but Speedy had raised his hand.

"Señor Bardillo," said he. "Look! It is the blood of the bird. It is on my hand; I have not missed. Look on the stones and you find more blood. I have drawn it. The knife has found the body of the pigeon!"

"Stop!" commanded the chief.

The riders reined back their horses, one of them so close that the beast reared.

"Fetch the knife!" ordered Bardillo.

A panting *mozo* brought it in haste. Silence had descended on the plaza again.

The great man, taking the little weapon, stared at the point. "I think it is true," said he. "There is blood on the point of the weapon! Come to me, Pedro."

Speedy approached him.

"There is the blood that I wiped from the stone where it fell, señor," said he.

"I see blood on your finger," said the other. "Wipe it away, now!"

"It is done," said Speedy, obeying.

The chief looked closely at the two finger-tips that had borne the stain.

"I thought that the clever rascal might have stained the knife with his own blood," said he, "but now I believe he has told the truth. By all the saints, that was either a very wonderful or a very lucky cast. Who are you, Pedro?"

"Ah, señor," said Speedy, bowing with his usual humility, "I am one to live as your gracious kindness permits me and teaches me."

Bardillo smiled faintly.

"He is something above the ordinary peon, Marañon," said he. "Get him some clothes. After he has washed away the grime, send him to me. There is some little mystery about him."

_____ 12

WHEN BARDILLO had passed through the postern and back into the house, the others

84

swarmed after him, Speedy among them, and Marañon walking behind him.

In the inner patio they paused, and Marañon said, "Now, hombres, it seems that you are to have a new companion. You, Clemente, and Juan, may think that you have reason to be angry with him. But there is no anger among the men of Bardillo. You know that of old. Don't venture to forget it now. Some of you have shed your blood already for Señor Bardillo, but his justice is, nevertheless, the same for every man among you. This new man is like the others. Do you understand?"

All answered in the affirmative, Juan cheerfully enough, and Clemente, last of all, remarked, "Pedro, here is my hand. We forget everything and commence again, do we not?"

"Don Clemente," said Speedy, "you are a brave man and a kind man. You forgive me my trick, and I shall try to make up for it another day with a good turn."

"Teach me the same trick to use in my time of need," said Clemente, "and I ask nothing better."

"I shall teach you every turn of my hand," said Speedy courteously.

"Good," said Marañon. Then, beckoning to Speedy, he said, "Pedro, come with me."

He led the young fellow into the house, up and down corridors and steps until he came to a door, which he pushed open. Within there was a small room with one narrow window, hardly a foot and a half square.

For furniture there was a cot, a sheepskin rug on the floor and another on the bed, a stool, and a small table, on which stood a washbowl. There were some pegs along the wall. A battered hat hung from one of these. A pair of boots slumped in another corner.

"One of our men used to have this room," said Marañon cheerfully. "He was with us a long time, and was one of the best of the lot. No man ever rode better, I can tell you! His end was strange, for the bullet that killed him struck him in the middle of the back. We are sad still, but with you in this room we'll be more cheerful about him before long. What is your last name, Pedro?"

"Garona, señor," said Speedy.

"Pedro Garona," Marañon went on, "you have begun very well. You have the eye of Señor Bardillo on you. You need only, for a few days, keep your eyes wide open, observe everything, speak little, and think much.

Copy the actions of the men about you who are oldest and wisest. If you are in doubt, come to me to ask my advice. Live cheerfully, obey readily, keep faith, avoid brawling. Do these things and you are in the pleasantest company in Mexico. Break any of these laws and you will find yourself entangled in a jungle that is filled with tigers."

"Señor," said Speedy, "I learned when I was a boy to judge a wise man by his face and by his words. I follow you in everything."

"I'll send you a *mozo* with clothes that ought to fit you," said Marañon. "And there'll be water to wash yourself. Señor Bardillo will send for you when he needs you!"

So Speedy found himself alone in the room and looked curiously about him. He realized, as Marañon had pointed out, that he was in a veritable den of tigers, and there would be no way but death for him if the least hint of his true character should appear. He walked on a tightrope that might break under him at any moment.

However, he put such thoughts out of his mind as far as this was possible, and started to prepare for his change of clothes by stripping off his clothes. Then he fortified himself against the cold mountain wind which was blowing through the narrow casement into the room by performing some odd gymnastics.

He had barely finished this performance when there came a knock at his door, and a *mozo* walked in to find the newcomer to the *casa grande* panting in a cold room as though he had just run up several flights of stairs.

He put down the clothes and a bucket of tepid water; and then he hurried out to tell his fellow *mozos* that the stranger who looked so slender was, in fact, deep of chest, and that he was made of such rippling muscles as one sees in the panther as it crouches, ready to spring.

Speedy, in the meantime, had scrubbed himself thoroughly, glorying in the strength of the dye which clung to his skin so well in spite of soap and water. He was sure that not ten men in the world had the secret of its use, or the trick of the chemical which, when one chose, washed it away like so much surface dust upon the skin!

When he came to the scrubbing of his hands, he took particular care about cleansing beneath the nail of the forefinger on his right hand, for under the nail there was a deep but narrow prick, such as the keen point of a knife might make between nail and flesh. Such an incision was this beneath the fingernail of Speedy—such a one as could be used for the squeezing forth of a few drops of essential blood, after which the bleeding would be stopped at once by the pressure of the nail.

Speedy, as he regarded that spot beneath the nail, smiled a little. Yet, with all his forethought, his trick might have failed had it not been that he had thought of smearing some of that blood hastily over the point of the knife!

The wit of the great Bardillo had been quick enough to hit upon the proof at once. And there it had been, the precious, thin smear of blood in addition to what Speedy had squeezed out upon the surface of the stone, as though the drops had fallen from the wounded bird. The chief was convinced.

That Bardillo was a fellow to be watched. He would take some circumventing, unless his eyes were well closed in a false confidence.

There was something about this entire adventure that Speedy liked not at all. It was true that, as usual, he was preying upon thieves, but then, on the other hand, he had managed his entrance into the house by winning the respect and the admiration of the whole band of thieves. He might balance against this the fact that he had been in danger of being flogged to death. But for all that, his conscience was not entirely quiet.

He went on with his scrubbing, dried his body with a cotton towel, and then began to dress. Complicated clothes were these that he put on. A weight of metal ornament made them hateful to him, and the tightness of the jacket was disgusting to him for he liked nothing that did not leave every muscle free to obey his will.

He was dressed, however, eventually, and now he made a few steps up and down, then went through a few movements to discover just how far and with what ease he could step or bend this way and that.

He had hardly finished fully this when there was another tap at the door. It was the *mozo* returning, with word that the great Bardillo wished to see his new recruit.

It was a great spread of rooms, halls, and corridors through which that guide conducted him. Already he had mapped down in his mind the tortuous route by which he had entered the place, but he wanted to get hold of a good chart of the place. Let him be twenty-four hours in the house, however, and it would be strange if he did not know every corner of it down to the bottom of its cellar, no matter how deep.

The *mozo*, walking with him, brought Speedy to a farther corner of the big house and rapped at a door, whereupon a voice bade him enter. He pushed back the door.

"Señor, I bring you Pedro Garona," said the *mozo*.

Speedy stepped forward cheerfully enough, and saw that the robber chief stood beside a big window with a deep casement on the farther side of the room, a window through which so much light came that it blotted out with shadow everything else that was inside; at least, during the first moment. Then, as his eyes grew instantly more accustomed to the light, he saw in a corner the last object he wished to find there—the face of a man who knew him, who hated him, and who had reason for his hatred!

_____ 13

THE GREAT BARDILLO, therefore, meant far less than that lean pain-stricken countenance of the man in the shadow. As Speedy shut the door behind him, he expected the man to whip out a revolver and open fire, but the man with the one arm remained as expressionless as a mummy, while his hollow eyes followed the movements of Speedy across the floor.

Bardillo had turned from the window. His look was stern; for that matter, sternness was his habitual mask.

"Now, Pedro," he said, "I want to talk to you."

"Yes, señor," said Speedy.

"What's your last name again?"

"Garona, señor."

"Where have you lived?"

"North of the Rio Grande most of my life," answered Speedy.

"Oh, in the States, then?"

"Yes."

"Why did you go there?"

"My father took me there when I was a child."

"Why did he take you there?"

"He had killed a man, señor."

The chief nodded.

"He had killed a man, then, so he ran across the Rio Grande."

"That is true, señor."

"And why did you come south, then?"

"Because, unfortunately, I killed a man, señor."

"Your father went north because he killed a man; you came south because you killed a man?" As he asked, the chief laughed. "There is killing in your blood, Pedro, is that it? How did you happen to kill this fellow?"

"It was because my knife's point happened to strike through his eye to the brain."

"That was the only reason, eh?"

"The only reason, señor."

"You're sorry for it, then?"

"Well," replied Speedy, "when I saw him drop dead I knew instantly that now I must go to Mexico. That was something I had been wanting to do for a long time."

"What made you want to come here?"

"My country, my people, my blood," replied Speedy.

The chief stood a little straighter, and his eye flashed.

"There is something to you; there's a substance to you, Pedro," he declared. "What was your life in the States?"

"A wretched life, señor."

"You say that with a good deal of feeling."

"Because I suffered a great deal, señor."

"What made you suffer?"

"A wife, señor."

Bardillo laughed outright. "What was the matter with her?" he asked.

"Señor," said Speedy, "I endured what I could endure."

The bandit was apparently more and more pleased with his new man. "When you are working for me, Pedro, what do you expect?"

"Trouble," said Speedy. "Much trouble, señor. Long rides in the cold. Long rides in the heat. To starve often, lying among the hills. To endure gunfire. To be hunted and hated. I expect all of these things to happen to me."

The other, as he heard this catalogue of evils, could not help smiling a little. "Then what folly made you come to me?" he demanded. "What will you gain to make up for all that you lose?"

"Well," replied Speedy, "if I am treated like a wolf, I gain the right to be a wolf, also. If men snarl at me, I can use my teeth, too. I have a chief above me and another man or two, his lieutenants; outside of them I am free to do as I please. And what is it that I please to do? That which a hawk desires, señor; to sail through the sky with my eyes turned down, looking for smaller birds. If I find any very large ones, an eagle or two, I whistle and my companions join me. We drop down and make the feathers of the eagle fly. We eat eagle meat that day. That is the life for me, señor, and for the sake of it I have come to you."

The great Bardillo actually grew rosy with pleasure as he heard this speech. Finally he said, "Pedro, I have nothing to say to you for the present. Live in the house. Be happy. Get acquainted with the men. You will go far with me, Pedro."

"Ah, you are very kind to me," said Speedy.

"Tell me, furthermore," said the chief, "if you are treated well in this place or if you have complaints. The new are on a footing with the old in my band. We are a democracy, Pedro."

"Thank you," said Speedy.

"You are free to go now," said Bardillo. "There is only one thing remaining. I grant one gift to every man who comes to me after drawing the blood of the pigeon. What gift will you ask for, Pedro?"

Speedy appeared to hesitate. Then his eyes lighted.

"I can tell you that, señor. I came to the town in the service of a swine of a gringo. I was like a servant to him. The people of the *fonda* laughed at me. I ran away from his service. Now, señor, I am no longer in rags. Grant me one great wish."

"You want a brighter scarf, is that it?" asked Bardillo.

"No, no, señor. I am happy with these clothes. They are the finest that I have ever worn. But now let me ride out and strike the men of the town silent with awe. Let me ride down the main street of the town. And let me be upon the back of the great horse of the señor himself!"

Bardillo started.

"You mean on the back of Nighthawk?" he asked.

"Yes," said Speedy, bowing to the floor.

"That's a great deal to ask," answered the chief.

"Alas, señor, you send him out every day into the pasture with two men," said Speedy. "It is only to ride him through the main street of the town, that the people who laughed at me may now see that the great señor himself has placed his trust in me! How else can they learn that so well as when they see me sitting in the saddle of the great señor and upon the back of his horse, the great stallion. They will say to themselves,

'One minute ago we mocked him: but now see what a thing it is to have found the favor of Señor Bardillo!' "

Bardillo's frown, as he listened to this speech, relaxed, and at length he broke out into a roar of hearty laughter.

"And why not?" he said half to himself. "You shall do as you please, then, Pedro. Go down and get the stallion when you please, and tell them that you come from me with that order."

"Suppose," said Speedy, "that they doubt you have given such an order, señor?"

An evil gleam shot from the eye of Bardillo. "In that case," said he, "I don't know what to say. Perhaps you will know how to convince them that you really come from me?"

Speedy bowed again.

"You give me permission, in other words," he murmured, "to go and take the Night-hawk if I can?"

"Yes," replied Bardillo. "That's the permission I give to you."

"I will go," said Speedy. "And ten thousand thanks, Señor Bardillo. I am your servant. I am covered with a hundred thousand obligations, and I depart to find the great horse. Ah ha, señor, you cannot tell how my

97

heart laughs out in my body when I think of sitting on his back!"

Bardillo, in fact, began to laugh a little as he heard this flowery farewell, and he was still laughing when Speedy reached the door, opened it, and backed out into the hall.

He had hardly turned down its shadowy length when the door opened again and the one-armed man stepped out behind him. He made a gesture, and Speedy paused for him to come up.

There was a casement at this point for the sole purpose of lighting the hallway, and Speedy stepped back in front of it. The one-armed man walked straight up to him.

"You remember me, Speedy?" he asked.

"I remember you dimly," replied Speedy.

"As a friend or an enemy?"

"That's hard to tell," answered Speedy. "You're simply back there somewhere in the shadows of my mind. I think I never saw you for a long time together."

"It was not a long time," said the other slowly. "It was a very short time indeed!"

His somber face seemed to shrivel with the great excess of his malice.

Speedy waited. All his nerves were tingling; his whole brain was thrillingly tuned for an eventuality.

"Do you not remember, Señor Speedy," went on the one-armed man, "the name of Benito Vizcaya?"

"That name I've forgotten," said Speedy, shaking his head.

At this the other grew livid and, turning away from Speedy, he made two or three short turns up and down the hall as though gradually to master his emotion.

Then, coming back, he scrutinized the young fellow's face even more closely than before, saying, "Señor Devil, do you remember the Pass of Las Hayas?"

Well did Speedy remember that pass, and from the very first he had recalled everything.

Benito Vizcaya went on: "I shall tell you a little to refresh your mind. The thieves had taken a good booty, and you had stolen it from them by your craft. You had taken it all and had ridden away. We followed. The others were weary. Their horses gave out. I, alone, I overtook you in the height of the Las Hayas Pass. I saw you fleeing like a dog before me. Then you disappeared farther along the trail. I followed fast. Suddenly a tiger leaped on me from the brush at the side of the trail. Not a tiger, but you! I was dragged from my horse. I tried to fight, but the skill of a fiend, the fiend to whom you have sold your soul, was in your hands. My own strength you used against me. I felt a terrible pain, I heard a cracking sound as my arm was broken to slivers!"

He groaned, half closed his eyes, and his head jerked back. "I rode back down the pass. The bone was thrusting out through the flesh and the skin, and the cold entered the wound. It was the next day before I could get to a doctor. The arm was infected. It had to be amputated." He paused, breathing hard: "Do you know what that means, Speedy?"

"A bad thing," replied Speedy calmly.

"Bad?" echoed the man. "To be pointed out by children, to be scorned by women, to be braved by men who would have run from me in the old days—that is what it has meant to me."

"I believe you, Benito," said Speedy. "I see that the pain has written its own account in your face. And I want you to believe me in my turn when I say that I am very sorry."

"You lie!" said Vizcaya. "You rejoice in my agony!"

Speedy raised a finger. "I don't lie, Vizcaya," said he. "Of course, I remember the whole thing perfectly. Tell me, then, because I'm very curious, one thing."

"Why I did not denounce you to Bardillo in that room?"

"Yes."

"You forget," said Vizcaya.

"What, then?"

"You forget, as I lay in the roadway, in the broken trail of the pass, that you leaned over me and said, 'Perhaps I'm a fool to let you live. You'll certainly hate me, but murder is not the game I love. Therefore I'm going to let you climb back onto your horse and ride for it. Ride fast, because that wound is a bad one, even if there's not much blood from it!' That was what you said to me, and now I make an answer to you."

He paused at this point and drew himself up, with flashing eyes. "I saw you from a casement on the side of the house, señor. I saw you when you were making the trial of the pigeon, and I recognized the face that I have hated for so many years, and so heartily! I recognized you, señor, and knew at once that you were at your old game again—to plunder the thieves; to be the robber of the robbers; the bandit of the bandits. I saw at once that you had come here to prey on Señor Bardillo and the rest of us. For a moment I held my hand, because, to say the truth, I could not believe that any man would be so foolhardy as to adventure in such a place as this, surrounded by such men.

"So I waited, but presently I saw you enter the room of Bardillo. I saw that you not only had passed the ordeal and made yourself safe in the house, but that you were likely to win the complete favor of every one at once. When I saw that, I was about to cry out your name; then I remembered what you had said when you leaned above me in Las Hayas Pass: 'Murder is not my game!'

"That is what I say to you now, Speedy. Murder is not my game. I shall give you a chance for your life, as you gave me a chance to save my arm. It will be not much of a chance, but it will be something!"

He paused, and, compressing his lips, looked at Speedy with an odd mixture of hate and envy, admiration and rage.

_____ 14

"A SMALL chance is a great deal better than no chance at all," said Speedy calmly. "And after the pain that you have had because of me, Vizcaya, I'm astonished to find so much generosity in you. Few men would do so much. Every day of your life you must have been saying to yourself, that to see me burned alive would be a proper pleasure."

"Perhaps," said the other, his smile growing ghastly, "I shall have that pleasure. In the meantime, I show you that murder is not the game I love."

He drew in a quick breath, and then rattled out the following words: "I shall go back into that room. I'll tell Bardillo that I rushed out after you because it seemed to me that I had suddenly remembered your face. I'll tell him that now I feel almost sure that I can place you in my mind—but not quite; not quite. Maybe he will ask me if it is good or bad, and still I will say that I cannot quite tell. Only that you are blazed in my memory by some powerful recollection.

"I hold him in talk this way until he burns with curiosity, and then, at the end of five minutes—five minutes from this moment, señor—I bring out a single word that will shake the house of Bardillo to the foundations. Speedy! That is the word that I will speak. In ten seconds the alarm bell will be ringing, the horn will blow from the window, and the men of Bardillo will be after you, my friend. Twenty wild riders! And you can save yourself as well as you may! Five minutes, señor, and then the game begins. It is not quite murder, however. There is not much difference, but a little. Perhaps you, too, will get through the trouble, and be able to face life after today with one hand, as I do!"

With that he turned suddenly on his heel and walked back toward the door of the room.

Minutes, for Speedy, were instantly of such vast importance that even seconds counted heavily. He used some ten of them to speculate quietly on the strangeness of this speech, which matched the oddest he ever had heard. Then he turned and ran.

That finery which he had put on he had cause to regret now. It was one thing to have bare legs and sandals as light as paper on the feet. It was another thing to be booted, spurred, and encased in heaviest cloth. Yet he made good speed down the corridor, down the stairs, and suddenly into the blazing light of the patio.

While he ran he balanced his chances. They were small enough, if he strove at once to get away. They were infinitely smaller if he attempted to gain the stallion, but now the gambling instinct was aroused in him to such a point that he could not possibly keep from making the attempt.

As he hurried into the patio, the very *mozo* who had loosed the pigeon appeared, and stopped with a grin and a nod to see the new hero in his new uniform.

"Amigo, where is the great stallion of the señor?" asked Speedy.

"In the pasture," said the *mozo*. "Yonder in the pasture, señor!" And he waved a hand toward the gate on the opposite side of the court.

"Good," said Speedy. "Now, then, do you wish to earn my friendship?"

"My father before me," said the *mozo*, "knew that friendship is worth more than gold."

He smiled a little at the double meaning which he conveyed with the word.

"It's a true saying," said Speedy. "Go to the inn. There find the young American. Say to him one word. Can you say one word of English?"

"It's an ugly language," said the *mozo*, "but I could try."

"It is an insult," said Speedy, "that is summed up in one word. The instant that you have said it, turn and run. Begin by explaining in Spanish that you have come from the house of Bardillo and from me. Tell him, further, that I have sent him a message, and that the message is 'Ride'!"

"Ride?" asked the peon.

"Yes. That one word. You understand?"

"I understand," said the *mozo*. "When he hears the insult, will he be very angry?"

"He will be on fire," replied Speedy. "But what do you care for the anger of the gringo once you are back in the street?"

"I care less than the snap of my fingers!" declared the peon. "I hurry to tell him, señor!"

And off he fled at full speed.

Even more rapidly, Speedy was through the opposite postern, and saw before him the rolling green hillsides beyond.

There strayed the cattle of Bardillo. There strayed the horses. And yonder was a tall brown stallion led by one man, while another sat the saddle of a second fine horse nearby.

How many minutes had passed up to this time?

Speedy went up to the men. One was that same Clemente who had quarreled with him at the first postern and Speedy would gladly have had any other man of the lot to deal with. Forewarned is forearmed, and Clemente had had plenty of warning concerning the magic which the slender hands of Speedy were capable of working.

"Clemente," said Speedy, "I have just left Señor Bardillo, and he gave me permission to take his own horse and ride it down the main street of the town in my new clothes. I'll lead him back to the stable for a saddle and bridle."

The stallion, as though he suddenly recognized the voice of the speaker, lifted his head with a jerk and turned toward Speedy. He was by no means a beautiful animal, but he was a running machine. Every bit of him was formed to drive him at sustained speed. Other animals had appealed to the eye of Speedy before this day, but never had one stirred him so completely.

Clemente, as he heard Speedy's remark, turned in the saddle and looked down at the swarthy pirate who was holding the lead rope in one hand and a rifle in the other.

"Well, José?" said Clemente.

José shrugged his wide shoulders.

"Are you a banker, Clemente?" he asked.

"A wise man asks wise questions," said Clemente.

"Well," said José, "if you had a bank and a stranger came in and asked you for half the money in your safe, do you think that you would give it to him at once?"

"I'd see him burn first," said Clemente, eyeing Speedy.

The time was sliding past with dizzy speed. At any moment now he expected to hear the terrible clanging of the alarm bell and the great, braying voice of the horn.

He stepped forward and laid a hand on the rope. "Amigos," said he, "I am sorry that you will not believe me. Tell me one thing."

"I could tell you ten," said Clemente grimly.

"Tell me this one thing," said Speedy. "Is it not true that this is the Nighthawk?"

"Perhaps," said the other two with one voice.

"If that is the Nighthawk," said Speedy, "do you think that I would be such a fool as to try to ride him without permission from the señor?"

José grunted. "That's true enough," said he. "That's true enough, I suppose. He would not throw away that uniform and be flogged till his bones were bare just for the sake of playing a prank."

"What do you know of Pedro?" said Clemente. "You don't know much about him, but you do know Bardillo. It's better to be too good a guard forever than a careless fool for half a minute."

"That's true, also," said José, in a quandary. "Take your hand from the rope, Pedro!"

A great many things can be done with a rope, and Speedy did one of them. He pulled against the horse enough to give more slack to the loop. Then he snapped the rope back with a flashing movement of his hand. It flicked through the fingers of the surprised José, burning the skin.

He leaped back with an oath; Speedy leaped at the same moment and caught his knees on the round, firm barrel of the stallion.

"*Hai!*" shouted Clemente, and jerked out a revolver.

Speedy flattened himself along the side of the big horse, hooking one foot over the back bone and winding a hand into the mane of the great horse. The latter, obedient to the merest touch, instantly swerved away, presenting a sheltering side toward the gun of Clemente.

"He's tricked me, curse him!" shouted José. "*Hai*, Clemente!"

He got that far when the alarm bell began

to beat with a rapidity that shocked the mind and the very nerves.

"Who is loose now?" said Clemente. "Pedro, off that horse or I'll shoot you, and the horse, too, if I have to."

"Something terrible has happened at the house," said José, seeming to forget all about the stallion. "Listen!"

The deep, braying voice of the horn was added to the bell's, and all the air was filled by the clamorous vibration. José began to run at full speed straight for the house.

Clemente still handled his rifle as though he intended to use a bullet on the insolent Pedro, but the outcry from the house was too much for his nerves. At length he turned the head of his horse to follow José, shouting as he did so, "Keep the horse safe, Pedro, or Bardillo will have your head."

Off he rode, while Speedy sat up straight, with a great sigh of relief, and turned the head of the brown stallion away from the house of Bardillo.

_____ 15

IF HE had had one chance in a hundred before, he might be said to have one chance in twenty now that he was actually on the back of the horse and riding away from the house of Bardillo. An unsaddled and unbridled horse beneath him, and he himself was by no means an expert rider! However, he found to his great joy that the Nighthawk was as tractable to the touch of a hand on either side of his neck as though he were a circus pony.

In the meantime, Speedy had brought the stallion to a full striding gallop. Looking back, he saw that the gate was open. Clemente and his horse had been turned back, and were now leading a charge of half a dozen riders, who must have been supplied from a store of everready horses kept under saddle and bridle. At any rate, a fine and colorful procession it was that charged down the hill.

However, Speedy could at least be sure that his friend Al Dupray, was enjoying freedom from interruption and suspicion. Dupray would have plenty of time to saddle his horse and ride hard, as he must be sure to do as soon as he received that message in one word.

Speedy himself must ride hard. He was followed by men as tireless as time and as savage; they could outride him, and they might be able to find horses for remounts here and there, but Speedy's only chance lay in the long, iron-hard legs of the Nighthawk, and soon the big fellow began to stretch himself. The grass flowed beneath them in a blur, like a stream of water.

He found a hill shoulder in the night, and there he dismounted at last and let the stallion graze. Twenty times he had been in easy rifle distance of death, and twenty times they had tried to close with him rather than risk a bullet that might strike the horse instead of the rider.

The green grass was no longer at hand. They had ridden into a lower and a far hotter belt of hills, where there was good, tough bunch grass, the best of grazing.

He tore up a quantity of this grass, and, twisting it into knots, he rubbed down the big horse, scrubbing him until his skin was dry; even taking particular care to go over his face, rimed and water-marked by the salty evaporation of much sweat; and the great horse held out his head and pricked his ears for the grooming.

One good grooming is equal to one good feed in the twenty-four hours, Speedy had heard. He was no expert, but he was working according to the best authorities. And now his own weariness amounted to nothing. It was simply the horse that counted.

He sat down and watched the stars slowly climbing out of the east. The stallion he had hobbled with the end of the lead rope. The scattering trees, all stubbly second growth, stood up like an army of spears about him, black and thin. There seemed to be peace in the world.

After all, nothing was gained by keeping a needless watch. He lay flat on his back, and, in spite of the chill in the air and the ground, he was instantly asleep. An hour was all that he would ask from this resting spot.

But the full hour was not out when the horse sniffed at his face. Leaping to his feet, he saw a file of riders, a half dozen of them, coming across the brow of the hill, not a quarter of a mile away. One after one they came, with their long rifles balanced across their saddle bows.

They saw him at the very moment when he was loosing the hobble knots, and down they came with a charge that sent him flying onto the back of the stallion, and so scurrying off through the brush and trees, where the mustangs were hard to outdistance, for they ran like rabbits, dodging all obstacles,

with their wild riders whooping and screaming like Indians.

For three days he wandered, resting the
horse at every possible chance, working to
find a safe way north out of the hills. The
only food he had was on the third day, when
he trapped a squirrel. He made a fire with
dry wood that gave out little smoke, roasted
the little morsel, and devoured it. It was
tough meat, but delicious to the tooth of the
hunted man. His only other provender was
the bark that he chewed to keep away the
sense of biting hunger.

Toward the close of the third day he ventured into a northward running ravine that
sloped out toward the desert, and came almost to the mouth of it when a line of riders
whirled out of nothing and charged upon
him.

He fled with the Nighthawk, the bullets
nipping the air, and singing at his ear.

It was a very different game, this, because
it showed him that the hunters had received
desperate orders from Bardillo. They were to
take no chances on losing this thief of thieves,
this Speedy, this frigate bird who preyed on
hawks of the air. They were to catch him or
kill him, even if in so doing they had to kill
the stallion, too.

Other horses could be bought. But there was only one Speedy to be dreaded and destroyed. He accepted that compliment with a grim shake of the head as he sent the long-legged flyer back into the heart of the ravine, and steadily on, until he was again on high ground, from which he could watch the barren sunset sinking in the desert.

After that, for another day, he walked, never mounting the back of the horse, because even the iron strength of the Nighthawk was giving way in this life of constant alarms.

Speedy trapped a mountain grouse, and ate that, too, as if it were the food of the gods. The fifth day he was still walking. Yet every time, as he came to the edge of the hills, he saw the blurred forms of distant riders drifting here and there. Twice that day he had to mount in haste and flee from sudden attacks. One bullet clipped the shoulder of his gaudy jacket. That was all.

So, on the sixth day, in the gray of the morning, an emaciated form rode out from the hills. There was a thin mist rising, to make the hour yet more dim. Riders drifted here and there, eyeing him from a distance.

Aided by the mist all that day, he fled north through the line of guards. Sounds whimpered and mourned in the air about him, little deadly messengers of lead that searched for him with undying greed.

Those sounds also fell away, and still he thought he heard the cry of "Speedy!" behind him, pronounced as the Mexicans always did that nickname, putting the accent on the last syllable.

He looked back. Only dimly and far away he saw the pursuers coming. He thought he heard them shouting, but no voice could reach him from them, and he knew that it was the fantasy of his own weary brain.

But he was through the line, and the horse ran strong and true, thin and weary as it was.

That northward march was a nightmare. They were in sight every day, those hovering riders, continually challenging, continually striving to close with him. Every night he shook them off and found rest and food for the horse, while he himself drowsed in catnaps. No other man in the world could have endured that terrible fatigue. Now the agony of starvation was upon him. No matter how tight he drew his belt, there was no help for him.

Then something in the hot midday stung him under the left arm. Afterward he heard the report of the rifle, as the hot blood gushed down his side.

He turned and saw the rider, who had dismounted to take the long chance, now climbing back into the saddle and spurring toward him to finish the kill.

What black madness and sleep had come upon his brain to allow an enemy to close in on him like this? He sent the stallion on, and the gallant horse responded to his voice and touch.

As he rode he stripped away the gaudy jacket, tore out the lining, tore up the shirt and undershirt, and, still without making a halt, he bandaged his wound.

It bled through the bandage. Nevertheless, he lived through that day, and dropped the hawklike, hovering line of riders far behind him. Suddenly they disappeared; yet he had not increased his pace.

At the very moment of their disappearance he saw before him a narrow strip of yellow, muddy water, twisting between low banks. Then he realized. It was not placed there by evil chance to block his way. It was the Rio Grande, and on the farther bank was safety for him!

The stallion swam across. On the farther bank Speedy fainted.

117

The damp cold of night air was in his face; voices were close to his ear when he came to himself again and heard a man saying, "A damn greaser with a hoss that he's gone and stole. That's all he is. Leave the rat here to die, and we'll take the hoss."

But another voice answered: "Look there at his skin! Where the blood's washed it, and the bandage has rubbed. It's white. He's only stained his skin that color!"

Speedy's dim eyes saw that a match had been lighted close to his wound. He sat up.

"Hello, and how's things?" asked the bearded ruffian who had spoken first.

"Things are looking up," said Speedy. "How's things with you, partner?"

"Well," said the other, "I ain't been clawed by any greasers lately, like it looks you've been."

"Who did this to you?" snapped the man in whose fingers the match had burned out.

"Why, there was quite a pack of them," said the young man.

"Greasers?"

"Yes."

"I'd like to get my hands on 'em! Know their names?"

"They're not hard to find," said Speedy. "Ever hear of Bardillo and his gang?"

118

He drew a gasp of astonished interest in reply.

"And who are you?" demanded the bearded man, lighting a match on his own behalf and letting it shine into the starved face of the young fellow.

"Why, people call me by any name that's handy," said the latter. "Speedy is a name that a lot of folks use."

The match dropped, a yellow streak of light that vanished as it touched the ground.

"Speedy!" said two deep voices, hushed with awe.

_____ 16

It was a full two weeks after this, in the middle afternoon, that Al Dupray stood in front of the invalid, Joshua Crane, with Sue Crane at the back of the wheelchair, looking out of frightened eyes at her lover. For the words that Dupray uttered were enough to frighten older and braver souls than her own; enough, for one thing, to silence the terrible tongue of Crane.

Dupray was saying: "That was how I happened to take the trail at all. I never would have dared to go. I never would have known how to tackle the job, except that Speedy was along. He fought the whole thing out with me. He got south to the town of El Rey. Then, in his makeup as a Mexican, he got into the house, too. I know that much. The people in the town told me—he got in and joined the gang of Bardillo.

"Then the pinch came. I don't know exactly how. But the pinch came, and with those devils closing in on him, I suppose, he still thought about me before he thought about himself. He thought about me, I say, and sent me his last message, which was one word—'Ride'!

"And I rode. I'm not Speedy. If I'd been in his boots and sent him such a message, he would have ridden, all right, but he would have ridden straight in to help me. He would have jumped the wall, tunneled underground, done something to come to my help. But I'm no Speedy. I rode to save my neck. And I barely got away with it, at that.

"I reached the river. I asked questions and sent messages, but no Speedy had crossed the river. No Speedy had come north toward this town.

"Then I got word that Speedy had been spotted. A rumor floated up from El Rey that he'd stolen the Nighthawk from Bardillo."

"He got the Nighthawk?" cried Joshua Crane.

The young man paused, and with scorn and rage he eyed Crane.

"You see what it means?" he demanded hoarsely. "Even after he'd sent me word to run for my life, because he saw danger closing in, he must still have been working at his scheme to get the horse. Why? Because I'd asked him to. Why had I asked him to? Because you made that the price of Sue! Blood! That was what you wanted! And now one of the finest fellows that ever walked the face of the earth—he's gone."

He hung his head and groaned.

"How do you know that he's dead?" asked Joshua Crane. "The fellow that wore that disguise and made a fool of Joshua Crane—it'll take nigh onto all the greasers in Mexico to kill him, young man."

"The news came just a couple of days ago," said Dupray. "The rumor came up from El Rey that Speedy had been shot!"

Joshua Crane put up a gnarled hand and pulled his hat from his head. He said, with bent head, "I kind of see that blame is comin' my way. I've been a hard man to you, Dupray, and a hard father to Sue."

He had raised his head as he said this. Now, in the midst of the only contrite speech that human ears had ever heard him utter, he fell silent. With mouth agape, he stretched out a gaunt arm and pointed to a rider who was coming up the driveway, having just rounded the last turn.

He came on slowly, on a horse that wore neither saddle or bridle, but only a lead rope, knotted about the neck. And he seemed painfully thin, that rider, for the slant afternoon light struck against his face and threw cadaverous shadows under the cheekbones.

"The Nighthawk, by the eternal!" cried Joshua Crane.

"Speedy!" cried Al Dupray, and ran wildly toward the horseman.

_____ 17

FROM THE south came a rider on a long-legged thoroughbred. From the north came a rider on a roach-backed mustang. A splendid fellow was he of the south, a tall man with wide shoulders; his saddle, bridle, golden spurs were all the best that money could buy. A shabby, almost ragged rider was he from the north, but, as they looked at one another across the gully, each knew that he was staring at one of the most formidable men he had ever seen. Only one man had either met more significant; and in each case that exception was the same. It was the force of that unseen third that was bringing them together over a course of many hundreds of miles.

They rode down the banks of the gully to meet in the center of the dry ravine. It was like the naked face of the desert as far as the eye could reach, with only a few greasewood bushes, things that looked like puffs of smoke lying on the ground, rather than substantial vegetation that throws a shadow.

But there is always life in the desert, though it may be hard to find. It is usually deadly or made to flee from death or to pursue it.

There are many rabbits, swifter than any jacks or hares in the world, mere tufts of gray fur with an understringing of light bones and hardy sinews. There are coyotes as well, neighbored by famine that sharpens the wits and steels the patience; and there are the big lobos, the geniuses of the lot, that flourish because their brains are mighty and their souls are great. And always, far above the desert, those small specks and larger ones are floating, the buzzards that wait on the wing for death to arrive.

On an errand of death, likewise, these two riders had come together. The third man had to die; their wits and their hands would devise his destruction.

When they reached the bottom of the shallow draw, the Mexican raised his right hand in a brief salute. "Señor Dupray?" said he.

The frog-faced man from the north looked with unsmiling eyes at the Mexican, and then answered in the same tongue, "I'm Dupray. And you're Bardillo."

"If there were shade here," said Bardillo, "we could dismount and sit while we talk."

"It's just as well not to leave any footprints," replied Dupray.

The Mexican smiled a little and glanced toward the distant, naked horizon.

But Dupray added, "The job we're on doesn't admit any chances. We have to look sharp from the start."

"Well," said Bardillo, "I believe in care as much as you. When men hunt Speedy, they take their lives in their hands."

"Yes," said Dupray, "they take their lives in their hands. The minute we begin the

hunt, there's no insurar
world that would gi
single one."

"True," said B.

His long face gro
emn, and his eyes flasi.

"But what are the chan.
if ours are so bad?"

"He has an even chance aga
us," said Dupray.

"And we each have only half
against him?" said Bardillo.

"We each have half a chance to b.
his," answered Dupray, with much certai.

"Señor Dupray," broke out Bardillo, "if i.
comes to that, I can have twenty or thirty
tried men on the hunt."

"I could have as many as that," said
Dupray. "But numbers are not what count.
Once there was a time when every one of my
men was more valuable than anything money
could buy, but they've fallen off from the
old standard."

Bardillo stared at him, asking, "What do
you mean by that, señor?"

"I mean," said Dupray, "that once Speedy
invaded my camp and made a fool of me,
my authority is gone. I can still pick up men
to follow me, now and then, but, after a job

...ey melt away. They've lost their ...ere was a time when the name ...was enough to bring a hard man a ...d miles. But that time has gone. ...y has done it."

...dillo flushed and was silent for a mo-...t. Then he added, "Since Speedy walked ...o my house and took my great horse, the ...ghthawk, away with him and since I ...unted him through my own hills and he ...rode through my lines—since that time, my men have fallen away from me, too. I have the remnants, but they are hardly worth keeping together. Once I had men who would ride through the gates of hell and bring out a handful of flames! That was the sort of men I had around me, señor."

"I had the same," said Dupray. "They had wits like coyotes and the craft of foxes, but they won't come back to me until the world knows that Speedy is dead and that I had something to do with his death."

"So!" said Bardillo. "The same is true of me. If I can send out word that I've managed the death of Speedy, then I know that my men will come back; perhaps better men than the old ones."

Dupray nodded. "If we can arrange the

trap and take Speedy," said he, "then I want you to get the credit, Bardillo."

"Hah?" exclaimed Bardillo. "All the credit for me? Is that what you mean?"

"I mean that," answered Dupray, though he made a wry face in speaking the words.

"But," said the Mexican, "one of your reasons for wanting him dead is that your men may know that you've had a hand in it."

"True," said Dupray. "But my chief reason for wanting him dead is to please myself. My share in it has to be as secret as possible."

Bardillo shrugged his shoulders, as one bewildered.

"I have a nephew, my sole relation in the world and my sole heir," Dupray went on. "He owes everything he is today to Speedy. It was Speedy that saved him from being hanged and brought him out of jail; it was Speedy who brought up the stallion from your own house for the sake of Al; it's because of Speedy that Al is now a respectable rancher. Even his father-in-law looks up to him a little, simply because Speedy is his friend! If he knew that I'd laid the weight of a finger on Speedy, Al would hunt me down. Now I've told you frankly how the matter goes. If we corner Speedy, you have the credit for it. I give you that as freely as the air you breathe, I insist on it!"

Bardillo jerked up his head with a smile.

"It is not difficult to persuade me," said he. "There is no good reason why we should not work together, particularly as you want me to have all the credit."

"Credit?" said Dupray, his fat, round face wrinkling with incredible malice. "I only want to see his blood run and look down into his eyes when they're as blank and empty as the eyes of a dead fish. You understand, Bardillo?"

"A good hate is more warming to the soul than a long draft of wine," said the Mexican. "My hate for him has made me thin. My ribs stand out like the ribs of a hungry wolf; but your hate for him keeps you fat. We shall be able to work together, Dupray. First, we try to find his trail. Do you know where he is, now?"

"He may be anywhere," said Dupray, gloomily. "He may be singing songs as an entertainer in a Mexican Café; he may be reading fortunes in a gypsy crew; he may be a juggler in a circus; he may be riding the rods of a freight train, or the blind baggage of an express, traveling simply because it makes him nervous to be still for too long at a time. He may be playing cards with as crooked a gambler as himself. Wherever there are men who live by their wits on the stupidity of ordinary men, there you're apt to find Speedy living on the crooks as the crooks live on the honest men."

Bardillo stared, but nodded.

"I've heard all of that before," said he. "And I can't understand. Why is it? To punish the criminals and save the honest men?"

"No!" shouted Dupray, in a burst of emotion, "but simply because there's only one bread, one meat, one drink for him."

"What is that?" asked Bardillo, frowning with wonder.

"Danger!" cried Dupray. "Danger is what he lives for. Always danger! Is it dangerous to rob a robber? It is! That is why he robbed you; that is why he robbed me! Curse him!"

He had to stop speaking for a moment, because he was choked by his passion. Then he resumed, while Bardillo was silent also. "As for finding his trail—look!" He pointed up.

"What do you see, Bardillo?"

"Nothing but a buzzard in the sky."

"Could you trail that buzzard through the clouds, then?"

"Why, no, of course not."

"How could we bring it down to the ground?"

"With a dead bait," said Bardillo instantly.

"And that's what we'll have to do with Speedy," said Dupray. "But not with a dead bait—a living one!"

_____ 18

BARDILLO CONSIDERED this suggestion for a moment. "A living bait?" he repeated. "Well, and who will be the bait?"

"How can I tell?" asked Dupray, with irritation. "If I had a perfect scheme and a perfect trap for him, would I have asked you to meet me here?"

Bardillo, offended in turn, was silent, but at length he said, "We must use our brains together. It is a problem, like the problem of a mathematician. We shall accomplish a scheme together."

"Perhaps," muttered Dupray tartly.

"This," said the Mexican, pursing his thick and projecting lower lip, "is the chief thing to remember, as it seems to me. He loves danger more than he loves life. Is that true?"

"That is true," rumbled Dupray, his head hanging thoughtfully to one side, his brow puckered.

"And if there's a criminal to be thwarted, that is the special game of Speedy?"

"Why do you ask?" snapped Dupray. "What has he done to you? What has he done to me? It speaks for itself."

"It speaks for itself," said Bardillo, growing calmer, as the other grew more and more excited.

"Lost causes are what he wants," said the great Charles Dupray. "The more completely lost, the better he likes 'em. There was John Wilson, running amuck as a gunman. He tamed Wilson and made a good rancher out of him. Why? Partly because the man's wife asked him to help, but chiefly because he'd thought of a way of scaring Wilson into good behavior. That way was to ride him up to my camp. Both their necks were inside the noose—but still Speedy got them safely away! We have to tempt him, Bardillo. That's the bait!"

"What's the greatest temptation he could have?" asked the other.

"The most dangerous task in the world."

"And what would be the most dangerous thing in the world for him?" went on Bardillo. "To come into your camp, or into mine. Is that true?"

Dupray shrugged his shoulders.

"Invite him up? Speedy is not a fool," said he. "He's almost a fool, throwing away his life every day, as he does, but he's not as gross a fool as that."

"We'll give him a reason, then, for going up to your camp. A good, sufficient reason."

"What reason is sufficient to make a man commit suicide?" asked the other.

"He has many disguises," suggested Bardillo.

"I know most of his parts, and he knows that I know 'em. Even if he put on some new disguise, I'd recognize his voice, if I so much as heard him whisper in the dark, and he knows that I'd recognize him, too."

"All the better," said the Mexican. "Then he'll have to go to your camp without trying at a disguise."

"That may be," said the other. "Yes, when the sun sinks at noon and the moon dances jigs with the Great Bear. What sort of nonsense are you talking, Bardillo?"

"It's not nonsense. The greater the danger, the more he'll be tempted, and that I know. Let me tell you what happened in my house. When he appeared before me, one of my men recognized him and warned him that in five minutes he would warn me. Yet Speedy did not use those five minutes in getting as far as possible from the house. Instead, he used up the time in merely stealing the great horse from my men. He stole it, and he rode off while the alarm bell was beating. *Hai*, Dupray, think of the nerves of that man, like steel, enduring the passing of the minutes, while he tried, a man on foot, to capture the stallion, though I had two guards with it."

"How did he manage to take it, then?" asked Dupray, his eyes wide with curiosity.

"Don't ask me," groaned the other. "I go more than half mad, when I think about his name even. Only, once he is challenged to go to your camp, knowing that you would know him even through all of his disguises, I think that the more he pondered on it, the more he would be attracted by the thought. The danger would lure him, like an imp of the perverse. I am sure of it. There remains only the bait to be found. As for that, you still have men with you?"

"Only one worthy of the old days," said Dupray, gloomily again.

"Who is that?"

" 'Bones' is his nickname, the only name I have for him."

"What is he like?"

"Bones? Bones is the cruellest fiend north or south of the Rio Grande."

"Well, all the better, then. Does Speedy know him?"

"He wanted to cut Speedy's throat when Speedy was with us in my camp."

"Still, Bones may be the very man for the thing I have in mind, Dupray."

"What is it?"

"We send out word into the world where Speedy lives—the world of tramps and drifting criminals, eh?"

"Yes, that's his world," agreed Dupray.

"Then, we send out word among those people that Speedy is wanted in a certain town, where a certain man would give a great deal to talk with him. In the meantime, we provide the man. Then—"

"You think that Speedy will be lured on by any such idea as that?" said Dupray, sneering. "I tell you, Bardillo, he might come to look the place over, but he would come like a shadow, with the eyes of a hawk and look over the man and the place with the eyes of a hawk before he let himself be known. You could never set a trap around a bait as clumsy as that."

"Let me finish, Dupray," answered the other. "My idea is simply this: we hire a trustworthy man, who will send out word that a reward will be given to the man who brings in Speedy. When Speedy arrives, the hired man speaks to him like this: 'Señor Speedy, we have a desperate need of a desperate man. No one but you will do. We need a man who will adventure into the camp of Charles Dupray. We send for you, because we know perfectly well that you have done the thing before.'"

"And Speedy," broke in Dupray, "simply answers that he's not such a great fool as to try a thing like that, eh?"

"Speedy," went on the Mexican, "may be surprised, and may say so, but he's sure to be interested. What is the reason for the errand to the camp of Dupray? Why, the reason is that our agent—he should be a lawyer, by the way—has word that a client in the East, a very rich man, is casting about for an heir, and finds that all of his next of kin are dead. But he has seen a picture of Bones—would that do? Could anyone have been apt to see a picture of Bones in a newspaper, say?"

"His face has been in the papers often enough," growled Charley Dupray. "What of that?"

"Well, then, the rich man has seen a picture of Bones in the newspaper. And he has recognized in it a great likeness to the features of others of his family."

"A pretty family, then," said Dupray, "because Bones earns his nickname. He's an ugly, skinny, buck-toothed devil."

"All the more reason to be vain. Ugly men are always sure to think of their personal appearance a good deal."

"True," said Dupray. "Bardillo, I begin to understand. We hire a lawyer, who gets in touch with Speedy and tells him that the disposal of a very considerable fortune hangs upon getting word at once to Bones. But Bones is wanted by the law. He cannot be advertised for openly. It is a secret messenger who must strive to find him. And that messenger must find him in the camp of the outlaw, Dupray. Then Bones must be persuaded to come down to the town. Is that it? To come down to the town, and then he will be put in the way of getting his hungry hands on his mysterious patrimony, eh?"

"You have the idea," said Bardillo.

Dupray shook his head, but presently he

began to frown once more with profound consideration.

"I don't know," said he. "It may be the very trick that'll catch him—the thing that will pull that buzzard down out of the sky!"

"I'm sure of it," said Bardillo. "I begin to feel the thing working in my bones, as if I were Speedy!"

"To bring good news to Bones, the throat-cutter," murmured Charles Dupray. "There's a fellow, at least, that I could count on. I tell you that he'd give up ten years of his life for the hope of putting a knife into the heart of Speedy. That's why he's stayed with me— because he was with me, he was in the same hut with Speedy and Wilson the night they came!"

Dupray began to laugh a little, swaying from side to side in his saddle, in the excess of his mirth.

Bardillo said, in the most businesslike manner, "It begins to seem that we have a trap to lay and bait for it, then?"

"Besides," said Dupray, "I know the very lawyer in the very town who will take my money as a bribe and do my work, no matter what it is. I know the man, Bardillo. I know the man."

"Shall we ride on, then, together?" asked Bardillo.

"We'll ride on together," answered Dupray. "Bardillo, we should have met face to face before this. But it took the devil himself walking the earth to bring us together."

They rode up the side of the draw. A strong, hot wind came up from the desert and rained a volley of flying sand in their faces, but they paid no heed to it. Happiness and the hope of a great triumph were shining in their faces.

_____ 19

IN THE offices of Raymond & Raymond, lawyers, in the town of Rusty Creek, Mr. Henry Raymond, a member of that firm, leaned back in his chair, on a day, and, resting his heels on the edge of his desk, he stared out through his office window and off into the sky.

When he saw a shadow appear on the outside of the clouded glass of his door, with a long practiced movement he jerked his feet from the desktop, unclasped his hands from behind his head, and swayed forward over his desk. When the door opened, he was in the midst of heaping papers, writing busily.

"One moment, please!" he called in a cheerful voice.

Then he turned, still holding his pen, took off his glasses, and peered with a sleek smile at the stranger.

This stranger was a fellow of middle weight, slenderly built, and very roughly clad. His skin was as brown as a berry; his eyes were very dark and bright; and what was the distinguishing feature of a most unexciting appearance, otherwise, was a certain electric tingle of physical well-being that was exhaled from the youth and touched Henry Raymond even at a distance.

The stranger had his hat in his hand. He might be twenty-five. Raymond's plump forehead gradually clouded. He reserved his own pleasant facial expressions for creditors and clients who seemed likely to be able to pay a large bill. He did not get many clients in the course of a year. When he did, he knew how to put the screws on them and extract all that was possible.

"Good morning, Mr. Raymond," said the stranger.

"Good morning," said Raymond. "Is there anything that I can do for you?"

"No, sir," said the other. "I came because I was sent for, I think."

"Sent for?" said Raymond. "Some mistake, I'm afraid. I haven't sent for you, son. Who said that I did?"

"A fellow by the name of Lank Wallace," said the young man.

"Lank Wallace? Lank Wallace?" said the attorney, frowning as he concentrated on the name. "No, I never knew a man by that name. Where did he reach you?"

"In Fort Craven," said the man.

"Fort Craven? Let me see—why, the only Fort Craven I know of is fifteen hundred miles from here!"

"That's about the distance," said the youth.

"The devil!" exploded Raymond. "You mean to tell me that an unknown person called Lank Wallace called on you in Fort Craven and told you that I, Henry Raymond, wanted to see you? And you came fifteen hundred miles on account of that message?"

"Well," said the other, "it wasn't exactly like that. I was ready to hop off in this direction, anyway."

"Ah, hum," muttered Raymond. "I see. One of the knights of the road. Is that your occupation?"

"You mean—am I a tramp?"

"That's a hard word," said Raymond carelessly.

"I'm a tramp most of the time, if you mean by that, a man without any steady occupation," said the young fellow.

"Tell me," said Raymond, "what Lank Wallace looked like? What sort of man was he? This is one of the strangest stories that I ever heard. Let's have the truth. It will serve you better than any lie, I can assure you!"

"Why," said the other, "Lank Wallace was about six feet three. He had ears as big as your hands, and a nose bigger than both his ears put together. His shoulders were stooped a little, and he had the largest hands that I ever saw."

"That's a pretty picture," said the lawyer. "Lank Wallace, eh? Why do you say 'was' when you speak of him?"

"He used to be, but now he's only 'was,' " said the stranger. "He was making the trip southwest with me, but on the way he started to play tag with a railroad detective, and the detective won the game."

"You mean—"

"Tagged him with a .45-caliber chunk of lead, right between the shoulders. Yes, he won that game."

"By heaven, he murdered Lank, eh?"

"Nobody could murder Lank," replied the stranger slowly. "Wallace was wanted for too many things that meant anything from life to a hangman's rope. But the detective didn't know that. He simply took a chance and happened to be right."

"Ah ha," exclaimed Raymond. "Something will happen to that railroad detective one of these days."

"Something did happen to him, just after he killed Lank Wallace," said the stranger.

"What?"

"Why," said the other, looking Raymond steadily in the eye, but speaking very slowly, "why, he had a lot of bad luck all in a bunch. He had about enough bad luck to last him the rest of his life."

A glint of appreciation appeared in the eyes of the lawyer.

"What kind of bad luck do you mean?" asked Raymond.

The other looked steadily back at him. "Oh, just bad luck," said he.

Raymond twisted a little in his chair, like one who is close to interesting information that still cannot be fully revealed.

"All right," he said at last. "You can keep

your secrets. I suppose you used a gun on the big cop?"

"I never carry a gun," said the youth mildly.

"Well," muttered Raymond, "let it go. But tell me, what about the message that this late Lank Wallace gave you from me?"

"Why," said the other, "he said that you wanted to see a fellow named Speedy."

Raymond started. "Speedy?" he exclaimed. "Ah, I see! It's true that I've offered a five-hundred-dollar reward to anybody who'll bring in Speedy. Mind you, though, it doesn't go except to the man who brings him in! That is to say, to the man who marches him into this office."

"Five hundred is a lot of money," said the young fellow. He nodded his head, as though considering the sum.

"If you know anything about where I can get in touch with him," said Raymond, "I'd shell out a few round dollars for that, too; or else you might be able to go wherever you've heard he may be and bring him here to me. Though I guess," he added with a laugh, "that it would take a dozen like you to get Speedy."

"Oh, no," said the youth. "I'd be enough."

143

Raymond stared. Then he laughed again, derisively.

"You'd be enough? For that manhandler?"

"Yes, I'd be enough. I'm Speedy, you see," said the youth.

Raymond leaped from his chair.

"Why don't you say that you're the devil on wheels, while you're about it?" he demanded angrily.

Then, suddenly, he began to remember the descriptions of this famous man, as he had heard them—a fellow not over twenty-five, looking perhaps three or four years younger, a face unseamed and unwritten upon by time, of middle height, and of a slenderness that quite belied the sinewy strength he had shown so many times, with features of an almost feminine delicacy and beauty, a very suntanned skin, a gentle voice and manner, and eyes very dark, and yet very bright.

As he summed up these remarks, he could see that the ragged young fellow now standing before him answered each particular, and yet he burst out, "It's not possible. You're not Speedy—the Speedy who's wrecked so many gunfighters and who—"

He paused again. The other was shaking his head in a deprecatory manner.

"I'm Speedy," he repeated, in the pause.

"You're Speedy?" said the lawyer. "Well, do something to prove it. I mean, I've got to have some proof. This is an important business that I want to talk to you about!"

"Well," said Speedy, "I don't know what I can do."

"The real Speedy," said the lawyer, "can do anything with his hands. He's magic. Throws a knife straighter than crack shots throw bullets; juggles half a dozen things at once; spins a crystal ball on the tip of one finger without letting it fall off."

"Well," said Speedy, "if that's enough, here's the crystal."

It appeared in his hand at the same moment, though Raymond could not see from what spot it had been produced.

The young fellow balanced it on the tip of a slender forefinger and, with a twist, started it spinning. His somber, long-lashed eyes were lowered, while he considered the spinning ball.

"Go on, now that you've got it going. Read my mind for me, Speedy, because, by thunder, I see that you're the man that I want!"

"You cross my palm with silver, first," said the other.

"Here's a dollar," said Raymond, chuckling. "This is rich. Go ahead, Speedy, and let me have a look at the inside of my mind."

"I'm to read your mind, your thought at this moment?" asked Speedy.

"Yes," said the lawyer.

There was a pause, while Speedy continued to stare steadily into the flicker of light in the center of the crystal, a shining streak like the glimmer of a little polished sword blade, trembling to and fro.

Then he began to speak, in a quiet monotonous voice.

"You are thinking," he said, "that if I'm fool enough to do what you propose to me, it will be a tidy sum of money in your pocket."

He caught the ball in the palm of his hand and made the big crystal disappear again into nothingness—not up his sleeve, surely, but where? The magic of that hand was far swifter than the gestures of the swiftest eye.

Raymond's exultation had disappeared, as he listened to the answer.

He was so taken by surprise that he did not even have wit enough to protest at first. He could only gasp out, "How the devil did you know that—"

Then he paused, agape, realizing that he

had committed himself with those few words too far to draw back.

But Speedy looked up at him with a peculiarly quick, flashing smile that had no malice in it.

"It's all right, Raymond," he said. "I know that you're not in the deal. I know that somebody else is behind it. What is the main idea, anyway?"

20

IT SEEMED to Raymond that he was truly trapped between the devil and the deep blue sea. He had before him a man whose formidable qualities were famous all through the West; and he himself had been suddenly tricked, thrown off his guard, and forced into a confession which promised to ruin everything. However, he did not instantly give up the game.

Henry Raymond was one of those liars who weave only a certain percentage of falsehood into their remarks. So skillfully is it done that even the most expert eye is often deceived and it looks as though all is the one true, real, artistic pattern. Now, when he was cornered, this talent came to his aid. He saw, with a flash of genius, that his partial downfall could be turned into his salvation, if what he had heard of this Speedy were correct.

He burst out, in a tone of hearty relief, "Well, it's a dirty business, and I'm glad that you saw through it, Speedy. I don't think that I could have gone through with the rotten game, anyway!"

"Dupray, eh?" asked Speedy gently.

"Sit down," said Raymond, himself rising and striding up and down the room. "Sit down, Speedy. I'm going to show you the whole cursed business. I'm going to make a clean breast of it. It's not the first time that I've soiled my hands for Dupray. But it's going to be the last time."

He stopped and faced Speedy suddenly, as the latter leaned lightly against the desk.

"Speedy," he blurted out, in a passion of remorse, as it were, "you'll be thinking that I'm a hound. You'll be about nine parts right, too. But what's important to me, just now, is to do you right in this business. It is Dupray. But how in the devil did you guess it? Or can you really read the mind?"

"I only look in the crystal," said Speedy with the faintest of smiles. "I only look in the crystal and try to understand what I see there—and what I see is that Dupray is dreaming night and day about killing me."

"He hates you, Speedy," said Raymond. "I never heard of anybody hating another man the way Dupray hates you. You broke up his gang for him. I think that's the chief reason."

"I didn't break it up, exactly," said Speedy. "I gave it a jolt, though. That's one reason he hates me. The other reason is more important, though."

"What's the other reason?" asked Henry Raymond.

"Well," replied Speedy, "it's the reason that the wolf hates the dog, and the dog hates the wolf. We're different kinds."

Raymond stepped closer, summoned a frown as though he were making a point to a jury of twelve good men and true, and raised his voice and let it ring.

"Speedy," he said, "Dupray would sell his soul to the devil to put a knife through your heart."

Speedy nodded. "And just now," he commented, "Dupray will make his big effort, eh?"

"I think he will," said the lawyer.

"The hate has been piling up in him, piling up like water, and the dam is apt to break. But that's all right," said Speedy. "I knew that the crisis would come, sooner or later, and then one of us would have to die. I'm sorry about it, though."

"Sorry? To kill a beast like that, Speedy?" asked Raymond.

"I'll tell you why," said Speedy. "His nephew, Al Dupray, is a friend of mine. A great friend. And if his uncle's blood is on my hands—well, that's the end of things between Al and me, of course."

Raymond sighed and shook his head.

"It's a mighty hard one," he admitted.

"Yes, it's hard," replied Speedy. "But I have a feeling that the finish has come at last, for Dupray and me. One of us has to go."

"If that's your feeling," said the other, "then back up out of this job, Speedy. Because Dupray has laid the trap for you."

"What trap, man?"

"Why, there's a sick man back East with a few millions lying around loose and no heir in the world except one of the men in Dupray's gang. You understand? Dupray knows about it. But he won't pass the word to Bones—that's the name of the crook who could be the millionaire!—and no one else can get to Bones to let him know about his good luck. You see? As a matter of fact I've got the whole correspondence here, all the letters and telegrams that Littleton—that's the millionaire—has sent to me."

He reached into a drawer of the desk and tumbled a confused mass of documents onto the face of the varnished wood.

"There you are—all that!" said the lawyer. "Littleton sent his own personal counsel out here, all the way. When the man couldn't locate Bones, he turned the business over to me. Well, I've located Bones, easily enough. I thought that my only job was to get word to him, in one way or another. Then, in comes Dupray himself and tells me how I can be worth ten thousand dollars to him."

The glance of Speedy fell upon a line of a telegram which was only partially exposed, saying, "Time remaining short. Hurry. Inquiry following."

"Ten thousand dollars?" said Speedy. "Is that the price he pays for me?"

Raymond flushed a little.

"He gave me five thousand as a retainer," said he. "And he gave me a promise of five thousand more. Do you despise me, Speedy?"

Speedy shook his head.

"It's all in the line of business," said he.

"I don't despise you, Raymond. If you've been working with crooks like Dupray, you've probably simply decided that the only thing for you to be concerned about is doing your job in the most effective way."

"You put it kindly, but I know what I think of myself," said the lawyer. "However, the point now is, how can I help you, Speedy?"

"Help me?" said Speedy. Then he added, a little coldly, "I haven't paid you any retaining fee, Raymond."

The lawyer flushed again.

"Perhaps you'll trust me to give you my best advice, free of charge, Speedy. I'm not quite as bad as you may think."

Speedy waved away the thought of such a condemnatory attitude on his part.

He said, "What's exactly the plan of Dupray?"

"Well, his plan is exactly this: the fellow back East, Littleton, is lying near dead, waiting to get word to his heir out here in the West. That heir is a crook working in Dupray's gang, wanted by the law, or the rope, maybe. Dupray says that the one thing to do is to get hold of Speedy and say to him, 'Everybody knows that you got to Dupray's gang before. Well, try the same thing again, and make yourself even more famous. Get to Bones, tell him about his inheritance and do it fast, because there's a dying man back East, waiting from hour to hour and fighting for his breath.' "

A shudder ran through the body of Speedy. He closed his eyes and puckered his brow with pain.

"That poor devil Littleton!" he muttered.

A single flash of triumph appeared in the face of Raymond, as he saw that one part of his lie, at least, had succeeded.

Then Speedy added: "And the gain of Dupray is that when I start hunting for Bones, he'll be on the lookout?"

"That's it. He's expecting you now. He's on the lookout every minute. Oh, he's waiting like a cat for a bird!"

Speedy nodded.

"It's not a bad scheme, take it all in all," said he. "Brains behind it, plenty of brains, and it might have worked, too. However—"

He turned toward the door and laid his hand on the knob of it. Bitter disappointment darkened the brow of Henry Raymond.

But, with his hand on the knob of the door, Speedy paused and shook his head. "That Littleton, that poor devil," he murmured. He turned suddenly around.

"Look here, Raymond," said he. "How old is Littleton?"

"Forty-three."

"That's young enough. What's the matter with him?"

Raymond made a wry face and laid a hand over his heart; he made the hand flutter like a falling leaf.

"Not a bit of good. Heart's no good. Littleton just lies and gasps," he said. "He ought to have been dead weeks ago. But you know how it is. Will of iron. He won't die until he knows that he's found the man who'll get his money. You see?"

Speedy groaned aloud.

"I wish that I hadn't heard that!" he said.

"It's a bad business," sighed Raymond.

"Because," said Speedy, "it means that I've got to go, whether I want to or not."

"Go where?" asked Raymond innocently.

"To the Dupray camp to find Bones. Any idea where the camp is now?"

"To the Dupray camp? To find Bones? You're not crazy, Speedy, are you? Don't you understand what I said, that Dupray will be on the lookout every minute?"

"Oh, I understand," said Speedy, almost wearily. "I understand all that, but Littleton, that poor devil of a Littleton."

He sighed and shook his head again.

"Bones is a cold-blooded cutthroat," he said. "But I've got to try to get the word through to him!"

_____ 21

HIGH UP among the mountains, where peaks gave back on three sides and on the fourth the hills sloped away toward the plains, set in at the foot of the loftiest peaks, there was a lake. It was as blue a lake as one could find in all the ranges of the Rockies.

It had the appropriate setting of a belt of meadow grass around one side of it, with a mighty array of trees bordering the opposite shore. One could sit beside that lake all the day long and every instant see changes, as clouds blew over or as the water trembled in the wind.

Charles Dupray, by the side of the lake, sat on the top of a large boulder, but he was not looking at the beauties which that mirror revealed. Instead, he was puffing at a pipe and looking down at a letter which he held tightly in his right hand.

It was not a very long letter, but the bandit read and reread it with singular enjoyment.

"Hey, Bones!" he called at last.

There was a lean-to built against the trunk of a giant tree, and out of the lean-to appeared a tall, gaunt form, stooped in the shoulders, narrow of chest, prodigiously long of arm and vast of hand.

The outthrust of his upper teeth kept him smiling continually, but his eyes were as steady and bright and evil as the eyes of a snake.

"Well?" said Bones.

"Where's Bardillo?" asked the leader.

"I dunno."

"Don't you?"

"No. I ain't a watchdog over no greaser," said Bones.

"Vincente Bardillo's something more than a greaser," suggested the great Dupray, and frowned.

When Bones saw that expression of anger appear on the flat frog face of the leader, he shrugged his shoulders and subsided.

"Yeah," he said, "I guess it's all right. Bardillo's a good shot, anyway. So's that Diego Marañon that he's got with him. They were shooting at rocks that they threw up for each other last evening. They can shoot, what

I mean. Only, nothing's coming of all this here business."

"You mean that Speedy won't come here?"

"That's what I mean."

The other smiled.

"Go get Bardillo for me, Bones," said he.

"Sure, he's just over the hill, maybe," said Bones.

He strode off, lifting himself rapidly along the slope with his gigantic strides; he loomed vast on the top of the hills, then disappeared in two steps. Presently he returned, striding as rapidly as before; behind him came the two Mexicans, Bardillo almost as tall as Bones, but much heavier, and Marañon shorter, older, grayer.

When they came up, Dupray nodded to them.

Then he said, "It's all right. Speedy's coming."

"The devil he is!" exclaimed Bones.

Dupray looked at him with a grin.

"Listen to this," said he, and read aloud:

Dear Dupray: Speedy arrived. That keen devil saw through the outside layers of the scheme. He knew that something was in the air. I was cornered and had to confess that I was working with you. But

I made out that there was a fellow in the East called Littleton, a man dying of heart disease, and fighting off his death until he hears that his heir, Bones, has been located. That picture of the dying man was too much for Speedy. He knows that you're on the lookout for him, but he's made up his mind to try to get past you to Bones, and take Bones East to Littleton. You won't believe it, but it's true.

I've told Speedy just where to find you. He's going ahead slowly, watching every step of the way, because he expects that you'll tackle him almost at any point going up to the camp. I'm sending this letter ahead by the relay that we arranged. It ought to get to you twenty-four hours before Speedy is anywhere near. He's a cool devil and quick as a flash. However, the idea of the dying Littleton was too much for his tender heart, and the fool has gone off on his last adventure. At least, it ought to be his last if you do your part as well as I've done mine.

Another thing. He knows that you're in the deal, but he doesn't dream, so far as I know, that Bardillo and Marañon are also on the reception committee.

Bones ought to be grateful for another chance to cut his throat, and I hope that Bones has his way because, if Speedy comes out of this alive and finds out that when I pretended to confess I was only telling a more complicated lie than before, he'll never go off my trail until he's broken me to bits. Yours hopefully,

Henry Raymond.

"What do you think of that?" asked Dupray.

"I think," said Bardillo, "that any lawyer who writes words like that, even in code, is a fool!"

"Raymond is not a fool," said Dupray. "But he's not as bright as he thinks he is. However, that was a useful set of lies that he told. Speedy is coming; Speedy knows that I'm trying to trap him, but Speedy does not know that Bardillo is on the ground with Marañon, and Speedy does not, most of all, realize that the man to whom he's bringing the great news is part of the trap that'll catch him. See that, Bones?"

Bones actually smiled in earnest, his lips stretching, and his upper teeth thrusting out with a white sheen. "I've always kind of had an idea," said he, "that I'd have the carving of that bird before the finish of things. I've always sort of had a hunch that he'd be my meat."

Dupray grinned in turn contentedly.

"Bones," he said, "you're a comfort, is what you are. But let me tell you all, no matter how many advantages we have, Speedy is still something to be handled with care."

Bardillo waved his hand and his long face lengthened still more, his thick lower lip thrust out.

"There's no danger that we'll be overconfident," he said. "Speedy is fire that's burned us all, but this time I've an idea that he's riding to his finish. Eh, Marañon?"

The older man looked up with a start, as though recalling himself out of distant thoughts.

Then he remarked, "There's this much for us all to say: Speedy is so accomplished a man that the killing of him will bring honor to all four of us. It will be a great day for us all. Bardillo, we ought to hurry forward and meet him on the way."

"Where?" asked Bardillo.

"At the crossroads hotel, down there at Clive's Corner," suggested Dupray. "That's the place to wait for him."

"I don't know the place," said Bardillo.

"I do," said Dupray. "We have plenty of time to get there and explore. I know the people. They know me. I've helped them with hard cash and harder advice. One of their boys wants to join me. I'll take him, too, when he's a little more seasoned. It's a perfect place. And I know every step and inch of it. Bones, rustle up the horses, will you?"

"I'll saddle 'em," said Bones, "just as if I was gonna go to my wedding."

He strode off, and Bardillo smiled upon Dupray.

"Charles," said he, "I think that Señor Speedy is riding on his last journey."

"The life he's been leading," said Dupray, "he had to come to the end of the trail sooner or later. What I'm wondering now is—which one of us will have the luck to send the right bullet into his heart or between his eyes?"

Marañon muttered something under his breath.

"What is it?" asked Bardillo. "Speak out, Diego."

"Why," said Marañon, "it's simply this. There are four of us, all acting together, all good fighting men, all armed to the teeth, and up the trail is coming one young fellow without even a revolver. Yet I suppose all four of us are more nervous than that young devil knows how to be!"

THE MORNING is delayed by the shadows of the mountains, and the night is hurried on; so it was that even before sunset, Speedy found that Clive's Corner was a dreary place. The white tops of the peaks were still gilded with fire, but the ravines that crossed at Clive's Corner were flooded with dimness. Looking up was like looking from the bottom of a well.

There was promise of a stormy night, as well. The wind was beginning to whine on a thin, high note that would have had peculiar meaning to a violinist.

Speedy gave a glance at the unpainted, unkempt shack known as the Clive Hotel. Then he shrugged his shoulders.

It looked to him like a proper setting for a murder. Then he went to the rear, found the stable, and, in the murky interior of the barn a shadowy figure cleaning the stalls with a fork. He came to the door and stood, fork in hand, looking down at Speedy. He was a big young man, but with a head that was hardly more than a handful and red hair that bristled. Small as his face was, it was all mouth and jaw. Nose and eyes and forehead were pinched together, crowding one another.

"Yeah?" said he to Speedy, and hitched at his one suspender.

"I'd like to put up here for the night," said Speedy.

"Would you? I reckon you might put your hoss up in the barn, anyways," said the lout.

Speedy looked at the other again. It was a magnificent body. A heavyweight wrestler might have been proud of that swelling chest and those mighty shoulders.

"Hotel's not crowded?" suggested Speedy politely.

"Crowded? Ain't had a visitor to pay a penny for ten days. Here, I'll take your bronc."

He took the reins and led the mustang into the barn. Speedy did not follow, but lingered on the threshold to peer into the shadows and make out the lay of the land. It was an old custom which had now become a fixed habit with him. Small details, well imprinted on the mind, had saved his life a score of times. The same sort of information might save him again, on this night, for he knew that he had entered into the territory of the enemy.

When he was sure that he had probed the dimness long enough to have made out the main features of the barn, he went to the back door of the hotel and knocked.

A woman's voice called out for him to enter, and he stepped into a kitchen where a brawny woman of middle age or more was rolling out biscuit dough into a thin slab.

"Yeah?" she said, looking up at Speedy through some ragged frontlets of streaming hair.

"I'm looking for a room for the night," said Speedy.

She continued to stare at him for a moment. Then, leaning still on the rolling pin, she called out, "Hey, pa! Come here!" A dragging step approached from a front room, and then there appeared a man of fifty years with a dignified carriage and a tobacco-stained beard. He carried a knife in one hand and the stick he had been whittling in the other. He put knife and stick in the fingers of one hand, took off his spectacles, and stared at Speedy.

"Wants a room for the night," said she.

"Ad!" called the man. "Hey, Ad! Where are you. Oh, A-a-a-d!"

The woman had begun to roll the dough once more. The light, which struggled out of the smoked chimney of the lamp, only partially conquered the gloom in the room.

"Ad!" called the man again.

"Comin'!" answered a voice.

A door opened nearby, and let in the sound of the voice and heels scuffling along the floor.

"Comin', Mr. Clive!" called the voice again.

"You're always comin', and you ain't never here," said Pa Clive. "Here's a gent that wants to be put up for the night. Go and show him a room, get out the register, sign him up, and do what you had oughta do to make a gentleman comfortable."

He turned and addressed his remarks to Speedy.

"You take the way things is today, stranger, it ain't hardly possible to get no good servants. A gentleman, he can't hardly live a decent life, because there ain't no servants."

He smoothed his yellow-stained beard and looked more dignified than ever.

And Speedy followed Ad out of the room

165

and up the stairs. She was a poor nearsighted drudge with a mouth that was always hanging open and eyes that appeared stunned by all that they beheld.

The room was what he expected to find. There was a washstand with an oval linoleum mat in front of it, the linoleum surfacing long ago worn through and the tough inner fibers showing. There was a cot decorated with two brass knobs at its head, only one knob was off. There was no table of any kind; there was no closet. Nails, hammered into the walls, could serve all purposes for accommodating clothes.

Ad, the hotel drudge, fumbled for and found the lamp, lighted it, regulated the flame, and then shaded her eyes with a fat, greasy, shapeless hand. She stared at Speedy, mouth open, eyes bewildered.

"Might you be wantin' anything, mister?" she asked.

He asked for hot water and was glad to see her out of the room. When she disappeared, he went to the window and looked out. The kitchen was in a penthouse at the rear of the building, and the edge of that sloping roof was about six feet away from the edge of the window.

A man might stand on the window sill and

jump for the roof, if he were pressed to leave that room otherwise than by the door. Again, an active man could hang from the window sill at the length of his arms, and swing himself across the space, if he were very agile. Landing in that way there would be much less noise. Landing on stockinged feet as he, Speedy, knew how to land, there would be no noise at all, no more than is made by a prowling cat.

When he had finished this survey and noted again the distance and the angle toward the barn, he regarded the dark masses of the pine woods that marched down toward the hotel on all sides. Above there were the vast slopes of the mountains and the shining summits high above the place.

There was something suggestive about this picture, but he did not stop to work out a meaning for it; Ad, the drudge, had just come back carrying some lukewarm water in a pail. She brought a piece of yellow laundry soap, as well, and with this he scrubbed himself thoroughly.

Then he went downstairs and found Mr. Clive waiting for him in the sitting room. Mr. Clive had put on a coat, in the meantime, and combed his beard, but had not washed it. He was revealed sitting close to a lamp on a center table, with a large volume spread out before him on his crossed knees.

He looked up, took off his glasses, located Speedy, put on the glasses again, and resumed his apparent study of the book. He turned two pages together—a fact that the unerring eye of Speedy at once detected—and continued to peruse, as though lost in the contents.

Speedy stood before the darkening window and teetered up and down on his toes.

Presently the volume closed, the pages slipping loudly together.

"That's a bright man that wrote that book," said Mr. Clive. "A mighty bright man, and yet he went and made his mistakes, too."

Speedy glanced toward the book and saw the title in large letters: *The History of Abrams County* by Fletcher Phineas.

"Mistakes, eh?" Speedy murmured.

"Lotta mistakes, too. There's what he says about old man Wheeler. Wheeler didn't kill Traxton with a shotgun. Wheeler, he would've despised to use a shotgun on man-size game. No, sir, I could tell you what I've seen in my time."

"I'd like to know," said Speedy.

The host settled back in his chair, and

thrust his thumbs into the armholes of his waistcoat.

"Seventy-two ain't young, would you say?" he asked.

"No," said Speedy.

"I've seen old man Wheeler, when he was seventy-two years old, stand out under a tree and take up his old Kentucky rifle, his hands wobbling till he found the bead. Then, him and his old arms and his hands and the gun, all turning into one rock, I've seen him shoot, and I've seen the squirrel fall a hundred feet out of the tree. You go there to the window, will you?"

It was only a half turn of his body for Speedy to look out at the window again. "See that sugarloaf?"

"Yes," replied Speedy.

"Got a big old bald-faced pine right on a line with the sugarloaf?"

"Yes."

"Well, sir, that's the very tree that I seen old man Wheeler shoot the squirrel out of, just to prove that I ain't no liar."

He said this proudly, and then he added, "But you take a man like that Fletcher Phineas, he was young and he was smart. He was educated pretty good, too, as a matter of fact. He was pleasant and he was agreeable, too, but he made mistakes. When he says that old man Wheeler shot Traxton with a shotgun, he was wrong. I didn't see the body, but I know Wheeler."

Speedy nodded absently.

Mr. Clive went on: "But I was sorry for Phineas. He was young, that was mostly the trouble with him. And Bill Cather, I've always said, was dead wrong, he was just kind of hasty, when he went and killed Phineas for the writing of this book."

"Why did he kill Phineas, then?"

"Why, it was for something like saying that Bill Cather had a father that had done time, or something like that."

"It wasn't true, eh?"

"Why, it was true, all right, but, as Bill says, he didn't mind his old man being in jail, as long as he didn't get into a book about it. Bill took to brooding on it, and pretty soon he just had to go and kill Phineas. It was too bad. Me, personal, I always spoke up and said that it was too bad."

Speedy nodded.

"What happened to Bill Cather?" he asked.

"To Bill?" said the hotel man.

"Yes."

"Why, I dunno. What should've happened to Cather?"

"I mean to say," asked Speedy, "what happened to him after the killing of young Phineas, who wrote that history of the county?"

"What happened to Cather after that?" said the other, still somewhat puzzled. "Why, nothing happened to him. What would've happened to him?"

"I thought he might have been run in for murder," suggested Speedy.

"Murder?" exclaimed the host.

Then he put his head back and laughed heartily. He finished laughing with moist, bright eyes.

"You ain't been in these mountains long, have you?" he asked.

"No," replied Speedy.

"Well," said the host, "it wasn't murder, at all. Nobody ever did claim that it was that. It was just self-defense. Phineas, he must've taken and made a move toward a hip pocket, or something like that. Nope, it was just self-defense, of course, but I've always held that it was mighty hasty self-defense on the part of Bill Cather, because everybody knowed that Fletcher Phineas never carried no gun."

23

THEY HAD their supper in the kitchen. The wind had come up higher and was thrusting and prying through every crack in the battered old house, putting fingers of ice into the rooms. The kitchen, heated by the big stove, was the only comfortable quarters for these reasons, and the host, with apologies, had suggested that they should have the meal in the warmth.

So they sat down as the dark lowered outside the misted windowpanes.

The big fellow from the stable appeared, Alfred to his mother, Alf to his father, and the three sat down with their guest while the hotel's drudge, Ad, labored back and forth, waiting on the table.

It was a queer meal. It had begun cheerfully enough on the part of all except Alfred, but he sat bolt upright in his chair with fire in his eyes and his jaws gripped hard together. Food he would hardly touch.

"Take a look at Alfred," said his mother. "Will you, pa?"

"Suppose that I take look," said Pa Clive. "He's big enough to be seen, I guess, the first shot?"

"Yeah, he's maybe big enough to be seen," said Mrs. Clive. "But don't you notice nothin'?"

"Well, what?"

"He ain't eatin'!"

"Leave me alone, ma, will you?" demanded Alf. "Keep your yapping to yourself."

"What kind of impression you gonna make on the gentleman, Alf?"

"What the hell do I care what kind of impression I'm makin'?" demanded Alf angrily.

All at once, as he spoke, his eyes started from his head, and he looked hastily down at his plate, as though he were afraid of a rebuke in more than mere words.

"Alf," said his father sternly, "I wouldn't sometimes think that you was a gentleman's son. I wouldn't sometimes think the blood what you got running in your veins. That's what I say, and that's what I mean."

He had laid down his knife and fork noisily, as he made this declaration. Now, as he resumed them, the gentlemanly Alf buried his face in his coffee cup and sipped noisily.

He was heard to mumble, after this, that he wasn't trying to step on the toes of no strangers nor he didn't mean no offense, neither, only pa and ma sort of nagged him on and made him forget himself.

Dinner came to an end; Speedy declined to remain for a second cup of coffee and withdrew, as he said, to study more of the history of the county.

As he left the table and passed into the next room, Mr. Clive said in a subdued voice, but with the air of a connoisseur, "A right quiet-spoken kind of a young gent. I wouldn't be surprised that he was something or other of a pretty good family. He seemed to kind of have an eye for things."

"He's ate after some good cooking, is what he's done," said Ma Clive. "I'll tell you what, he's ate after good cooks."

"He's ate after good cooks," agreed Pa Clive. "You could see—like the way that he laid into the venison steak. You see, he knew venison from beef, maybe!"

He nodded, pleased with himself.

"Alf," said his mother, "are you trying to break your neck or are you just lookin' at the cracks in the ceiling?"

Alf slowly raised his backward fallen head and stared straight before him.

"I wouldn't've never thought it," said he.

"I didn't know that you bothered yourself thinkin' none, most of the time," said Pa Clive severely. "But lemme hear what you gotta say."

"Nobody would ever think it," said Alf.

"Think what?" asked his father.

Alf shook his head and sighed.

"Don't play the fool. Nobody would think what?" asked his gentle mother.

"Look!" said Alf.

But he was pointing his hand, like a gun, at nothing.

"Look at what?" asked his father.

"You know about Speedy?" said Alf.

"Speedy? What are you talkin' about? The man-eater that they talk about?" asked Mrs. Clive.

Alf raised his great hand and presented the flat of it to her.

"Him!" he said.

"Him?" murmured Clive. "What you hushin' your mama for?"

"Whisper," said Alf.

Pa Clive whispered, "What's it all about?"

From the next room came the sound of a guitar being tuned. An old one had hung many a year from a hook on the living-room wall.

"It's about him," said Alf.

"Alf, don't go and make a fool out of yourself," said his father. "What's about him?"

"Speedy!" said Alf.

"Speedy?" gasped his mother. "You mean to say—"

"Five thousand dollars is what I mean to say!" said Alf.

"He's gone out of his head," said the father, his voice dying away to nothing, as he leaned across the table.

"I ain't crazy," said Alf. "Do I know Charley Dupray when I see him? I do! And he was here not half an hour ago. He's still here—outside."

"Dupray!" said Mrs. Clive, and rose as though she saw a ghost.

"It's all right, ma," said Alf. "It ain't us that he'll harm. It's Speedy that he wants. And Speedy is him that's in that room, twiddlin' at a fool guitar!"

24

PA CLIVE laid hold on the sides of the table with both hands and with such force that his arms began to shake. "Who told you that was Speedy?" he asked.

"Who do you think?" demanded his son in return.

"Dupray!" whispered the father.

"Nobody but him!" said Alf.

"Five thousand dollars!" murmured the father.

"Dupray'll pay that if we help him to the scalp of Speedy," announced Alf.

He passed the tip of his red tongue over his thick lips. His eyes rolled, as though he saw some delicious dish before him on the table.

Ma Clive rose up from her chair. Her voice shook and quavered and grew dim as she murmured, "Pa, you ain't gonna do it. You ain't gonna sell—"

"Shut your face!" hissed pa. "Five thousand dollars! You said five thousand, Alf?"

"That's what Dupray said. And here's what he paid."

He cast one furtive glance toward the door of the living room from which there now issued the first strains of "Ben Bolt," sung in a low, but very true and resonant voice, accompanied by the guitar.

"Five thousand dollars!" whispered Pa Clive.

And in the meantime, his son suddenly produced a sheaf of bills and, wetting his right thumb, proceeded to count them.

"Here's twenty-five hundred dollars," he said. "That's the advance payment."

The long, lean claw of Pa Clive reached for the stack.

"I'll take charge of that, my son," said he.

The great fist of Alf closed over the money. A deadly glare shone from his eyes.

"That's mine," he said. "That was give to me, not to you."

"Alf," whined the mother as she felt the eye of her husband fall bitterly upon her, "what you talkin' about? What you thinkin' about? Ain't there any proper respect in you?"

"Say, ma," exclaimed Alf, keeping his savage eye still fixed upon his father, "who should I be respectin'? An old bum like that, or twenty-five hundred bucks? You can have him, if you want, but I'll have the coin."

He grinned vastly, pleased with himself and his clever ideas. Then he stuffed the money back into his coat.

His father had turned gray with rage and hatred. He trembled from head to foot, and said, "You wouldn't think that Alf was no gentleman's son, but looks like he's all your child, ma! Besides, I dunno that I'd let a thing like this take place in my own house!"

His wife, in the meantime, stared with haunted eyes at the coat pocket inside which the money had disappeared. Her own scruples had been removed by the sight of the money.

"Five thousand dollars, all in one heap, all in one family," said she, "ain't to be sneezed at. They ain't, is a fact."

"Where's that fool of an Ad?" asked Pa Clive.

"She's outside fetchin' in some wood, is all," said Mrs. Clive. "Pa, don't you go and do nothin' wild!"

The host had pushed back his chair, though a rising note of the plaintive ballad which was being sung in the next room drowned out the sound.

"I gotta mind," said Pa Clive, "to go and tell him, is what I got a mind to do."

His son swayed forward, as though ready to leap to his feet and hurl himself at his father.

Instead, he lifted one huge, grimy forefinger, and merely said, "Likely Dupray is listenin' in at the window, right now, and hearin' what you got to say."

"Set down, pa," said Mrs. Clive, perspiring profusely, and wiping her wet face on the sleeve of her dress.

"I won't set down," said Pa Clive.

He turned away. With two enormous strides, his son was before him.

"You think that you're gonna rob me out of the only decent chance that I've ever had to make a man out of myself, do you?" demanded Alf. "You think that you can rob me out of that, you damned old goat? I'll take and wring your neck for you, if you come between me and my chance!"

"Alf, Alf, for goodness' sake," whispered the mother fiercely.

And yet there was a certain glitter in her own eyes as she looked from her son to her husband.

"Stand back outten my way," said the father, his voice weakening, "and lemme get at that stove to fetch some coffee. Gonna try to order me around in my own house?"

Alf, hearing this excuse, stepped back, but still kept himself formidably posted between his father and the door to the living room.

Pa Clive went to the stove, picked up the blackened coffeepot, and carried it back to the table.

"I dunno that I want this stuff," he said, poising the nozzle above his cup. "Ain't there no corn likker left in that there jug, ma?"

"There's wasn't no more'n a drop left to moisten my throat with it, after you and Alf took your swigs before lunch," said Ma Clive.

Her husband gave her a bitter glance.

"A fine life I lead here," he declared. "A damn fine life. But there's gonna be an end, there is."

He filled his cup and carried the pot back to the stove, without offering any coffee to either of them.

"There's gonna be a change, a big change," said he, slamming the pot back into place and returning to the table. His voice changed. "What's the scheme, Alf?" he muttered.

"The scheme?" said the son. "What for should I tell you, and let you blab it?"

"I was only riled a little," said the other. "It ain't for me to take away that luck that comes to my house, is it? Besides, I reckon that I get the other coin, when the job's done?"

"I reckon you get it," said the son, unwillingly. "I dunno why, though. A lot of help you're likely to be."

"Your pa's got a brain, when it comes to scheming things up," said his mother. "Don't you go and be too fast and ready with your tongue, Alf."

"Well," said Alf, "maybe he could be useful, if he wouldn't be shootin' off his face all the while. Maybe."

"Where are they?" asked the father, his eyes gleaming as he leered at Alf. He poured off a steaming draft of the coffee and, poising the cup high, he went on: "Seems like I'm getting warmed up to it. That Speedy, if it's him, he ain't done nothin' but raise hell all over the map of the world. There ain't any reason why he should keep on livin'. There ain't any reason as good as five thousand dollars, I reckon. Where's Dupray?"

"Him and the rest, they're outside," said Alf. "They're waitin' for me to call 'em. That's all."

"And what's the scheme?"

"It's an easy scheme, and it's a good one. All we gotta do, is just to ask him in here, after we got 'em posted. Four of 'em, and all dead shots. And outside will be one. And three inside, with me and pa. We can do our bit of shootin', too, when the pinch comes."

Mrs. Clive grunted.

"The floor will be a terrible mess!" said she.

"Ain't there soap and water and scrubbin' brushes?" demanded her spouse savagely. "Ain't there all of those things, I ask? And don't fresh blood wipe up like nothin' at all?"

She sighed.

"Maybe so," said she. "Maybe so. I ain't gonna be here when the shooting comes, though."

"We don't want you," said her son. "Where's that big fool of an Ad, too?"

She came in at that moment, carrying a high-heaped load of wood. Her face was very pale. Her eyes were starting from her head, only her lids were lowered and she was looking at the floor.

She put down the wood with a crash beside the stove. All three of the others jumped.

"You clumsy fool!" said Alf.

She dusted her hands, and said nothing. Still her eyes were not raised, and still the others could not see the gleam that was buried in them.

"You go on to bed," said Mrs. Clive. "I'm gonna go to bed, too. The men, they got something to talk over."

"Have they?" muttered the girl with a sneer.

"Yeah, they have, and this here is the only decent, warm room for 'em to talk in. Come on. We'll go up the back way."

The thick, wide shoulders of Ad shrugged as high as her ears, and she shuffled toward the door as the ballad singer in the next room swung into that sentimental old passage:

Oh, don't you remember sweet Alice, Ben Bolt, Sweet Alice with hair—"

It seemed to strike the ear of Ad for the first time, as she neared the door, walking behind her mistress. She stopped short and her head jerked high. For a moment, she stood there, listening, with wonder and awe and a strange doubt in her face.

Mrs. Clive turned back to her.

"Gonna stand there all night? Whatcha thinkin' about?"

"I was thinkin', was the scraps carried out to the pigs," said Ad.

"Damn the pigs," said Mr. Clive angrily. "G'wan and get out of here!"

The two women disappeared, and a moment later the song in the living room ended.

"Well," said Pa Clive, setting his teeth and turning on Alf.

"Yeah, I'm gonna go out and tell 'em that the coast is clear," said Alf.

He stepped to the back door, then turned about. "You ain't gunna go and make no fool of yourself, pa, are you?" he asked, scowling.

"You mean, tell Speedy of the plan? Is he worth five thousand dollars, or the half of what that would do to put this family back where it belongs? No, sir, he ain't. He's gonna get just what he's give to others, many a time before this day!"

"Yeah, he's give it, and he's give it plenty," said the son.

He opened the door, paused an instant with the wind rushing into the room about his bulky figure, then stepped out into the darkness, and closed the door behind him.

Pa Clive, with a shudder that might have been caused by the cold, went to the stove and extended his hands over it. He rubbed those hands busily. Then, as the warmth seemed to be penetrating into his chilled body, he lifted his head, listening to the distant roar of the wind through the big pine trees.

Usually, it was a pleasure to listen to the howl of the gale when one sat comfortably in a kitchen, with the fire burning well in the stove. But tonight it seemed as though the full power of the storm were beating against his face and stirring his heart.

He turned from the stove, drew himself up to his full height, and struck an attitude of such gravity as he deemed fitting to a gentleman.

At that moment, the back door opened again, and they came in.

25

SPEEDY WAS no longer in the living room. He had plucked at the rusted strings of the old guitar and sung his songs for a few minutes, and now he went up the stairs to his room, not taking a light with him, but using his memory only to illumine his way through the dark. Twice he had covered those stairs and the twisting hallway, but he had used every faculty, and now he could recall every foot of the way, the very look of the banisters, the width of the landing where the stairs turned, and the very height of the ceiling in the hallway above.

So he came, unerringly, to the door of his room, opened it and, passing inside, saw the pale outline of the window in the starlight, found, and lighted the lamp.

Then he sat down and, drawing up the stool close to the window, he looked out at the stormy night. The wind blew from the other direction just now, so that it did not strike against the window and, with it open, he felt the tremor of the wind rather than its direct force. He watched the clouds tumbling across the sky. The stars were like flying sparks.

Someone knocked at his door. He called out, and in came the burly servant, Ad. Her eyes were on the floor, a glowering look was on her face as she brought in a pitcher of drinking water, placed it on the washstand, and turned to go.

Speedy stood up and, even when her back was turned to him, he stopped her with his eye.

At the door she turned back to mutter, "Good night."

"Good night, Ad," he answered cheerfully.

She had the door half open, but closed it again, as though compelled by the unexpected kindness in his voice.

"A bad night for sleepin', though," said Ad, "what with this wind, I mean—and—"

She stopped herself, and hastily pushed open the door again, but Speedy was saying, "I can sleep through worse storms than this, when I'm in a house filled with honest people, Ad."

She was half out in the hall, when she turned back with a start and a grunt, like that of a horse when it has been struck by a whip.

"What?" said she. "Whatcha say?"

"I said honest people make safe nights," said Speedy.

She gaped at him.

"Yeah, maybe," said Ad.

"But," said Speedy, "I can see in your face that there's trouble in the air."

"How can you see that in my face?" asked the girl.

"You know, Ad," said Speedy, "if one knows how, one can read thoughts in the eyes."

Narrowly, he watched her while he said this.

She was startled again and swung the door shut behind her, planted her fists on her wide hips, and faced him with an air of surly defiance.

"Now you go ahead and tell me what I'm thinkin' about now!" she exclaimed.

He watched the savage, brutal glare of her eyes for an instant.

"You're seeing me dead, Ad," said he.

Ad's resolution and defiance were gone instantly. She shrank back, cowering, as though a gun had been pointed at her.

"Ah," she gasped, "how did you know that?"

He controlled the disgust and the horror that were rising in him. There was something in the air, and he could guess that she might open the door of the mystery to him.

"I know it," said Speedy gently, "because I could see the workings of the mind behind your eyes."

"I never heard nothin' like it!" breathed the poor girl. "Did you read somethin' in the eyes of Alf, too, when you was settin' at the table opposite to him?"

Speedy nodded gravely.

"You did?" gasped the girl. "Whatcha see in his eyes, then?"

Terror and curiosity kept her gaping at him, and hanging on his answer.

"I saw," said Speedy deliberately, "the gun that he was thinking of."

She caught her breath, and he knew that his second guess had reached the center of the target.

"It's spooky," muttered Ad. "I never heard of nothin' like it, nowhere. I've heard of fortune-tellers, but they all talk about things to come, that don't never come at all. Oh, I know about 'em. But you—you seen the gun in the eyes of Alf?"

"Yes," said Speedy calmly.

"How could you set there so still, then?" she asked, more amazed the longer she thought of it.

He shrugged his shoulders.

"Maybe," said she, "you didn't see who he was gonna use that gun on?"

"On me," said Speedy, stepping out under her own guidance with that stroke of guesswork.

The result was the complete collapse of Ad's nerves. She gripped at her own fat throat with both hands and moaned, "D'you mean that you really know they're gonna murder you?"

His blood may have chilled as he heard

her speak the word, but he showed nothing in his face. There was much more to be learned from this creature, if only he could keep on using her in the right way. One wrong guess, and her belief would be at an end.

"I know that they intend to murder me," said Speedy.

"You was talking about the honest men in the house a minute back," she exclaimed, confused and doubting.

"Because," said Speedy, "I wanted to see if you would lie to me about them. But you couldn't lie, Ad. No matter what your tongue was saying, the truth was in your eyes as clearly as in a glass."

"It kind of staggers me," said the girl. "You ain't gonna just stay here, are you?"

"Why not?" said Speedy. "Why should I leave?"

"With six bloody murderers ready to kill you—six of 'em right here in the house?" exclaimed the girl.

"You know, Ad," said Speedy, "that a man can't escape from his fate."

"Well," said she, "I'd take a pretty good chance at it. I'd get on a hoss, if I was you, and I'd try how fast four legs could gallop me away from this here Clive's Corners!"

"Would you?" murmured Speedy. "Well, Ad, the truth is that a man has to meet the dangers that luck has stored up for him. And some of those men are dangerous enough."

"You know who they are?" asked the girl.

He actually shaded his eyes with one hand and concentrated his stare upon her.

"I can see their faces very dimly in your eyes, Ad," he declared.

"Here? In my eyes can you see it?" demanded the girl.

"In your eyes, because they're the windows of the mind, Ad," replied Speedy. "You're seeing those faces as you speak of them and, therefore, I can see them, too.

"I can see the chief man of all, the one that the others look toward. He's not very tall. His shoulders are wide. He has a round face, like the face of a frog—"

"The saints forgive us all!" gasped the girl. "It's enough to take and make a body religious, is what it is, to hear you talk."

"There's another man," said Speedy, "who's very tall, with buck teeth and a smile on his mouth but none in his eyes."

Of course, Speedy knew if Dupray was there, Bones was reasonably sure to be with him.

"Oh, my poor heart," said the girl. "It's pretty near cracking, it's so excited. I never was so scared in my life, just seeing the spooky way that you look through things. When you look into my mind, don't you see the big greaser with the great big chin, though?"

Speedy started. Then he peered into the stupid, frightened eyes of the girl again. Mexican? A big Mexican with a heavy chin!

And then, very clearly, the image of the great Bardillo recurred to his mind. Bardillo, joined with Dupray! The world could hardly have furnished two more perfect devils to work in conjunction against him!

"Yes, of course, I see him," said Speedy. "I see his wide shoulders and his narrow hips."

"Oh, save me!" cried the girl. "It ain't to be believed. You can look inside of the minds of folks, just as easy as nothing at all. I seen you do it, and I can swear to it, now! I've seen, and I know!"

She broke out again: "D'you see the older Mexican with the tall man?"

Speedy could guess at that figure easily enough. If Bardillo was there, accompanied by an older Mexican, it must be none other than that grave and wise counselor of villainy, the great Marañon.

"The man with the gray beard?" said Speedy calmly. "Yes, I can see his face, too, and even the purple pouches under his eyes. I see him quite clearly, now that you begin to concentrate your own seeing on his face."

Ad shook her head violently from side to side for a long moment.

"I ain't one to believe no foolishness," she said solemnly, "and I ain't one to pay out money on fortune tellers. But if you was a fortune-teller, I wouldn't dare not do what you told me to do. I wouldn't dare. That's certain!

"Ain't you gonna do nothin' but stand there and wait for 'em to come?" she asked after a moment's silence.

"I'll do something at the right time," replied Speedy.

A footfall sounded on the floor.

"They're comin' now," moaned the girl, flying into a panic. "They'll think that I been telling you and warning you. They'll never know that you been warning yourself! Tell me what to do! They'll murder me, too!"

"I won't let 'em touch you," said Speedy calmly. "There's only one man coming. Get back there, so that when the door opens you'll be behind it."

She obeyed, in terror, turning her face to the wall, and throwing up her arms against it, in order to press flatter.

A moment later, there came a soft knock on the door. Speedy, who had pulled off his boots, was sitting on the edge of the cot, as the door opened, and the full dignity of Pa Clive appeared against the velvet blackness of the hall.

26

"HULLO," SAID Pa Clive. "Turnin' in?" Speedy nodded and smiled. "Why," said Pa Clive, "we was just gonna have a taste of whiskey punch downstairs in the kitchen, and we sorta wanted to have you with us. It ain't a warm or friendly thing to keep the guests away from the punch bowl, on a night like this here!"

He stood smiling, a picture of benignity, rubbing and wringing his hands at the thought of the benefits which he was to bestow upon the stranger.

Speedy, considering the dignity of that hypocrite, smiled again and nodded.

"I'll have my boots on again in a minute," said he, "and then I'll be down with you. Thanks a lot."

"No thanks, no thanks at all," said Pa Clive. "Wantcha to be happy is all I wantcha to be in this here hotel. We'll be expectin' you down right smart, then?"

He paused in the door, turning sidewise, smiling and nodding at Speedy in the most inviting manner.

"I'll be with you before long," said Speedy, picking up a boot.

"That's it, that's it," said Pa Clive. "Come right on down."

He closed the door behind him, very, very gently, and then his footfall went slowly down the hall and his voice rose in a booming bass, as he sang, "Tenting tonight."

Even the icy terror of Ad was dissolved by this. She turned to Speedy, gasping, "And them waitin' down there to murder you, and him singin' for joy because he's already countin' the murder money in his palm. Oh, what a snake and a sneak he is! You ain't gonna go down, are you?"

"I'm goin' down," said Speedy. "I told him that I'd be down there before long, and I'm going."

She retreated to the door.

"Whatcha gonna do to 'em?" she breathed, all her fears for this mysterious man dissolving as she faced the perfect calm of Speedy.

"I haven't quite made up my mind, yet," replied Speedy. "But I know that I'll have to go down. Ideas will come to me after I'm there, perhaps?"

She opened the door.

"The saints be good to you," she muttered, "or the devil, because it's more like that it's him that helps the likes of you!" And she went hastily off down the hallway.

Speedy moved quickly the instant the door shut after her. The window was already open, and now he stepped to it and leaned out. He could survey the side of the kitchen in this manner, the drawn, yellow shade made brilliant by the lamp that was shining inside the room. There was no one outside, that he could see.

He slipped through the window and, hanging from the sill by his hands, he began to swing his body back and forth in a slow oscillation, whose arc became wider and wider with every movement.

He had gained a sufficient impetus presently, but he waited for a few more seconds, until a fresh uproar of wind struck the house and set it trembling and rattling. Then he loosed himself and shot through the air toward the edge of the kitchen roof.

In his stockinged feet he landed lightly upon it and clung there, balancing with some difficulty as the force of the wind struck against him.

From the eaves, he dropped again, without sound, to the ground and stepped to the window.

There were a half dozen small rents in the shade, and through those gaps he peered until he had seen every corner of the kitchen. It was a death trap, well prepared for him.

Facing the door through which he was expected to enter, stood the great Charles Dupray, his hands empty, but how quickly they would both be garnished with weapons, the instant that there was need!

To his left and ready for the same target, was Marañon, holding a double-barrelled, sawed-off shotgun. He alone would be a sufficient engine to sweep away half a dozen lives, if men tried to crowd toward him.

At the central table was Pa Clive, with a cup of coffee actually before him, from which he sipped. But he sipped with the cup held in the left hand, and in his lap was a big Colt.

His son stood back against the wall, with a

naked revolver in his ample grasp, and the great Bardillo was beside him. All five were in readiness to blast the life from the body of that kindly invited guest.

Speedy smiled faintly.

But he missed the cadaverous frame of Bones. Where could that giant be?

Speedy stepped to the corner of the kitchen wall and just outside the kitchen door, he saw his man. They had posted Bones as the rear guard, in case Speedy should manage to rush through the converging lines of fire and get out the doorway.

Speedy shook his head. There was a subtle and unbelievable compliment in the implication that, in spite of the death trap's completeness, they had decided that it might be possible for him to live through it and escape through the doorway.

What a weight of armament was prepared in there—and against a man who had empty hands!

But fate had kindly posted in reach the man he had to speak with.

Like a cat, he stole down behind the lofty outguard, crouched behind him and, reaching stealthily forward, caught the butt of the riot gun with which Bones was armed, and quickly snatched it away from him.

There was not a sound. Bones, wheeling about and grasping at air, found the terrible twin muzzles planted against his breast and the slender form of Speedy behind them.

With his head, Speedy gestured to the side.

"Move!" he said.

And Bones, turning a little, stalked in the indicated direction, across a windswept space and into the shelter of the wall of the wood-shed.

"We can talk here," said Speedy.

And Bones, halting, faced back toward the other.

"Well," said Speedy, "it was a good idea, and pretty well worked up, but they'll have to wait a while for me, those fellows in the kitchen."

"How'd you find out?" demanded Bones.

"How do you think, Bones?" said Speedy.

"Some fools would say it was your mind reading," admitted Bones. "But I ain't a fool of that kind. Watcha gonna do with me?"

"Mind reading was the trick, nevertheless, Bones. Oh, it's just a trick, but it works as well as though it were a real power, most of the time. Now, Bones, I want to talk to you a little. I haven't much time—they may get impatient in yonder!—but I've brought you a message."

"Yeah?" said Bones.

"This is the way of it," said Speedy. "You have a relative in the East. A cousin. He's dying of heart disease and wondering if he'll live long enough to hear that you've been located. For you're to be his heir, Bones. His name is Littleton, and there's a lawyer named Raymond, Henry Raymond, who'll give you all the details of where you're to go and what you're to do. The law wants you, and so you'll have to move with a good deal of care. But there's a fortune waiting for you."

"Hold on," said Bones.

"I'm telling you the truth," said Speedy.

"You mean," said Bones slowly, "that you come up here and waded through this bit of hell tonight just for the sake of bringing me good news?"

"I'll be honest with you, Bones," said Speedy. "It's not entirely for your own sake that I've done it. It's rather for the sake of that fellow Littleton, who's gasping his life out, waiting to get in touch with you. I'd like to know that that poor devil had some comfort before the end."

Bones made no answer.

"I'll tell you," said Speedy, "that I can't waste time talking, Bones. I've got to be on my way again. The message had to come to you. Luckily, Dupray seems to have guessed that I was on my way. Raymond is a crook of the first water and must have kept in touch with him all the time. But I've found you, and you know the news. The only thing that's left is the address of Raymond in—"

"I know him," said Bones, in a deep, husky voice. "And I know that the whole job is a plant."

_____ 27

"A PLANT? The whole job?"

"Yes, Speedy, a plant. But look here! Somehow, it kind of flabbergasts me—I mean, you coming up here through hell fire for the sake of bringing the yarn to me. That's what I can't get over. Maybe not so much for me, but for Littleton. What's Littleton to you?"

"Why, he's a sick man, Bones. That's all."

"He ain't even alive; he ain't nothing to you anyhow. You know what you come into—you know them that are in the kitchen?"

"I've just finished looking at 'em," said Speedy.

"Hand-picked, except old man Clive," said Bones. "The choice of the world, when it comes to murder and such, and you run the risk of all that, because you get your sympathies worked up for a sick man, do you?"

"Heart trouble is no joke," said Speedy.

"Neither is Dupray and Bardillo a joke," said Bones. "Why, Speedy, I aimed to cut your throat myself, is what I aimed to do!"

"Who planned it?"

"I think it was mostly Bardillo's idea. I heard him and Dupray talkin' it over."

"What did they say?" asked Speedy.

"The whole picture was that you'd have to be tempted into doing a job that looked dangerous," replied Bones. "And the meanest, most dangerous job that they could think of was to line you up to take a message right to Dupray. Him that would be waiting to kill you! So they picked me out, and said that I was the heir of Littleton. Then they hired Raymond, the crooked lawyer, to advertise for you and offer rewards to anybody that would get word to you that he wanted to see you. That's all there was to the game. And it worked. What a fool you were, Speedy, to be took in that way by those skunks!"

"Yes, I was," agreed Speedy, but without bitterness. "One of these days, I'll be a fool just once too often. This time I was pretty close to it."

"Speedy!" Bones suddenly exclaimed in a low voice.

He made a sudden gesture; Speedy whirled, crouching to the side as he did so. No human being could have moved more swiftly, more adroitly. But the gun butt was already suspended over the head of Speedy and crashing down. It struck him as he dodged, only a glancing stroke from the mighty hand of young Alf Clive, but, had it landed full and squarely, it would have shattered his skull like a shell. Even as it was, it knocked him into a pit of darkness.

When he came to, he was sitting in a chair in the kitchen of the Clives', hand and foot, leg and arm, head and shoulder lashed with many weavings of small twine to the chair in which he sat.

He lifted his head and saw Pa Clive facing him.

The older man nodded and smiled on him. "There you be, Speedy," he said. "There you be, out of the dark and back with us once more, and all of us mighty glad to look at you!"

He laughed as he said this, and stroked his beard.

"That'll do from you," snapped Dupray.

"All right," said Clive. "I ain't one to talk out of my turn. But there's Speedy—many a man has hunted him—many a man has tried to get at him—and how many ever had him cornered before this? Tell me that. But my Alf, he went out and got him with his two hands, is how he went and got him!"

Alf smiled and lifted those two immense hands as they were mentioned, examined them with his own eyes, and then looked proudly around the room.

"He did a mighty good job," said Dupray. "One that I won't forget!"

Bardillo waved a hand impatiently toward the host.

"We'd better finish off this business right away," said he.

"It's all right, Bardillo," said Speedy. "Don't be in such a hurry. I won't talk, because I know he wouldn't believe me even if I told him."

"Wouldn't believe what?" said Dupray, scowling.

"Nothing," said Speedy. "It's all right."

"Sure it's all right," said Dupray.

"We're losing time," broke in Bardillo. "You've got him. Let's put an end to him and get on."

"What's the hurry?" asked Dupray. "He ain't done much to you, Bardillo. But he's done plenty to me. He's blocked me, checked me, and made a fool of me. And now I want to enjoy this for a minute or two. I don't want to be hurried about it. He's going to die, and I want to taste his death. I want to linger over it."

"I hate him," said Bardillo deliberately, "as much as one human being can hate another, but he's dangerous, and we had better use the good moment to put him out of the way."

Dupray did not even glance at the speaker, but feasted his eyes on Speedy.

"I gotta have my way about it," he said. "I've waited and prayed for this day to come. Speedy is here in front of me; he's helpless. Give me time, Bardillo, because I have to have it."

28

BARDILLO SEEMED no more contented after the
remarks of Dupray, but he prepared to sub-
mit, as to the inevitable. He merely said to
Marañon, "It's a bad business. Every drop
of blood in me is against it."

"But look," said Dupray. "Here he is,
tied so that even if he were a snake he could
not wriggle loose. He has no friends near
him. Every one of us has a reason for getting
rid of him. How could he possibly get away,
Bardillo?"

"There might be twenty men closing in
around the house for him," suggested
Marañon.

Dupray shrugged his shoulders and smiled.

"You don't know him as we do?" said he.
"He works alone. He plays a lone hand.
Sometimes he may ride with one other man,
but that's all. Bones, what happened to you
out there?"

"Why," said Bones, "the idea was that I
was to guard the door against anything from

the inside, not the outside. I was watching the door, not the whole forest around me. And pretty soon comes a tug from behind and I turn around and my gun's in the hands of Speedy, and pointed at my chest. He fetched me off to the woodshed."

"They were talkin' plumb agreeable when I come up," put in Alf. "I dunno what the hunch was that made me turn and go out there. It was the long wait for Speedy that made me sort of think that he might be up to something, I guess. So I went out, sneakin', and seen the two of 'em behind the woodshed."

"What were you talking about, Bones?" said the chief.

He looked with a cold eye upon the big man, and Bones answered, "What would he be talkin' about, anyway? What would anybody be talkin' about that was on your trail?"

"Didn't he tell you about the sick man and the millions?" asked the other.

"Sure he did," said Bones. "But he wanted a big return for that. He seemed to think that I might have some idea where your money was cached away. That's what he was talkin' about so fast. I'm to get the Littleton coin, and I'm to tip him off where he thinks that your cache might be. Kind of weak-witted, ain't he, to think that the money would still be in the cache, if I knowed where it was?"

"Even if you knew," put in Speedy, as though anxious to defend his reputation against this attack, "even if you knew where it is, you'd be afraid to touch it, on account of Dupray. Don't talk bigger than you are, Bones!"

"I'd be afraid to touch it?" said Bones. "I gotta mind to go and bash in your face!"

He stepped closer and balled up his big fist as he spoke. A sympathetic smile appeared upon the face of Alf, for one, but Dupray raised a warning hand.

"Back up, Bones," said he. "There's plenty of time for all of that. Speedy, you started out after my cache, did you? I mean, what people call my cache. You really think that I've got money buried away, do you?"

Speedy shrugged his shoulders. "Everybody knows that you have a fortune and a big one laid away, Dupray," said he. "There's no doubt about that. You've taken money by the hundreds of thousands, and jewels, solid gold and all that. Now, you never spend a penny, so the stuff must be somewhere. It won't evaporate. Eh, Bardillo?"

The Mexican started.

"Why do you ask me?" said he.

"All right," replied Speedy. "There's no use talking about it, I suppose. Only—"

He shrugged his expressive shoulders again.

"I don't follow this," remarked Dupray, frowning at Speedy and then at Bardillo.

"Bardillo's a hard fellow to follow," admitted Speedy. "When it comes to that, he's a damned hard fellow to follow, I'd say."

He smiled and nodded at Bardillo.

"I don't know what he's talking about," declared Bardillo, frowning.

Alf Clive put in: "There's some more money to be paid down. You've got your man, Dupray. I guess that I get the other half of that coin now?"

Dupray turned to Bardillo.

"I've paid my half," said Dupray. "You can pay your share now, partner."

Bardillo nodded, but he made a grimace as he did so.

"Fifteen hundred dollars, eh?" said he. "That's half of three thousand."

There was a howl of protest instantly from Pa Clive.

"It was five thousand!" he shouted. "Half

of five is twenty-five hundred! I'll have twenty-five hundred, Bardillo."

"Will you?" said the Mexican softly and dangerously.

Dupray grinned broadly. Pa Clive turned to the American bandit with appeal.

"You know, Dupray, that it's twenty-five hundred comin' to me. I ain't gonna be robbed. Not in my own house!"

He stood up, irritated, trembling with the apprehension of loss.

"Oh, it's all right," said Alf, "You'll get enough, pa. You didn't do nothin'. Me, I done all the work! I got him, didn't I? I turned him in, when he'd've got clean away. It was me, wasn't it?"

He jabbed a thumb at his great chest as he said this and rolled his little eyes around the room to collect applause that he felt was due him.

Dupray answered, "You did a good job, Alf. You're going to do other jobs, and better ones, too. I have my eye on you, young man. I'm goin' to take care of your future all right."

He spoke this quietly, but with a certain savage feeling, looking not at Alf Clive, but at Speedy.

"Now, Señor Bardillo," said Pa Clive, "I

211

know that you ain't gonna back out of the bargain. I know that you're gonna be a man of your word."

"Your son has been paid," said Bardillo. "When it comes to you, why here's fifteen hundred, and that's enough."

The emotions of Pa Clive became so great that he almost stifled, trying to shout out a protest.

Speedy remarked, "Well, you ought to be a little more generous, Bardillo, considering everything. You know how much coin you'll soon have in your hands."

Bardillo scowled at the prisoner.

"What money?" he said.

"Come, come," said Speedy. "I don't have to tell you that, I hope!"

Bardillo laid down a small sheaf of bills upon the kitchen table.

"There you are, Señor Clive," said he. "Not a penny more out of me. It's more than you deserve."

Pa Clive extended his hands to the entire universe, that it might take note of the injustice that was being visited upon him.

"It ain't right," he exclaimed finally. "It ain't honest. Alf, look! He's only give me fifteen hundred for my half. And I give my house to 'em for a trap. If it wasn't for my house, they wouldn't have Speedy. Alf, ain't you gonna do nothing about it? Your own father, your own flesh and blood!"

"Aw, shut up, will you?" said Alf genially.

"Yes, be quiet," commanded the great Dupray.

Old Pa Clive sadly gathered up the money and stuffed it into his coat pocket.

"We've been cheated out of a thousand dollars this here day," said he.

His eye reddened as it turned upon the others.

"All that I hope," he said savagely, "is that you don't have no good luck, no more; and that Speedy gets away, and that he cuts you up, every doggone one of you. I been cheated. And a time'll come, gents, when you'll find out what it means to rob a Clive in his own house!"

"That's enough out of you," said Dupray. "Fifteen hundred is too much, anyway. The other thousand, Bardillo, the other thousand can go to Alf, here."

"Good!" exclaimed Alf.

"What other thousand?" demanded Bardillo, scowling blackly.

"The other thousand that goes to make up your half," said Dupray quietly and coldly.

213

"I've paid twenty-five hundred for my share. D'you think that your own share is going to be any less?"

"He's ridden a long way," put in Speedy.

Dupray turned to the prisoner.

"You've gotta be talkin', still, don't you?" he remarked.

"It's true," said Bardillo. "I've ridden a long distance. I contributed the idea, also, that brought about his capture. You have a hundred reasons for wanting him out of the way. To me, he did only one injury. You must be just, amigo."

Dupray nodded, as he listened.

"I kinda like to hear you," said he. "I kinda like to hear the way you try to slide out from under, but it won't work, Bardillo."

"It won't work, Bardillo," said Speedy. "No matter how you feel about it—and, of course, you're right—he'll make you pay!"

"Make me?" said Bardillo, starting as though he had been struck.

"Come, Bardillo," said Dupray, still perfect master of himself. "You see how it is? Speedy is trying to make bad blood between us. That's his idea of a way to get free. We're to quarrel, and he comes off scot-free."

He chuckled and stared at Speedy.

"That's the idea, Speedy, I suppose?"

"Oh, no, Dupray," said Speedy. "Bardillo won't fight. He's as fast with a gun as you are, and a straighter shot, too. But he won't fight. Not yet!"

"What d'you mean by that?" demanded Dupray sharply. "You talk as though you and Bardillo were in cahoots. You talk as though you knew something about him; you've talked that way ever since you were fetched in here!"

Speedy stared at him and shrugged his shoulders.

"Go on and answer, Speedy," said Dupray. "It won't cost you anything."

"It's no good," said Speedy. "If you're too blind to see for yourself, why should I tell you?"

"Too blind to see what?"

"Why, you old fool," exclaimed Speedy, as though his patience were exhausted, "d'you think that it's just an accident that Bardillo and I are here together? Is that a chance that's likely to happen, I ask you?"

"Now, what's he driving at, Bardillo?" asked Dupray.

"How shall I tell?" answered Bardillo, with a clouded face.

"Bardillo is really wonderful. Look at him,

Dupray," said Speedy. "He keeps his face—no, not entirely. No, he begins to redden a little. But, on the whole, he keeps his face wonderfully. That's the sign of a good conscience, I suppose, in the eyes of the world."

"What are you getting red about, Bardillo?" asked Dupray.

"I?" said Bardillo, growing hotter than ever and crimsoning to the eyes. "I ask you, what does this badgering mean, Dupray?"

"That's not so well done," said Speedy, tilting his head critically to one side. "Not nearly so well done. You shouldn't try to bluster with a fellow like Dupray, Bardillo. Dupray isn't the sort to be talked out of face."

Dupray turned on Speedy.

"Speedy," he said, "what the devil are you driving at with all of this?"

Speedy shrugged his shoulders and relaxed in the chair that held him.

"If you're so blind that you can't see that Bardillo and I were to play the game together," said he, "why should I tell you about it?"

THE WIND chose this moment to leap on the house and shake it as a cat shakes a rat and the voice of the storm wailed down the chimney. A puff of smoke and ashes sifted through the cracks of the stove and hung in the air as thin clouds.

It seemed that the stroke of the wind was strangely appropriate, considering the sudden tension which had been placed upon the nerves of all the people in the room.

Even Pa Clive stopped moaning about his losses.

"What game, Speedy?" asked Dupray, in the most coaxing of voices.

"What game?" echoed Speedy. "What game d'you think? The game of getting at your hard cash, the stuff you've put away."

"There's no stuff put away," said Dupray, turning literally gray-green with excitement. "You mean that Bardillo had a deal with you to hunt."

"It's a lie!" said Bardillo.

"Of course," said Speedy. "You've won, Bardillo. It was a pretty double cross that you worked!"

"Scoundrel!" shouted Bardillo, half maddened by the cunning series of lies in which he was being involved.

He suited his action to his word by snatching out a revolver and covering the prisoner.

"Don't shoot," said Dupray.

Bardillo, turning his head, saw that the revolver of Charles Dupray was leveled on him. Big Alf had drawn a weapon, also, and Bones was turning the double muzzles of his riot gun toward the Mexican.

Only Marañon had remained cool and collected.

He spoke now for the first time.

"Friends," said he, in a voice so calm that it was almost dull and lifeless, "we are not children. It's simple enough—what is in the mind of Señor Speedy. He is cornered. He has no hope. Therefore, he tries to make great and sudden trouble between old friends. Señor Dupray, you will believe me, if you think for a minute."

"Of course, I'll believe you," said Dupray. "Of course, we're friends; only, I want to hear a little more from Speedy before he gets what's coming to him."

"Don't ask me," said Speedy. "I've talked too much already. I never hoped to convince you, Dupray. You're too bull-headed. You've made up your mind that this Bardillo will play fair with you, and nothing that I could say would ever change you."

Dupray wagged his frog face slowly from side to side.

"What would you try to convince me of, Speedy?" he asked.

"I'm through arguing. I never wanted to argue from the first," replied Speedy. "You've got me, Dupray. Go ahead and finish me, or let Bardillo do the trick. He's anxious enough to, for fear I should talk some more about him."

"Dupray," gasped Bardillo, "I must kill him. I cannot stand here and listen. My breath leaves me. I choke."

"Sure. And so do I," said Dupray. "He's going to die, and he knows it. But before we bump him off, let him talk a little. Put up the gun, Bardillo, will you?"

Bardillo, after a moment of silent struggle with himself, put away the weapon and turned his back sharply upon the others.

He muttered something about being unable to watch, and Speedy remarked, "That's a good stroke, Bardillo. If you can't keep your face, it's always better for a fellow to turn his back."

"What's that about a double cross that Bardillo has worked on you?" demanded Dupray.

"Why," said Speedy, "I suppose he thought that it would be better to keep all the money in his own hands. Marañon, there, would never ask for a full share. He's simply an old retainer. When Bardillo gets his chance to work the game that he knows so well how to work—why, he won't need my help. It was only to get you flattened in the first place that made him suggest the deal to me."

"Are you going to listen to that barking dog?" exclaimed Bardillo, but still without turning to face them.

"Yeah, I'm going to listen," said Dupray. "It's sort of amusing to hear him lie, eh?"

"Oh, go to the devil," said Speedy, apparently growing weary. "Why should I talk to you? I only wish him all the more luck. I hope, when he has you stretched out, that he takes off your skin an inch at a time and burns it in front of your face."

"Thanks," said Dupray.

"That will make you talk fast enough," continued Speedy.

"Talk about what?" asked Dupray.

"Why, what do you suppose? About the place where you've hidden your stuff!"

"I was to be caught and flayed alive till I told where I'm supposed to have cached my savings, eh?" murmured Dupray. "That's it, is it?"

"Ten thousand devils!" exclaimed the Mexican, whirling at last.

"It hurts when your ideas are put out in plain view like that, Bardillo, doesn't it?" murmured Speedy cheerfully. "But tell me, old fellow, why you didn't go through with the original scheme with me? We could have worked it, easily enough. I was ready. You were ready. Dupray was suspecting nothing. He only thought that the hunt was for me; he never dreamed that he was the choice!"

Dupray lowered his head and thrust it forward as he stared at Bardillo. "That's it, Bardillo," said he. "Why didn't you go through with the first idea, the main idea?"

Bardillo caught a breath.

"Dupray," he pleaded, "is it possible that you'll believe this devil?"

"I don't know," said Dupray. "I'm just thinking about it."

"You ought to keep your back to us," said Speedy. "Your face shows too much, and Dupray isn't blind."

In fact, the face of Bardillo was crimson and pale in blotches, so wildly had his temper risen. But the contorted features might have been the expression of any one of half a dozen evil emotions.

"It's not so pretty," murmured Dupray. "Damn it, Bardillo, I'm thinking that there's something in what Speedy says."

Marañon broke in: "Gentlemen, you're not going to be foolish? You're not going to be talked into trouble that will give Speedy his chance? Finish him now—this minute! Then you'll see that his lies are as thin as air!"

"Of course," said Speedy, nodding and perfectly at ease. "Finish me off, and then I won't be able to show you what they're made of, Dupray. It's a pretty Mexican game that they've been playing."

"Bardillo!" exclaimed Dupray.

Bardillo did not answer. His heavy lower jaw was beginning to thrust forward slowly.

"Bardillo," said Dupray, "I have more than half an idea that Speedy has told me the truth!"

"Have you?" asked Bardillo, through his teeth.

"Turn your back, Bardillo," urged Speedy. "You're losing control of your face altogether. Turn your back and talk over your shoulder.

If you'd gone through with the first plan, we could have been rich, all of us. We could have roasted the information out of Dupray. But I'd rather die and rot than have worked with you as a partner, now that I see what you are!"

As this speech burst from him, the hand of Bardillo flashed again for a gun. There would be no stopping him this time, and Dupray merely cried out in a high, barking voice, "Take it, then!" and snapped out his own gun.

Bones, with a shout, at the same moment, leveled his gun, but he tripped in making a step forward; both barrels of the heavy riot gun roared in the air and, as the revolvers began to boom, the explosions blew out the light of the lamp. The flame leaped twice in the chimney and died like a ghost.

Someone shrieked; bodies fell heavily. Men cursed. The red tongue of fire licked and darted like the red of blood from the muzzles of the guns.

Speedy found himself picked up, chair and all, and carried swiftly forward. A door crashed open under the weight of the charge and, looking up by the dim light of the smoking lamp in the parlor, he saw that Bones was carrying him!

He was thrown down, helpless, to the floor. Then two slashes with a knife freed him; the great hands of Bones jerked him to his feet, and the voice of Bones was gasping, "Now, get out of it! I gotta go with you. My name's mud with Dupray, after this!"

"Get out of it! No, no, I'll get back into it," said Speedy. "I'll thank you later, Bones!"

He turned toward the kitchen door, as he spoke. Feet trampled furiously across the floor of the room; one voice was monotonously screaming on one note; the back door slammed. From the upper part of the house the voices of the women began, pitched high and small with the distance.

"It's too late for the best part of the fun," said Speedy, changing his mind. He went back deliberately and picked up the lamp from the table. "We'll have a little look inside," said he.

Bones, agape, muttered, "It's a bad chance to take, Speedy. There's no good will come out of it."

"Maybe not," replied Speedy. "But I've got to see who's down and who's up."

He carried the lamp to the door and, holding it high above his head, he let the light stream into the kitchen. What he saw was the last of a wild confusion.

The table was down. Broken chairs littered the floor. The rear door had been kicked open and still hung upon one hinge. In the far corner lay big Bardillo, crumpled against the wall, with Marañon kneeling beside his chief. Old Pa Clive, his hands stretched above his head, was still screeching like a madman. He ran blindly, staggering toward the light.

_____ 30

Pa Clive ran on as Speedy drew back from before his blind charge. He collided with the farther door, in his effort to get into the hall, he tore the door open, he dashed out and up the stairs, and all the while that meaningless yelling was dinning through the air.

Then Speedy advanced into the kitchen, Bones with him. The lamp was placed on the table and Bones relighted the lamp which had been put out when the riot gun was accidentally discharged from his hands.

The great Bardillo was not the only man who had been wounded. Other bloodstains led toward the door. But Bardillo was dying from a dreadful wound in the breast, and he kept one hand vainly covering the place, while the blood streamed out.

He retained his perfect calm. Recognition was in his eye as Speedy stood before him, saying, "What can I do, Bardillo?"

"There was a flask of whiskey on the table," said Bardillo. "It's fallen somewhere on the floor now. If it's not broken, I'd like to have a swallow of the stuff."

"Certainly," said Speedy.

Bones had already found the flask, unbroken, and was bringing it. He uncorked and placed it at the lips of the dying man, who took a deep swallow.

Then he closed his eyes for a moment, breathing rapidly. The bleeding increased perceptibly at the same time.

"We can make him more comfortable, Marañon," said Speedy.

Marañon turned a face that was pale with hatred toward Speedy, and said nothing.

"I'm very well where I am," answered Bardillo. "I've only a minute or two before the light goes out for me. Don't move me. Marañon, I'm sorry to be leaving you, but I've had all I could ask for out of living."

Marañon grasped in both of his the hand which his master reached toward him.

Bardillo looked toward Speedy.

"Tell me," he said, "how you knew that Marañon and I were hoping to get at the money that Dupray has hidden?"

"Everybody who comes near Dupray hopes the same thing," said Speedy. "That's not a novelty. I linked you up with me, in the lies I told him, so that he'd come closer to losing his temper. Finally, he lost it. But I'm not so happy to see you lying here, Bardillo, as I would be to see him. I'm sorry for you. I've an idea that I've done you a good deal more harm than you've ever done me."

Bardillo smiled. His eyes dimmed.

"I would have cut out your heart and carved it for dinner," said he, "with the greatest pleasure in the world. Don't speak of being sorry. Dupray turned on me, as I would have turned on him. There's nothing to regret, except that I got what I would have given to others—what I've given to others a good many times before this. Still, I must talk with you, Speedy."

"I will listen to you, Bardillo," said Speedy, "with all my heart. I tell you again, I'm sorry that this had to happen."

"I know that you're sorry," said Bardillo. "I've loved blood for its own sake all of my days, but danger is the thing that you've

227

hunted. Murder has never been your way. You've made Dupray a tool to kill me, and you've made me a tool to wound Dupray. I think he may die of that wound, too. I don't know, but I pray that he may. Hell would be an empty place for me, unless I could find Dupray there when I arrive. Speedy, I want to talk to you about yourself."

"Go ahead," said Speedy.

He drew closer and dropped on one knee.

Once again Marañon turned a look of hate toward the young American. Bardillo saw it and murmured, "Don't hate him, Marañon. He was beyond my reach and, therefore, he'll be a thousand light years beyond yours. Let him go his way. It's not for the wolves and the coyotes to bother the mountain lions, Marañon. Leave Speedy alone. Go back to El Rey. You can keep a few of the men together who used to follow me. Keep them until you've gathered as much of the money as you can. Then sell everything. You know where it is all kept. And now, Speedy!"

He turned his head toward the American, who leaned still closer, so as to catch every whisper.

Bones, fascinated by this mysterious scene that was like a reconciliation, leaned closer also, gaping horribly above them.

"Speedy," said the dying man, "I've wasted too much time. I'm going faster than I thought. But I want to give you my last warning. You've come to the end of your tether. You've ridden your last chase, and hunted down your last man. Let the devil burn colder in you, Speedy, or soon there'll be nothing left to burn. Your luck has been as wonderful as you are. But now, I warn you. I can see it with the eye of my mind. Be careful. Leave the man trail, Speedy. Settle down quietly, if you can. Find a wife. Leave—"

He choked. His head jerked back. A tremor went through his body. "Señor!" cried Marañon suddenly, in a shockingly loud voice.

"Hush, Marañon," said Speedy. "He cannot hear you."

He reached forward with delicate fingertips, and drew down the eyelids of Bardillo over the eyes that were still bright in death.

Then he stood up, but Marañon had flung himself down on the bloody floor beside his master and lay shuddering there.

Speedy beckoned to Bones, and the pair of them went quietly out into the night.

"That old Marañon," muttered Bones, "he seemed to sorter like Bardillo, after all. But it beats me, Speedy. Why would Bardillo want to give you a warning like that—just to throw a bluff? He can't know anything real, and he just wants to throw a chill into you?"

"Not that," said Speedy. "He was talking out of the bottom of his heart. They say that men can see through clouds and time, when they come close to death. And Bardillo was seeing something about me. Perhaps about Marañon, also."

Speedy laid a hand on Bones.

"I've been close to death before," said he, "but never as close as this. And you got me out of it!"

"No," said Bones, "you talked yourself out. I just loaned a hand at the finish. If I'd been any kind of a man, I'd've stopped big Alf when he knocked you down and started draggin' you back to the house. But I'll tell you how it was—I didn't exactly realize then what sort of a gent you was, Speedy, and how you was giving my life back to me and trying to tell me news that was good for me, at the very time I was layin' low to murder you!"

Speedy felt the tremor that ran through the body of the man beside him, and Bones went on:

"It wasn't till you sat there in the kitchen,

with the wolves all gathered around you, settin' on their haunches, their eyes shining at you, they was so hungry for your blood, it wasn't till just then, that I looked and seen the kind of man that you was. All man, all steel, and nothin' weak about you. When you talked, I didn't realize, for a long time, what you was up to, and how you was laying Dupray agin' Bardillo. I didn't, till just before the gunplay begun. When I realized it, I said to myself that brains like you had couldn't be put out with bullets. A second later the guns were roaring, and I grabbed you and carried you out. That was all. I just seen, in a flash, that it wasn't the right time for a man like you to die."

He ended this speech very simply, but a sort of wonder had come over Speedy.

After a moment, he said, "Let's get farther away from the place. A lot farther away. I can't stand the noise that the women are making."

They moved on toward the barn. "Does it seem to you," asked Speedy, "that the game's worthwhile, Bones?"

"What game? The crooked game?"

"Yes."

"I dunno," answered Bones. "It's the only

thing that I pretty near ever turned my hand to."

"What was it that started you?" asked Speedy.

"Oh, I was a kid, fifteen or so. And I thought that I was smart enough to play crooked cards, and I got called in the middle of a deal. So I tried a gunplay, and I dropped the wise guy, all right. I thought I'd killed him and rode for it, got away and before I heard that he wasn't dead, I'd done too much ever to go back inside the law again."

Speedy nodded in the darkness.

"How do you feel about it—the crooked game, Bones?"

"Why," replied Bones, "it ain't any shame for me to tell you the truth, Speedy. I'll tell you that I feel kinda sick and cold around the heart, most of the time, when I think of what's to come. But I don't let myself think much. Not a doggone lot, anyways."

"Suppose you chuck it, Bones?" said Speedy.

"Chuck it?" said Bones. "What else would I do? Where'd I go? No decent man would have nothin' to do with me."

"Do you know where John Wilson lives?" asked Speedy.

"Sure I know! Didn't the whole gang of us try to get you there?"

"Then go back to Wilson," said Speedy. "Tell him that I sent you, will you? Tell him that he's to put you up for a while, and he'll do that."

"I would've cut his throat, once," said Bones.

"That makes no difference," said Speedy. "He'll do what I ask him to do. Will you go there? I'll come back when I can. And then we'll try to arrange something for you. Any man who's sick of a wrong life ought to have a chance to lead a right one."

"What'll become of you? Where are you going now?" asked Bones.

"Dupray," said Speedy, "I've made a vow in my heart to get him, this time, and get him I shall, if I have to spend my life on the trail."

"Hold on," murmured Bones.

"Well?"

"Ain't you forgetting," said Bones, "the last thing that Bardillo said to you?"

"I'm not forgetting," replied Speedy solemnly.

"He said," went on Bones, "that you were at the end of your rope. He said it almost like he had a way of knowing."

"Perhaps he knew," agreed Speedy. "I can tell that. But the fact is that I have to take the trail myself."

"Well," said Bones, "I know that if Bardillo couldn't budge you, I can't say nothing that will."

"I've got to go," said Speedy. "There was never a devil in the world that's worked as much mischief as Dupray. He'll do it again, too. I can't leave his trail. It may be the end for me, or for him, or for both of us."

Bones sighed. Then he said, "What can I do? You won't take me with you on the trail, Speedy?"

"No," answered Speedy. "I can't do that. You were his man. You worked under him."

"That's true," answered Bones. "I'm best pleased to be away from the business. But I'm wishing you luck."

31

THE SUN was out of the zenith and beginning to go westerly, and the heavy shadows of the pine trees were growing longer when Alf Clive rode up the trail with a rifle balanced before him, the mustang between his legs looking hardly larger than a big dog, such was the bulk of the rider.

When he came to the top of the hill, he turned the head of the mustang and looked back across the heads of the trees toward the rolling ground beyond. Then he shrugged his broad shoulders and made a gesture of surrender with one hand.

"Hello, Alf," said a voice behind him.

"Speedy!" cried Alf.

He whirled in the saddle and raised his rifle. But it was some seconds after this that he saw the other behind the thick, high shrubbery along the road. Behind the man he could gradually make out the silhouette of a horse.

He was half a mind to send a bullet at the two figures, but second thought bewildered him, because it was plain that, if there had been mischief in the mind of Speedy, he had had plenty of time to shoot his quarry full of holes.

So Alf delayed the bullet and, while he was in the quandary, Speedy calmly led his horse out onto the road and mounted it.

"How are things with you, Alf?" he asked.

"What brung you here, and whatcha want with me?" asked Alf sharply, adding, "I got you covered, Speedy, and don't you try none of your doggone tricks, neither."

He tried to speak as fiercely as possible, but there was a great awe in his voice and face as he considered the other.

"Why, Alf," said Speedy, "I have nothing against you."

"Me that nearly got you murdered?" said Alf. "You ain't got nothin' agin' me?"

"Not a thing," said Speedy. "It wasn't you that nearly got me murdered. It was the five thousand dollars that Dupray and Bardillo offered. That was all. You did your job to get the money, and you did it very well, too. You got the money and that ends the business, so far as you and I are concerned. I have nothing against you, and I'm not on your trail."

Alf drew a great breath.

"They say that your word's better than anybody else's oath," he remarked.

"You can trust it now," said Speedy.

"Who you after, then?"

"Dupray."

"I was with him, and he up and left me," said Alf. "Went off, and said he'd be back. I've waited half a day, and he ain't come. He slipped away, after I'd been pretty useful to him, too! I was gonna work for him, but I ain't gonna be treated like a hound dog by no man, not even Dupray."

"That's the right spirit," said Speedy. "You lost him where?"

The eyes of the big fellow narrowed, but suddenly he broke out: "Well, why shouldn't I tell you? He done me dirt, runnin' off like that. And you could've popped me full of lead from behind that bush yonder. Well—I left him back yonder, where the woods peg out, and there's only a few big trees dotted around on the hills. Back there is where I left him. How'd you manage to trail us this far?"

"I used my eyes, and guessed a little now and then," said Speedy.

"Used your eyes?" murmured the other. "But look here, Speedy, it's three whole days that we been riding."

"That's true."

"We laid about a hundred trail problems that would've puzzled the devil himself. But—well, that was what Dupray said, that you'd find the way through in spite of anything that we did. You got me beat, Speedy!"

"Not at all, Alf," replied Speedy. "I simply kept on casting ahead, and I had luck in finding the trail again."

"Luck don't come a hundred times in a

row," said Alf, shaking his head and staring with a brutal wonder and envy. "I wish I knew how you done it."

He added suddenly, "How's things back there at home?"

"Not very good for you, Alf," said Speedy. "If I were you, I'd keep away from your father and mother, for a time. They seem to blame you for getting the twenty-five hundred while they collected only fifteen hundred. I think your father and mother don't deny that you may have had something to do with the killing of Bardillo."

"I didn't do no shooting at Bardillo!" said Alf. "I was only shooting—in the dark—at—at—"

"At me," said Speedy, smiling a little.

"Well," blurted out Alf, "I was scared what you might do to me, if you got away. You guessed that even in the dark, did you? You knew that I was shootin' at you?"

Speedy passed over the absurd question easily.

"I found blood here and there, Alf, along the trail. Was Dupray badly hurt?"

"Yeah, in the body, somewheres," said Alf. "I dunno just where. He didn't ask me for no help. He didn't say as it was hurting him much, neither. He just rode along and kept his mouth shut."

"He has courage," said Speedy, nodding his head. "But how did he look?"

"Why, just the same kind of frozen frog face that he always has," said Alf.

"Hold up through each day's riding?"

"He held up, all right. He's an Injun. He never gets tired on the back of a horse. Only this morning, he laid in his blankets kind of late. He didn't want no breakfast but coffee, and he went off finally, and told me he'd ride back in an hour. He didn't come. He went and give me the slip."

"Thanks," said Speedy. "That's all I want to know."

"And what do you make out of that, Speedy?" asked Alf.

"Nothing, except what I guess," answered Speedy.

"What's that?"

"Why," answered Speedy, "that if I were you, I'd put that twenty-five hundred dollars in some good ranch, take a mortgage on the rest, and try to settle down."

"Hey!" exclaimed Alf. "You can read minds, can't you? How'd you know I was thinkin' of that?"

"Only a guess," replied Speedy.

"When I seen you and Dupray and Bardillo at one another," said Alf, "though you was only usin' words, I begun to see that I could never rise to the top on that kind of a game. I'm just as glad that Dupray turned me off! So long, Speedy."

"So long," said Speedy, and rode his horse down the slope up which Alf had just come.

<hr>

32

HE RODE on for two hours into the midst of that rolling country, tree-dotted, beyond the edge of the woods, which he found exactly as Alf had described it.

There he camped. It was almost useless for him to search in detail, because the whole face of the country was covered with grass two and three feet high, and there were thickets here and there sufficient to have hidden regiments.

But there he camped, and ate hard-tack, drank from the canteen, and watched the sky from time to time with the patience of an Indian, who is quiet because nature is a book in which he is reading.

So Speedy was reading, and in the evening

he noted with much interest two or three buzzards up in the zenith.

That night he slept long and awoke in the rose of the morning. His face was wet with dew. He went down the hill to a brook, undressed, bathed, rubbed himself dry, dressed again, shaved, returned to his camp, and ventured on a very small fire to make coffee. That and a bit of hard-tack out of his saddlebag were his only food. For food bothered him on the march hardly more than it bothers a migrating bird.

At length, he resumed his survey of the skies.

There were more buzzards now, and they were circling quite a bit lower down, about one particular hill.

He waited until the sun was at nine o'clock. More and more buzzards were flying now in their grim circles, a dozen birds in all, the lowest of them very near to the ground.

Then he started, rode straight across country, abandoned the horse at the bottom of the hill which the birds seemed to have selected, and went up through the· grass as noiseless as a snake.

The grass cleared away a little toward the top of the hill, for here stood three immense trees, left from the primeval forest. Here the cattle that grazed on the range took shelter from the sun about noon.

As Speedy emerged from the tall grass, facing the three great trees, he noticed that half of the middle one had fallen. The remnants of the vast log were stretched along the ground in a mound of decay with the grass already closing over it. The great, broad stump of the ruined trunk rose a dozen feet from the ground.

It was beyond this tree that a horse was grazing and, seated on the ground with his back against the stump and just his shoulder visible, was Dupray. As his head turned, Speedy saw enough to recognize that unforgettable mask of a face.

He left the screen of grass and stole forward. That horse, yonder, might warn his master. If Dupray turned—well, Speedy, as usual, carried no gun!

So he stepped on the ground as a shadow falls, smoothly drifting forward. He saw a buzzard sail down to the ground and light on the fallen log, its horrible, naked red head thrust out. It peered at Dupray, whose weary voice said, "Not yet, sister. Not yet!"

Speedy stepped around the side of the great tree trunk and, with a flick of his toe, kicked away the gun belt which Dupray had unbuckled and laid to the side.

Dupray looked up and scrutinized his face with eyes that turned green with hate.

"I knew you'd come, Speedy," he remarked in the calmest of voices.

"I had to come, Charley," replied Speedy. "This had to be the last trail, either for you or for me. It seems that it will be the last one for you, though."

Dupray regarded him silently for a moment, utter devastation stirring slowly in his face.

Then he said, "You win, Speedy. You won from the first fall of the cards. And to think that I've had you spread out, helpless, tied! All you needed was one push of a knife! To think that I had you like that!"

"Nothing but luck. You can't beat such luck, Charley," said Speedy.

"Not luck, but your damned brain, like the brain of a rat and a fox rolled together."

"Don't be too rough, Charley," pleaded Speedy. "No matter what you feel about me, you might remember that I'm the friend of Al."

"The damned cur," said the robber, "he's throwed me over, his own flesh and blood, to herd with you."

"Rough talk, brother, rough talk," commented Speedy. "But tell me why you picked out this spot to come and die in."

"How did you find me?" asked Dupray with a snarl.

"I watched the buzzards gather. When Alf told me that you'd lain late in the blankets this morning, I could guess that the wound was making you pretty sick."

"Reading the minds of birds now, are you?" asked Dupray.

"I'd rather read your mind, man," replied Speedy. "I'd rather find out why you've come here to die."

"I come as far as I could crawl," said the other. "That's all. Speedy, if you're a decent man, you'll scratch a hole and bury me away from the buzzards."

"This is the heart of your range, partner," commented Speedy. "Oh, I'll bury you, well enough. Don't worry."

"Just hoist me up—it's no great trick, if you get me onto a horse first. Then dump me down inside the hollow of that trunk, there."

"How d'you know it's hollow?" asked Speedy.

"How? Why, they're always hollow when

they've stood as long as that," answered Dupray.

"Not always. Not by a long shot," replied Speedy. "You have been here before, Dupray. Wanting to die in that hollow stump like a sick owl—is it because you've got your stuff cached inside, the gold, the diamonds, and the sheafs of hard cash, Dupray? Is that the place?"

Dupray looked at him and smiled.

"D'you think I'm fool enough to use that sort of a hiding place, when I've got every hole in the mountains to use if I want it?"

Speedy nodded.

"Why not?" he asked. "The cattle tramp around here; they'd cover up the sign you'd make in coming and going. Not many people would suspect you of hiding away in an open hole like that. Yet a good wrapping with a tarpaulin would be enough to see it through the weather."

Dupray suddenly choked. His mouth opened. He bit at the air like a dog in agony. The spasm passed, and, with his head hanging over on his shoulder and his body slumped down to the ground, he gasped, "Speedy!"

The tramp leaned over him.

"Dupray," he said solemnly, "I thought I

245

hated you like a snake, but I can't help being sorry for you when I see you here. If you've got any word to leave for Al, tell me, and I'll surely carry it to him."

"Yes—for Al—closer!" said the dying man.

Speedy dropped to one knee and put his ear close to the lips of Dupray.

"What is it, Charley? Louder."

"This," said Dupray, and suddenly struck upward with a long bladed hunting knife which he had managed to get into his hand from the inside of his coat.

He could have driven it straight through the heart of Speedy, but savage venom made him try for the throat, and in his blindness, the crook of his arm struck under the elbow of Speedy.

The blow had failed, and Speedy was away like a shadow.

"Damn you!" breathed Dupray. "I'll get you yet and—"

In his frenzy he got to his feet, scooped up a revolver from the fallen belt, and fired. His bullet went wild, hitting the ground, as he pitched forward on his face. He was dead when Speedy reached him. Like a wild beast, he had used his death agony to maintain the fight.

In the deep pit of the hollow tree trunk, as he had requested, Dupray was buried, wrapped in thick folds of tarpaulins which Speedy had found inside and which covered many securely wrapped parcels, exactly as he had imagined. But the contents of those parcels now filled the saddlebags of two horses, and made in addition, a staggeringly heavy pack which he lashed over the saddles. The money and the jewels were the main items; but the weight of the burden was the massive gold, the gold that Dupray had loved to fondle and stroke like a cat beside a family hearth.

Then Speedy took his way down the slope. The evening was coming on, for he had been long in the hollow of the trunk. A fortune for a dozen men was weighting down the horses he led, but there was no content in his mind. It was blood money, won by crime, hoarded for no good end. To him, it would be of no use.

There must be another trail, still beyond this, perhaps another beyond that; always another, to the end of his days. And those days, according to the dying Bardillo, would not be long.

But somber moods could not last long with him. Plucking at his small guitar, he began to sing as he led the horses over the next hill and straight into the gold and crimson of the West.

33

In the dappling of shadow under a cotton-wood, Speedy lay, the very picture of that laziness and ease which had caused certain foolish men, long ago, to give him his nickname. All the lines of his slender body flowed as smoothly, with as soft an inertness as the lines of a panther stretched on jungle grass. Only the eyes of the panther will stay alert. And the eyes of Speedy were alert, also. He seemed to be almost unconscious, and yet hardly a leaf could stir on the tree above him without his knowledge.

He wore the clothes of a Mexican laborer— white cotton trousers so frayed at the bottom that they were rolled up to his brown knees, a shirt open at the throat, a rag of sash about his waist, and straw-soled huarachos like sandals on his feet.

A straw hat was under his head, and the wind ruffled in the back of his hair, sometimes moving it like a shadow on his forehead. He looked like a Mexican; there was a

Latin delicacy of feature. And when he half smiled at a thought, his smile was the white Latin's flash in a brown face.

He was aware of the coming of the two men, long before their shadows crossed him. From the corners of his half-closed eyes he was aware of them for what they were, twin brothers in bulky size, in brutal good looks. He was aware of the slight flaring of their nostrils, the stiffness about their mouths. Nature had given them some of these animal characteristics; whiskey had accentuated them. In the young eyes of Speedy there was the wisdom of old age; he noted above all the big hands of these men, and the guns that were strapped low down on their thighs. The left arm of one was slung in a bandage.

"We can talk private here in the shade, Steve," one of them was saying.

"There's somebody here already, Tim," said the other.

"There ain't anybody. There's only a greaser," said Tim.

"Sure, it's only a greaser." Steve chuckled. "Up, bum, and start movin'!"

The eyes of Speedy opened a little more, only a little. They were as bright and as coldly dangerous as ever the eye of a panther could be, before it leaps.

"He don't hear you," said Tim.

"I'll open his ears," said Steve, who wore the bandage. "Up!"

And he ground the toe of his boot into the ribs of Speedy.

Speedy sat up.

"No spik English, señor," he said.

"You no spik English? You get out, just the same," said Steve.

Speedy rose to his feet without touching the ground with his fingers, with a single easy movement of his body. He made no protest, and walked slowly off, his shuffling huarachos bringing up wisps of dust. He moved a little closer to the wall of the inn, and then slumped again to the ground, as a tired dog lies down, all in one move.

He had for shade, now, the shelter of a mesquite. But the mesquite foliage makes no more than a misting of the light, holding its little varnished leaves edgewise to the burning of the sun so that it will lose as little water as possible by evaporation. It was, therefore, almost in the full glare of the sun that Speedy lay down, with his straw hat again under his head. But the burn of that sun he could endure. He let the fierceness of it soak into his flesh, and smiled a little. He seemed sound asleep, in a moment; and when a whirlpool of dust was raised by the wind and walked toward him, he did not stir as it crossed his face with its vortex.

"Look at him," said Steve, "rolling in the dust and soakin' up the sun. Can he hear us?"

"What difference? He don't understand," said Tim. "Now, blaze away."

"I got the cablegram today," said Steve. "I can't go. You can."

Speedy turned his head a little. Through the lashes of his eyes he studied the pair carefully. And his ears strained. Some of the words that followed, he could hear clearly enough; others were more than half lost; others were mere murmurs that contained no syllables.

What he made out was that the cablegram called for instant action; that Steve could not go on the mission; that Tim would have to ride.

"And when I get there?" said Tim.

Steve raised his right hand and crooked the trigger finger in suddenly. Tim shook his head in violent disagreement.

And Steve exclaimed something. Speedy's ears caught: "—Materro wants. That's all."

It was perfectly clear. Someone was to be

shot. "Materro" wanted it done. And Tim was to do it.

Presently the two men walked down the street. Speedy went behind them as far as a cluster of men who were in front of the hotel, where they stood talking loudly, with many gestures. There the two paused to speak with friends, and Speedy brushed by Steve. In his hand he took away the cablegram form that had been in Steve's coat pocket. Turning into the next lane, he opened the paper and read:

ISABELLA ESCAPED AND PROBABLY ON SAILING SHIP BOUND FOR SAN GALLO ARRIVING PERHAPS BETWEEN TENTH AND TWENTIETH STOP FINISH NOW MATERRO

Speedy folded the slip again. The grisly thing went like a finger of ice over his brain. Was it a woman who was to be murdered? No, she was not to arrive at San Gallo until between the tenth and the twentieth. It was the ninth, that day. And Materro wanted something done at once. "Finish now." That was the word that brought death to someone.

He turned back from the corner in time to see Tim and Steve disappearing across the

street through the swinging doors of a s
loon. Speedy stopped to think.

If he were to prevent the killing, he mus
either keep Tim from leaving the town, o.
else he must follow the man and stop his
hand at the vital moment.

Follow him where? To San Gallo? Was
that the name of the place where the murder
was to take place?

Speedy went first to the stable behind the
hotel and got out his mule. It was a good,
tough gray, with the strength of iron in it,
and it was almost ideally suited for carrying
a rider over the thirsty leagues of the desert,
where the water holes were drying up. The
dry marches which that mule could make
were prodigious things. But it lacked speed,
of course, and speed was probably what Tim
would use.

Speedy looked the mule over with a sigh
of despair. It was not fast enough to head off
Tim. And he had not enough money to
change the brute for a good running horse.

However, he knew how to make the best
of a bad bargain. With the mule saddled,
and the narrow roll of his pack strapped
behind the saddle, Speedy jogged down the
street and stopped in front of the saloon into
which the two brothers had disappeared.

He dismounted, opened a large canvas saddlebag, and took from it a guitar. He was tuning it as he entered the swinging doors.

After the hot desert air outside, the moist coolness of the place passed like the touch of water over his skin. But a red-faced man with an enormous paunch shouted at him from behind the bar: "Out greaser! No greaser in this saloon!"

Speedy took off his straw hat and bowed. He commenced to back toward the door, still bowing, still smiling, but he backed very slowly.

"I, señor," said Speedy, "only sing and dance for the Americanos. I never raise my head to drink with them."

"Damn him and his singing," said the man with his arm in the sling. He was standing at a little distance down the bar, with a glass of red-brown whiskey, shining in his hand. "Throw him out, Barney."

"Yeah, get out!" roared Barney, the bartender. "Get out and stay out, unless you can sing like a regular bird. You take your chance. Want to try it? Get out now, unless you're pretty sure you'll please us, because if you don't, we'll *kick* you out, and when you light, you'll bust most of your bones."

Speedy no longer retreated. He even

stepped forward, and replaced the hat on his head.

"I am your servant, señor," he said, "and being your servant, I should not fear to please you. Is Mexican music what you want?"

"Yeah, give us a greaser song," said Tim. "Tune it up and let's have it."

Instantly, Speedy struck the resounding strings of the guitar, and then, plucking them rapidly, and not with too much strength, he started the accompaniment, and raised his voice.

"I'll give them a song and dance that will please them, now," he told himself. "But across the desert, there'll be dancing in more ways than one. I'll lead some people a desert dance there, all right, before I get through."

Tim and Steve instantly sidled between him and the door, to block his retreat. A glance at their faces showed that they were anxious for the song to end, not because they disliked the music but because they wanted the pleasure of beating the Mexican.

Speedy sang a song of the wine making, far south, of the purple dust on the grapes, of the juices that spurt out from beneath the treading feet of the wine pressers, of the fragrance of the new wine, of the nights pale and bright with stars, and the days white with a powerful sun.

He sang, and then, still keeping the accompaniment going, but making it suddenly loud, he started dancing. The straw huarachos, whispering and crinkling against the floor, flew almost faster than the eye could follow.

Steve and Tim, by the door, were eyeing the dance, as they had listened to the song, with sneering malice in their faces. But Barney, the bartender, leaned over the bar with a wide grin of pleasure, and presently began to beat time with the flat of his hand.

Finally, Speedy stopped plucking at the guitar and devoted all of his attention to the dance alone, spinning and whirling here and there on his flying feet, his arms outstretched to keep the balance secure.

In the midst of that whirling, he drifted close to the two brothers near the door, and with an unseen gesture, passed the cablegram back into the pocket of Steve.

Speedy went on spinning in the dance, until it carried him behind the big couple and the swinging doors.

Instantly the powerful hand of Tim collared him and hurled him staggering back toward the center of the long, narrow room.

"You can't run out on us, you sneak!" shouted Tim.

"Let him alone, Tim Lynch!" shouted the bartender.

But Speedy, coming out of the stagger from which he had nearly fallen to the floor, was continuing the dance. Even his smiling had not stopped, and as for the flash of his eyes, it might well be mistaken for the mere gleam of a singer's eyes, and not for the hate and rage that were burning in him like a fire.

34

THE DANCE ended with Speedy taking off his hat and making a wide and deep bow. He smiled on the bartender and he also smiled on the two handsome, brutal faces of Tim and Steve Lynch, that sneered at him.

The bartender beat more loudly than ever on the bar.

"That's the best song and dance that I ever seen!" he declared.

"Wait a minute," said Tim Lynch, still smiling, while his eyes surveyed the slender body of Speedy. "Wait a minute, will you? There's gotta be a vote on this here. You vote that it's a good song and dance, but if you're voted down, that greaser gets kicked out onto the street. How you vote, Steve?"

"Rotten!" said Steve, fairly shouting. "There wasn't no music to the song, and there wasn't no sense to it, neither. And the dancing was kind of out of step, seemed to me. Rotten, I'd say."

"That's what I say," remarked Tim Lynch. "There ain't any more music in that gent's throat than there is in my feet. Out he goes!"

And he made a sudden reach for Speedy.

He missed his hold, as though he had reached for a dead leaf, so lightly, so easily, did Speedy avoid that hand. But he had made one mistake. He had looked upon the man with the bandaged arm as a negligible property in the brawl, but now big Steve Lynch, his step lightened by malice, his eyes squinting, came swiftly in. He did not try to catch Speedy with his hand, but used his fist.

At the last instant, Speedy saw the flying danger come near. He could not avoid it entirely, and as he swerved, the heavy knuckles of Steve glanced along the side of his head. The weight of the blow flung Speedy back against the wall, his head and shoulders striking heavily.

Helpless as he was for the instant, serious damage might have come to him. But now Barney charged in between. He had taken this time to get around the end of the bar, and now he stood between Speedy and danger.

"You fellows can run the place down there at San Gallo," said Barney, "but you ain't runnin' my saloon. Not half! Leave him be. He ain't your size, and you've scared the poor kid to death and broke his head for him!"

In fact, the eyes of Speedy were a little distended and rolling. It might have been purest rage that worked in him, but the bartender chose to take it for fear.

Steve Lynch, in spite of the fact that one arm was bandaged, seemed eager to step in past Barney and get at the victim, but Tim restrained him.

"Take it easy, Steve," he said. "We've give the greaser something to think about. He ain't goin' to be so sure about his song and dance, from this time on. He's goin' to be scared, when he gets out among folks, and that's the way that a greaser had oughta be! Come back there to the end of the room.

I wanta talk to you some more, before I start."

He turned to Barney.

"Give us a couple of whiskies," he said.

The whiskies were forthcoming, and the pair of big brothers retired to the end of the room, while Barney, clapping Speedy on the shoulder, said, "Don't take it too hard, young feller. We got some rough gents in this part of the world, and the Lynch boys is among the roughest. Stand up and have a drink with me, and forget that clip you got alongside the head. Lucky it didn't land square, or there would of been a busted head for you, and no mistake."

Speedy stood at the bar, trembling. In all his life, anger had never come so near to mastering him, but anger now was the last thing that he dared to show. What was important was that he should learn all he could of the plans of the Lynch brothers, and discover, if possible, the identity of the person they were to kill.

So he stood at the bar, facing a little toward the other pair, and studying their faces through the shadow. Tim Lynch was lost to him, for the head of Tim was turned away from him. But there was a pale shaft of light falling from a window upon the face of Steve, and that light enabled him, now and then, to read the lips of Steve for a few instants. Speedy saw him say, "Crocker's gotta die; that's all. He's gotta die, and you've gotta kill him!"

It seemed from the shaken head of Tim that he dissented to this, and Steve leaned forward, his face partially hidden behind his hand, to argue the point.

The argument did not need to last long; Tim was readily convinced, according to the manner in which he soon was nodding his head.

Then Steve was saying, "The boys are all solid, now, except that old fool of a Danny. And you can brush him out of the way. Then get Lew Crocker and get him good. I wish I was goin' to be there—"

Again his hand partially covered his lips, and Speedy, burning with curiosity, quivering with eagerness, could make out no more of the words that immediately followed.

But he had learned a great deal.

At San Gallo, wherever that might be, Tim Lynch would find that "the boys were now all solid," and that it would be easy to kill a man named Lew Crocker, because Crocker's only friend was an old chap named Danny.

Why not call in the sheriff for this occasion? Surely the law was needed.

But Speedy, thinking the matter over as he sipped his drink at the bar, decided that he would never be able to interest the powers of the law. All that he had discovered was hardly more than hearsay. As a matter of fact, he had not even heard, but merely seen, some of the words on the lips of Steve. He would be laughed at. These fellows were known. They were familiar figures. He was a stranger and, to all appearances, no more than a "poor greaser." The sheriff would probably throw him out of his office, if he tried to tell his tale. Yes, or put him in jail as a mischiefmaker and hobo!

Speedy thanked the bartender and went out into the street. There, in the burning sunshine, he touched the swelling on the side of his head where the iron-hard knuckles of Steve had glanced.

What had happened to him today had never happened before in all his life. To the blunt and heavier strength of other men he had always been able to oppose a rapier deftness of hand and wit that turned blows and dangers aside. Now he had been bruised, humiliated, kicked about like a dog.

Somewhere there would be a counter-reckoning. The day might come when Lew Crocker, whoever he was, would have another friend than Danny, in the time of need.

A Mexican peddlar of a mule load of odds and ends came down the street, and Speedy turned in at his side. This was a fat fellow with a rosy face, and a wandering eye that searched all who came near, in his hunt for a customer.

"Where shall a poor man find a chance to work?" asked Speedy. "I hear of a town called San Gallo."

"That's no town," said the peddlar. "That is no place at all for our countrymen. It is a ranch where nothing but the gringos work."

"I heard of it," said Speedy sadly.

"Forty miles south, toward the sea," said the other. "I know it. I know all of this country better than a hawk knows it. A green lagoon is stuck into the side of the land, and at the end of the lagoon there is a ranch house. That is all. That is San Gallo. No town, but a ranch."

"And no Mexicans work there?" asked Speedy.

"Not one," said the other. "The gringos only—"

There was a heavy beating of hoofs.

"Out of the way, greasers," shouted a heavy voice.

And between them galloped Tim Lynch on a big black horse. The dust, cupped and flung upward by the hollow hoofs of the horse, hung in a blinding cloud, and through it Speedy dimly saw the man disappear, with the red of his bandanna fluttering rapidly behind his neck.

Speedy was on the back of his mule at once.

To follow that rider was almost like trying to keep the trail of a flying comet, but he would attempt the task.

He felt that already he had failed in almost every point. For one thing, he had wanted to keep Tim Lynch from leaving the town. For another, he had wanted to learn more particulars of the place that was now his goal. But all he knew was that San Gallo was a ranch many miles to the south, where a green lagoon thrust into the land from the Gulf of Mexico.

On that place he might find Lew Crocker, whose life was endangered. There was a woman, Isabella, who seemed to be connected with the story at some point. There was also Materro, a sinister influence in the background who could tell the Lynch brothers when to act.

The whole matter was a mystery, and Speedy had only the speed of a gray mule to use on the desert trail!

_____ 35

IT WAS time to make haste slowly, Speedy knew. He simply kept the mule to a steady dogtrot, with the dissolving dust cloud made by Tim Lynch vanishing before him.

Behind him, the little town dwindled, and then disappeared behind the first low swale of ground.

Before him lay open desert country, gray country, with dusty, sundried grasses growing in obscure patches, here and there, though now and again he saw a scattering of cattle grazing.

Twice he almost lost the trail of Tim Lynch, but he managed to spot it again, where the man had turned both times to the left onto smaller trails. He knew that track, by this time, and the barred shoe on the left forefoot. His confidence increased, and he kept the mule steadily to that trot.

The dust cloud that Lynch made with his

black had disappeared, and it did not grow up again as the miles drifted behind Speedy. Then he saw the trail leading down toward the pale gray-green willows of a watercourse.

He dismounted on the verge of them and went on foot. The pungency of tobacco reached him first. Then, on the bank of a semi-stagnant pool, he saw Tim Lynch stretched on his back with his hands under his head. The black grazed a patch of grass twenty steps away. The big horse was rather badly spent, and no doubt the pause had been made by Lynch to rest it at a halfway point down the trail.

The obvious thing was to take the horse and let the man proceed on foot. Cowpunchers are notoriously helpless when they have to walk. And certainly it should not take long after the arrival of Speedy at San Gallo to warn Lew Crocker of the danger that was now approaching him.

Yet it was a savage temptation to put hands on Tim Lynch here and now. Speedy fought that temptation back. Instead, he turned himself into a snakelike body that worked softly through the underbrush until it came near the black horse.

The cinches had been loosened. Speedy rose like a shadow, drew the cinches taut, and without stopping to tie them, whipped into the saddle. Behind him, he heard a shout, then a wild yell of rage. A gun barked. A bullet beat into a tree trunk near by. But Speedy already was flying the horse among the willows, back toward the point where he had left the gray mule.

He dismounted there, tied the cinches of the black horse, took the gray mule on the lead, and rode on again. He was far off on the head of a low hill when, looking back, he saw the big form of Tim Lynch issue from the trees and run in frantic pursuit, throwing up dust almost like a galloping horse.

Speedy laughed, as his eye for an instant caressed that laboring form. Much of the forty miles remained. It would be a very weary Tim Lynch who finally managed to reach San Gallo, if he did not give up the long trail in sympathy for his sore feet.

After that, Speedy headed due south, in the hope that he might eventually blunder onto the right way. Otherwise, after reaching the coast, he would have to wander up it until he found the house and the lagoon.

So he came down into the coast country, a land of chapparal with thorns like the claws of a tiger, cactus, pale-gray mesquite; a gray land, covered with sun-cured gray grass, pale with dust. Even the liveoaks were gray with a draping of the sad Spanish moss. Small, tough cattle, wilder than deer and savage as beasts of prey, grazed those miles. And sometimes Speedy saw them cantering with a long, stretching lope. He knew what that meant, and followed. He could see more and more of the cattle coming from several directions, aiming at a focal point. That point was a big stretch of stagnant water, a "tank" made by building a costly dam of masonry across the course of a creek, and so saving the winter rains for the drought of summer.

To that artificial lake, the cattle had to come from a great distance. All around it, the grass was eaten to the roots for a mile, and having watered, the wise range cattle went back again, at a trot or a gallop, steering for some distant grassy sections. For two days, three days, even four days, some cowpunchers swore, those steers would remain grazing on the dry, acrid grass before the need of water sent them back, red-eyed, toward the "tank."

Numbers of them were in the water, belly-deep, or lying down near the verge of the lake waiting until they could take a second or a third drink, before turning back once more toward their chosen grazing land. Myriads of sea birds, regardless of the beeves, covered the face of the lake, but they rose with a roaring of wings when they saw Speedy come near.

He rode into the lake, over the hardcaked and cracking ground from which the water had retired, over the soggy mud of the border, and then well out into the "tank." When he paused, the animals nosed the stale water once or twice, shook their heads in protest— and then drank deep!

Speedy was pleased. Mules are not dainty, but a horse that consults necessity rather than individual taste is the horse for the Southwestern desert. Looking over that ill-smelling lake, he felt the grimness of the country more than ever. What would have been an abomination in a luckier land was a treasure here. The cattle came to it. So did the beasts of prey.

He saw the trail of a jaguar, the immense print of the forepaw clearly marked on the soft mud at the edge of the water. A puma had been there, little wild cats had come down to lap the warm water, and deer, and hogs, and there were the tiny hoofmarks of the peccaries, all of these signs overworked by the complicated patterning where the sea birds had walked. One tragedy was there.

The carcass of a dead beef showed on the edge of the water, where the soft mud had pulled down some thirst-starved beast that stood still for too long, and let the muck underneath imprison its legs.

Speedy rode on. It was very hot. The heat waves that reflected from the surface of the earth made the air tremble. Only now and then the blue water of a mirage shone steady as a sapphire in the distance. But Speedy was not tempted. Those fair visions, he knew, were too beautiful for the country which embosomed them.

The sun was still well up in the sky, when he came to a hill which was reasonably high, for the midst of that low rolling or level country. He climbed it. At the top there was the outline of a trench that had been dug, and an embankment thrown up outside it. Men had been besieged here, perhaps, hundreds of years ago. Perhaps here the natives had surrounded a little party of armored Spaniards and held them while the sun did the work of death better than arrows could have managed it.

From that height, Speedy looked far out to the coast, and to the dull sheen of the sea beyond. He saw the wavering coastline, with one deep lagoon stuck like a silver dagger into the heart of the land, and a house at the end of it.

That was San Gallo, he could be sure. It was not forty miles, after all, and the big horse was still fresh enough.

Through that clear air, he could see a vast distance; he could mark the form of a horseman on a low sand dune near the in-jutting lagoon. He could see the piers of the old wharf, that looked like the upstanding teeth of a broken comb. All of this was very small and fine, something to be squinted at and guessed rather than seen. But very real was the sweet and dangerous air of adventure.

For that was the port to which "Isabella," who had escaped, was coming in a sailing vessel. Was she old or young? Young, said the heart of Speedy. Who was "Materro," who had signed the cablegram? Was it he who had imprisoned "Isabella"?

There was enough in the air to have made another man turn back, but Speedy began to sing. He tapped a big canvas saddlebag, and the strings of the guitar gave out a soft chord of accompaniment.

But there were preparations to be made. He might need a new identity in San Gallo.

So Speedy dismounted, took the roll from behind the saddle, and unfurled it. He shed his own clothes and gleamed for an instant in the flash of the sun like a ruddy bit of bronze, striped about the hips with white.

He put on a pair of corduroy trousers, much too large for him and a ragged blue flannel shirt, and a plaid vest into which two bodies as large as his own could have been slipped. He girded about his neck a tie of flaming crimson, with yellow spots in it, and put on his head a cap that puffed out behind and sloped forward into a very deep visor that made his face seem older and more lean and pointed. He got on his feet a pair of socks, and shoes over them. The uppers of those shoes were badly scuffed and worn, but his feet were fitted perfectly. Only the cleverest of shoemakers could have built those shoes so exactly, and made them so light and so supple between the ball of the foot and the heel. In those shoes a tight-rope walker could have performed.

Speedy put away his discarded clothes with care, and did them up in the roll. He carried several changes of outfit with him, for in his life of aimless wandering, when he was led across thousands of miles every year by horse or the iron trail of the railroad, he sometimes needed to change his skin, as it were. For he hunted neither man nor gold, but only the goddess of adventure; a fair face and treacherous eyes for a man to love.

She was not far from him now, he was certain, and that was why he laughed aloud as he sat in the saddle again, and sent the big gelding forward toward the ranch house. He felt that even if he encountered Tim, the ragged Mexican asleep in the sun would not be recognized in one who seemed like a gypsy of the plains.

In a draw he unsaddled the black horse and turned it loose. Then he rode on with the mule.

He saw that the ranch house was a typical one of that section of the country, as he drew nearer to it. The kitchen was at one end of the building, the bunk house was at the other, and these two extremities were joined by an open-faced hall in which dangled saddles, bridles, and a thousand odds and ends.

Speedy tethered the mule at the hitch rack, and went toward the front door. When he rapped at it, it was opened by a fellow with a concave face that bulged out at the forehead and at the chin. The central section of that face had been mashed by the kick of a horse.

The man waited for no questions, but simply said, "No handouts here. On your way, kid," and slammed the door.

<hr>

36

A LITTLE shudder ran through the body of Speedy as the door crashed before him. It might have been fear; it might have been anger; it might have been an excess of that same eerie emotion that had gripped him when, from the hilltop, he first looked down on the house and the harbor of San Gallo.

He went to the kitchen door, up two steps from the ground, and pushed it open.

"Hello, doctor," he said.

The cook turned slowly, an ominous slowness. He was a big bulk of a man with a swollen red face, and his sleeves were turned up over hairy arms to his elbows, and all his great body was encased in a canvas apron, fingermarked with grease. He looked across his shoulder at Speedy.

"On yer way!" said the cook. "If you want a handout, they's a place twenty-thirty mile up the coast where they feed bums."

"This looks all right to me, this place," said Speedy. "The place looks all right, and the cook looks all right."

The cook was stirring in a large kettle with a ladle.

"I'll give you a good reason for likin' this place better, kid!" said he.

He turned as he spoke, and hurled a dipperful of boiling-hot soup toward the doorway. His viciousness made him swing a little too far. Only half of the liquid passed out the doorway. The other half splattered over the wall, and made the cook shout with rage.

He would have felt much better if he had doused Speedy with scalding soup, but he had seen the stranger side-step like a dancer out of harm's way.

Speedy appeared again, smiling, lifting his deep-visored cap.

"You fellows are a jolly lot, down here," he said. "You like your little jokes, eh?"

"Little jokes? Damn you, we like our little jokes, do we?" shouted the cook. "I'll little joke you. Joe! Sailor Joe! Come here!"

"All right," called a distant voice.

A door slammed. Heavy footfalls came near.

"Take that bum by the scruff of the neck and throw him off the place," said the cook.

"Sailor Joe" was as big as the cook, pound for pound, but there was not a scruple of fat on him. His face was blackened by a beard that would not stay shaved; his brow was blackened by a scowl that would not clear away. Sailor Joe was a brute by nature, and there was so much of him that all the days of his life he had had his way.

When he saw Speedy, Joe laughed loudly, his face twisting crookedly to the side, his mouth sprawling open, his eyes disappearing. Then he strode for the kitchen door—and Speedy.

The latter backed down the steps, not in haste, but pleading as he went. The cook bawled in a huge voice, "Come on and see the racket, boys! Turn out!"

And promptly three men turned out of the bunkhouse door to see what was going on. One was the fellow with the concave face, one was an elderly cowpuncher, one a chunky bulldog of a brute.

It was the elderly puncher who cried, "What's the matter with the kid? Leave him alone, Joe! He ain't done nothin' but ask for a handout, has he?"

"Shut up, Danny," said the fellow with the concave face. "Leave Joe have his way. Kind of time that we let tramps know that they ain't wanted down here. Besides—"

The last words were drowned by the first roar of Sailor Joe as he advanced.

Speedy, still retreating, cringing, seemed to realize that he could not flee fast enough to avoid and escape the wrath of Joe. He tried to placate the sailor with words, but Joe, his fury mounting as he saw the chance of resistance diminish, suddenly charged.

He swung for the head of Speedy with all his might, the weight of his great body, the weight of his run all lurching behind the punch. And Speedy seemed to stumble as though fear had weakened his knees. His head swayed under the avalanche of that flying arm. His shoulder struck the ribs of Sailor Joe with a great resounding thwack as the Sailor charged on.

It was as though Joe had rammed his ribs against the stump of a tree. He bent over, with a gasp and a grunt, while the men of San Gallo whooped with delight, and Speedy seemed to stagger helplessly away, as though about to fall, wavering to this side and that, as Sailor Joe charged again, more blindly, with a redoubled force. In fact, the mere wind and coming of that danger appeared to overwhelm Speedy, so that at the last instant he slipped to his hands and his knees.

Sailor Joe tripped on him as on a stone!

His arms being thrown out for the purpose of seizing and destroying the smaller man, he was not able to use them to break the fall, and down came Joe with a terrible impact. He landed on his stomach and his face, while a dust cloud spurted out on either side of him. His body shook like a jelly, and he lay still.

Speedy, getting to his feet, brushed off his knees and gaped at the surroundings.

"What happened?" he exclaimed.

Several voices shouted with laughter at this.

"Joe's corked," said one. "He's all done in by that kid. You fell into some hot luck, kid, is all that happened."

"Luckiest thing that I ever seen," said another and in his delight, he kicked a pebble that sprang to a distance and scattered through a little tangle of tall grass.

Out of that grass slid, instantly, a sinuous shape that flashed in the sun and then coiled—a five-foot diamondback with its head drawn back and its supple neck ready to strike death into any enemy.

Sailor Joe began to quiver and writhe as consciousness returned to him—but not breath! He was unregarded in the presence of the snake, however.

"Right here by the house, where a hoss or a man could'a'been bit!" exclaimed the cook, pulling out a gun.

"Wait a minute!" cried Speedy. "No use in wasting a good snake."

He was rolling up his sleeve as he advanced toward the rattler.

"That snake," he said, "will eat a lot of rats and other vermin, if you don't kill it. Take the poison out of it and let it be, friends!"

"*You* take the poison out of it," said the cook. "Can you do that?"

They began to gather closely around the spot, while Speedy, rolling up his right sleeve, showed a forearm slender enough, to be sure, but rounded and alive with a sinuous interplay of lithe muscles. That arm was something like the body of a snake, the wrist like a snake's supple neck, the hand like a snake's head, capable of lightning movement.

The diamondback, as though it feared so many huge creatures approaching, turned and fled, but a long, eerie whistle came from the lips of Speedy and stopped it. It coiled. The whistling continued, running through cadences strange and unmusical to all the human ears that heard it, but it seemed to enchant the snake with delight. For the rattler stopped sounding its whirring alarm, raised its head, and began to sway it sinuously from side to side with the rhythm.

Speedy, while he whistled, now held out his hand, and bending over, he approached the snake little by little.

Sailor Joe had got staggeringly to his feet by this time, still gaping and gasping. He had lost a tooth, in the fall. Blood streaked his face and worked in small rivulets through the dust, but he forgot his own pains instantly when he saw the stranger and the rattlesnake.

"He's inside of the strikin' distance," said Sailor Joe. "He's goin' to catch it!"

"Shut up!" said the cook breathlessly. "Sure he's in strikin' distance. And he'll get it in a minute, or I'm a fool!"

"I hope," murmured Sailor Joe, "that that there snake pours a pint of poison into him, till he swells up and turns black and busts with it!"

Only the elderly man, Danny, showed any concern, for he said, "Look out, son! You may be fast, but a snake's a lot faster!"

The whistling of Speedy continued, and the undulations of the raised portion of the snake went on until there was a sudden pause in the music. At that instant, the snake struck. But it was a clumsy striking, with only a partial retraction of the head, and a rather aimless flinging forward of the body. Even then, it appeared to the watchers a movement faster than their eyes could follow. But Speedy had followed it both with eye and hand; he shifted suddenly as a dead leaf, struck by the wind. The head of the snake struck the ground beside his foot, and instantly Speedy had it gripped about the neck.

The long, brilliant body coiled at the same time, around the bare forearm of Speedy. A gasp of horror came from every throat. Fascinated, with bulging eyes, those hardy fellows stood around, and watched a knife come into Speedy's hands. He worked quickly, and rather gruesomely with the point and edge of it, in the mouth of that rattler. Presently he flung the snake away from him, and it flashed off like a whiplash into the grass.

"There," said Speedy. "That snake will eat a lot of rats and vermin, now, and it won't kill anything too big for it to swallow. Snakes and owls do a lot of good, they tell me."

"Where'd you learn that trick?" demanded the cook.

"Old tramp taught me," said Speedy.

"You pick up a lot of things on the road, if you keep your eyes and ears open."

"I've seen you before," said the cook. "Where?"

"I don't know," said Speedy. "Going by on the top of a train, maybe, or on the back of a good, fast mule."

The men laughed again at this.

"And where'd you learn to fall down and trip gents like that?" boomed Sailor Joe, reaching for the shoulder of Speedy.

He clutched the thin air, for Speedy had withdrawn a half step saying, "I'd like to get some soap and water to wash the snake off my skin."

"Maybe the snake's more under your skin than on it," suggested Joe savagely.

"Let him alone," said the cook, with authority. "The kid's earned a handout. I never seen such a thing in my life. Take charge of him, Danny. Chive, stay out here. I gotta talk to you about something."

37

THEY WALKED up and down, the man with the battered, concave face, and the cook, while the latter asked, "Watcha think of that kid? Seems like I've seen him somewhere."

"If I'd ever seen him—at work," said Chive, "I'd sure remember him."

"I never seen him at work," said the cook, "but I've seen him somewhere, seems to me. Something about him, it kind of struck inside of me. Maybe it was a long time ago. Seems like it was a younger kind of a face that I remember. How old would he be? Twenty-two?"

"Nigher to twenty-four," said Chive.

"Sure was funny, the way Joe happened to fall over him."

"There wasn't any happen to it," said Chive.

"You mean that the kid done all those things on purpose?"

"That's what I mean."

"Come along," said the cook. "You dunno what you're talking about. Joe could break him to bits, and the kid knew it, and he was so scared that he fell of a heap, was all."

"He seemed scared to you?" said Chive.

"Well, didn't you see his eyes, the way they bugged out, and the way he begged Joe to leave him alone? Scared? I never seen anybody more scared."

"You can make your eyes bug out, and

you can make yourself talk fool talk," said Chive. "But you can't change the color of your face. And his face didn't change none. A man that's real scared gets white around the mouth and in the middle of the cheek. He might not change any other place, but he gets white there. But the kid didn't get white no place at all. I took a look—see, and I seen."

"You're just nacheral suspicious," said the cook. "The kid just had a flock of luck, was all. He was scared to death, I'd say."

"All right," said Chive, "but lemme tell you something. When you tackle that kid, you tackle him with a gun. And you'd better be sure to get the drop, because if he's fast with a Colt as he is with a snake, he'll shoot the middle piece out of you before you get your gun talking."

"He was pretty slick with that snake," said the cook, agreeing slowly. "But you're wrong about the rest. He's got a wide-open eye. There ain't any meanness at all in him."

"A lot of females have wide-open eyes, too," said Chive, "and them are the kind that do you in, old son. Remember that. Suppose that this kid is just a nacheral-born actor, eh?"

"I'll take my chance," said the cook,

shrugging his big shoulders. "Now listen to me. I got something more to talk about than snake charmers. I wanta know how things are goin'."

"None too good," said Chive. "I try to keep the boys lined up. But it's a hard job. I'm mighty respectful to Lew Crocker, all the time, and I work hard to keep the boys lined up, but they're apt to get sassy. They know damn well that they're gettin' their extra money from Tim and Steve. And of course that makes them back-talk to Lew Crocker a good bit."

"The fools!" said the cook furiously. "They'll spoil everything!"

"That's what I've told 'em," said Chive. "I've told 'em twenty times that what they're to do is to pretend to be real, honest cowpunchers and pull the wool over the eyes of Lew Crocker—until the right time comes. But it's a rough lot that Steve got together here."

"Look here—is young Crocker gettin' suspicious?"

"He is," said Chive. "He'd a' fired the whole bunch of 'em, except for me talkin'. As cowpunchers, they're a pile of hams, these fellows. Sailor Joe can't handle any end of a rope, and the whole bunch are lazy and mean.

They've lived by their guns too long. I could talk Lew Crocker out of being suspicious, though, if it wasn't for old Danny. He's always out on the range where he can tell how these mugs are wastin' their time. He reports to Lew Crocker, and Lew gets hot. But he's a decent young gent. He's patient, and he tries to believe me when I tell him that they're goin' to work into shape and be the best gang of cowhands on the range. He's a pretty good sort, Lew Crocker is. You gotta hand it to Lew for the way he's taken hold of this ranch and kept it going after his old man died."

"Listen to me," said the cook.

"I'm listening," said Chive.

"Get over this idea of being fond of Lew Crocker. Who's paying you the real money? Or are you working for Crocker's fifty a month?"

"Damn the fifty a month," said Chive. "I know who I'm workin' for. I was only talking, was all."

"All right. It's time to quit the talking and get to work," said the cook.

"You mean—what?"

"Where's Lew Crocker now?" asked the cook.

"Rode down to the lagoon, I guess. Spends

some time every day, down there by the old harbor. Maybe he's got an idea that he's goin' to fix it up into a little port, once more, to ship the cattle out."

"He ain't goin' to ship no cattle, and he ain't goin' to make no port," said the cook calmly. "The reason he's down there, every day, is because he's gone and got word that something he wants is likely to come into sight off that lagoon."

"Is that why he's built the rowboat?" said Chive.

"Sure it is. But he ain't goin' to row in that rowboat. I think the time's nearly come for him to die, Chive!"

Chive started violently. He darted a hand up to his misshapen face, and lowered it again. His eyes were large, but gradually they began to narrow.

The cook, who was watching him closely, said, "You like this kid, eh?"

"I like him, but I like five hundred bucks a whole lot better," said Chive.

"There's goin' to be more than five hundred in this for each of us," said the cook. "There's more to this job than you think. Killing Lew Crocker is only a start, maybe. I've heard Steve do a little talking."

"About what?" asked Chive.

"About things that I can't talk about yet, but I know there's a big deal in the background, if only all the boys stick with Steve and Tim. You're a gent that they could count on, Chive. I've always knowed that."

"What'll we do with Danny?" said Chive.

"There ain't enough blood in him," answered the cook, sneering, "to make a good-sized stain on the floor."

"Can't we send him away someplace?" asked Chive.

"So's he could give evidence?" said the cook. "Matter of fact, Chive, the way I see this business is that old Danny goes off his nut and pulls a gun, and shoots his boss dead, and while Lew Crocker is fallin', he shoots Danny full of holes. And there you are with a story to tell any sheriff that happens along."

"Steve and Tim have done a lot of talking to you," suggested Chive.

"Yeah, here and there," said the cook.

"When does the shooting come?" asked Chive.

"Any day," said the cook, "when Tim or Steve get back and give the word."

38

WHERE WE find kindness, we are inevitably lured to expect and believe in honesty, also. As for Speedy, those swift, accurate eyes of his had already read the faces and in part the minds of the men of San Gallo. "Chesty," the little bulldog, Chive, the scarred and savage warrior, the two brutes, the cook and Sailor Joe, had all been sifted and appraised by Speedy. They looked to him like a gang of thugs. But Danny was a different metal. He was over fifty, yet still hardy. Time had drawn his face and puckered his eyelids, but it had not yet dimmed his gray eyes. His expression was sour enough, but his speech was drawling and very kind.

He had shown Speedy where to put up the mule, and they walked back toward the house slowly together.

"Things seem pretty peaceful down here," said Speedy. "I don't suppose that anybody would ever have to run for it, down here, unless the sea rose and came pouring in. Or do you have to fight rustlers, or something like that? Looks like you have a handpicked gang of gunmen, Danny."

Danny looked sharply at him, pausing. "Well," said Danny, "they may be gunmen, but I didn't pick 'em."

He scowled down at the ground.

"They look to me," said Speedy, "good enough for a murder, any day."

Again the head of Danny twitched, as he looked suddenly at Speedy.

"What you got on your mind?" he asked.

The glance of Speedy had not been so openly aware of his companion, but nevertheless, he had looked into the very mind of the cattleman, and he felt that he could place some trust here.

He fumbled for guidance, with his next words.

"Nothing on my mind, much," said Speedy. "Is this the whole layout? This the whole crowd, that I've seen?"

"All except the boss," said Danny. "And the Lynches."

"Yeah? And what's the boss like?"

"Lew Crocker? He's as clean a cut as you ever seen, is what he's like. A doggoned upstanding boy, and a good head, too."

We rarely praise honesty in others unless

we are honest ourselves. There was a certain heartiness in these words that won the trust of Speedy more profoundly than before.

"Young, clean-cut, upstanding," murmured Speedy. "It's a queer thing, Danny, that he'd go in for a crew like this!"

"Six weeks ago we had a different outfit," said Danny gloomily. "We had men that had been here for a long time, most of 'em. And then things started happening. Couple of 'em got into a fight in town, up in Porto Nuevo. They got cut up pretty bad, and we had to have a new pair, and the first that the boss picked up was Steve Lynch—his brother Tim fills in, sometimes—and Chive, the gent with the busted face.

"And the end of the month, two more of the boys stepped out of the picture. Seems they got boiled and left Porto Nuevo and didn't come back, or something, and one of them was cook, so we got the new cook, and Chesty, and that's the way it's gone. Seems like the gents at Porto Nuevo are layin' for the punchers from San Gallo, and it just happens that every time, lately, that we lose a good puncher, we get a gent that looks like a yegg to take his place. Just bad luck, I reckon. And they're bad cowhands, too, lemme tell you."

"Well," said Speedy thoughtfully, "when a crowd is not all of one kind, there's apt to be trouble."

"Aye," said Danny warmly, "there's apt to be trouble. They ain't my kind, none of 'em. They give me the cold shoulder. And they ain't Lew Crocker's kind, neither. And that makes trouble. The boss is getting sort of grouchy at 'em. Not that some of 'em don't work hard. There's Chive. He's a good cattleman. He knows his business, and he works mighty hard. So does Steve Lynch, and Tim, when he's here."

As they came back into the bunkhouse, they found that the other men had gathered there. Speedy said, quietly, as he came through the door behind Danny, "Well, when I feel bad weather in my bones, I keep my eyes open. You'd better do the same."

That was all that he ventured to say. It won him a curiously piercing glance from Danny, but Lew Crocker came in a little later, and the cook beat a gong to announce supper.

Lew Crocker was a fellow worthy of note. Sun-browned, lean, stalwart, he was as fine-looking a man as Speedy had seen in many a league of wandering, and he had the clean, clear eye of a man who has no shadows on his soul. That surety came to Speedy as he sat down at the foot of the table, opposite to Danny, and saw the master of the house at the head, speaking cheerfully to his men. He was not many years past twenty, and life as yet had not marked him except to place the one wrinkle between his eyes, the brand of labor and its pain.

What Speedy wanted, above all, was a chance to talk for two minutes alone with Crocker. In those two minutes, it might be hard to convince him of the extent of the danger that was threatening him, and its reality, but Speedy felt that the warning must be given soon.

Tim Lynch was not a fellow who would be permanently held up by the difficulties of the way, or by the lack of a horse. And at any moment he might arrive.

That was why the need of Speedy for speech was very great, but he had to talk in private. He could not call Crocker to the side without awakening suspicions in the others, and Speedy had reason to feel that the rest of the gang were well primed for action of any sort. The very way in which Clive and some of the others looked at the boss was proof that they were ready for action.

Yet there was no chance to talk before

supper. Though Speedy tried to hurry up to him, he failed. There began for him a long and nervous agony of strain, while he searched his brain for an opportunity to convey his warning.

It was a good supper. You can judge a rancher, very often, by his willingness to feed his men well. And with that as a criterion, young Crocker appeared a very fine master, indeed. Frijole there were, of course, that far south. And there was roast beef, and a strong soup, and heaps of fried potatoes, and stewed corn, and hot bread. The cook was an artist, in his way, and though he scowled at Speedy every time he entered the room, he could be forgiven. All cooks have bad tempers; that is a legend and a truism in the West.

There was not much conversation, though at one moment it touched on Speedy.

"You strange to this part of the world?" asked Lew Crocker.

"I've never been right here before," said Speedy. "But I keep on the wing, a good deal."

"Punching cows?" asked Crocker.

"No, sir," said Speedy. "I've never done that. I juggle a little," he continued, picking up an empty glass, a saucer, and a pair of knives, and making them whirl in twinkling circles into the air, as he talked. "And I do a few card tricks. If people want music, I whang a guitar, and sing to please their ears, or I dance to tickle their eyes."

He replaced the articles he had been juggling so skillfully. The sparkling eyes of the men flashed at him, as though he were a newly discovered treasure.

"And then," said Speedy, "I'm a mind reader, particularly when I work with cards, or a crystal ball. I tell the future, Mr. Crocker. And I pick up a few pennies that way. I'm handy to mend broken pots and pans, too. And I do other odds and ends to pick up a living. I can hook onto a freight car or catch the blind baggage when a train's traveling fast, and I'm at home on the back of a mule. And that's the way I get around the world."

"Other words," said Sailor Joe, "you're just a bum!"

"Be quiet, Joe," said Crocker. "He's my guest—he's the guest of all of us. And I hear that you charm snakes, too. What's your name?"

"I've been called a lot of names," said Speedy. "Some call me Sleepy, and some call me Slow, and some call me Sunshine, because I like to lie in it, and some call me Mississippi, and some call me Speedy—because I do little tricks with my hands."

The meal was ending. Chive produced a pack of cards, and tossed them to Speedy.

"Lemme see some of this fortune-telling. Start in with my past!" said Chive. "Doggone me, but I love to show up a faker."

"All right," said Speedy, taking the cards out of the case and pouring them from hand to hand with great adroitness, until they seemed a mere liquid flash in the lamplight. "All I can see is what the cards show me. I'll ask them a few questions."

He shuffled them, and dealt, with a rapid flick, four cards, all black.

He swept them up in a sudden gesture.

"All dark," he said, shaking his head. "Been anything shady in your life, Chive?"

"What do you mean by that?" asked Chive.

"Well, I didn't stop to ask the cards," said Speedy. "Some fellows are pretty sensitive, Chive, and they don't like to have the cards talk too much about 'em. But we'll see what this hand is saying."

He spread them on the board and shook his head over them.

"It looks," he said, "a lot like stripes and

bars. A lot like that! Prison, or just jail, Chive? No, prison, I'd say. For several years you—"

"You crook," said Chive. "Who you talkin' to? To hell with you and your cards!"

But there was a very loud and continued burst of applause from all the rest. Lew Crocker was smiling a little to one side of his face.

Chive stamped off from beside Speedy, but curiosity drew the cook into the same place.

"Never mind about the past," said the cook. "Tell me about the future."

Four diamonds came out of the pack— they seemed, in fact, to come out of the top of it, so expert was the manipulation of those flying fingers.

"Hello!" said Speedy, "what sort of a crowd is this? A jailbird—asking your pardon, Chive—and here's a fellow with a killing in mind! Or what would all of this red mean?"

"Killing?" growled the cook. "I never heard of such a fool idea! Your cards are crazy!"

"They may be crazy!" said Speedy, lifting his dark, innocent eyes to the cook's face. "I only tell you what they tell me. Let's see what else they say."

"Oh, the devil with 'em," said the cook. "This ain't fortune-telling. It's just talkin'."

"Try me," said Crocker. "Want me down there?"

"It's better," said Speedy.

Crocker came down and sat on the edge of the table, smiling.

"I want news," said Crocker.

"News about what?" said Speedy. "Money?"

"All right, try money," said Crocker.

A mixture of clubs and diamonds fell on the table, faceup. Again Speedy shook his head.

"It looks to me," he said, "as though the cards were saying that you're more likely to lose money before very long, than you are to win any."

"So?" said Crocker.

"You see how it is," said Sailor Joe. "The poor bum, he thinks people will believe him more if he tells 'em bad news. That's all."

"Try something else," said Speedy carelessly. "Women?"

"All right," agreed Crocker, laughing. "Try that."

Again cards fell.

"Hold on," said Speedy. "I hate to tell you what the cards are telling me. It sounds too much like the usual line of bunk that the gypsies talk. But—you see where the queen lies? As sure as fate, Crocker, a girl is coming to you—"

"What sort of a girl?" asked Crocker.

"Dark," said Speedy, half closing his eyes as though in the profoundest concentration. "Black hair and black eyes. An olive skin, but with a flush of color in it."

"By thunder!" breathed Crocker. "And coming to me, did you say? Do you mean traveling?"

"Why," said Speedy, "according to the cards—and that's why I hate to say it because it sounds so foolish—but according to the cards, the girl is coming to you across the sea."

Crocker leaped from the table to the floor and exclaimed loudly, "It's the most—" he began. Then he leaned against the edge of the table once more and said earnestly, "Tell me some more. What's to happen—"

"To the girl?" asked Speedy.

"Yes, yes! To the girl! Is there—is there—is there happiness ahead for her, Speedy? Ask the cards!"

Speedy dealt again, saying, "All I can see is what the cards show me, Crocker."

He stared at the fall of the cards and shook his head again.

"Well," he said, "I hate to keep giving bad news, but it looks as though—well, it looks as though there's a lot of trouble ahead for her."

"Trouble?" said Crocker very anxiously.

Speedy looked straight up into his face.

"Yes—danger," he said. "You see the ace of clubs beside the queen with—"

Chive swept up the cards.

"All nonsense!" he said.

"What do you mean by doing that, Chive?" demanded Crocker. "How dare you—"

"Why, chief," said Chive, "I don't want to see you cut up so bad about the chatter of a young crook with a pack of cards! Better take roulette seriously than the meanderings of a fortune-teller. But go on and let him gabble, if you want to."

"No," said Crocker. "I'm sorry I spoke like that, Chive."

"Oh, that's all right, chief," said Chive. "I don't blame you for getting sore. Looked like I was being fresh, or something."

"Just for a moment," said Crocker, laughing, "I was rather carried away; that was all. Sorry."

He tossed a dollar to Speedy, who caught it dexterously out of the air.

"Bad news or good news," said Crocker, "you hit on some things that may be true. Here's a little silver for you."

"Thanks," said Speedy, and as he leaned over in rising, his head came close to that of Crocker, and he added in the most careful of whispers, "Guard your life!"

They went on into the bunkhouse, again. And Speedy took note that the face of Crocker remained totally unmoved. But as they passed to the end of the room, Crocker said behind him, "Guard against whom?"

Speedy turned. His lips hardly stirred as he said, "All but Danny."

"You're a singin' and a dancin' man, eh?" said Sailor Joe. "Well, I can sing and I can dance a little, myself. Lemme hear what you can do, kid?"

"I'll get my guitar," said Speedy, "and do what I can."

He started for the door, and Crocker remarked that he'd get a breath of air.

Sailor Joe touched Crocker's shoulder.

"That Speedy is a hoss thief," he said.

301

"We'd better get him off the place before the night's over."

"Let's hear him sing first," said Crocker, and stepped out into the night.

<hr>

39

In the open night, Speedy saw the tall silhouette of a man as he returned from the shed, and the voice of Crocker said, "Speedy?"

"Yes," said Speedy, coming. "It's time for us to talk."

"About what?" asked Crocker. "What's the idea of this? What's in the air? Is it a lot of sham and nonsense?"

"If you'll listen hard, I'll talk fast," said Speedy. "I saw Steve and Tim Lynch talking today. And they were talking murder. I won't tell you all that happened. The main thing is that after a while I heard 'em name the man who's to be killed. And his name is Lew Crocker. Tim Lynch came toward the ranch to do the job. I managed to stop him on the way and steal his horse, but he's coming again, of course. I don't know when he'll arrive."

In the silence that followed, he could hear

the harsh breathing of Crocker, who broke out, suddenly, "They're two of the best men I have!"

"Sure they are," said Speedy. "They're the ringleaders."

The moon was sliding up out of the east, lifting a white pyramid of fire above its coming. A deadly light showed the two men to one another.

"Murder!" exclaimed Crocker. "Murder me? They'll get no loot out of me!"

"A fellow named Materro wants you put out of the way," said Speedy. "He cabled to Steve Lynch. I saw the cablegram. He said in the cablegram that this is the time to finish."

"Materro! Mateo! Materro!" groaned Crocker, striking the back of his hand against his forehead. "I know there's plenty of devil in him, but he couldn't—not murder—he couldn't buy a murder—"

"No," said Speedy, "maybe this gang of thugs would do the job for fun. Look at the layout. Look at the way they've shifted your old hands off the place, till only Danny's left. Don't you see that it's a plant, and that you're right in the middle of it?"

"Cold murder!" whispered Lew Crocker. His breath seemed to be stopped. "Materro!

The uncle! It can't be Materro. Not Isabella's uncle!"

"I saw his name signed to the cablegram," said Speedy. "Don't you see the lay of the land? Materro fixed Steve and Tim Lynch a long time ago. They've managed to run your old hands off the place. They've got the bag fixed and stretched for you, and they're ready to drop you in now. Isn't it as clear as day? Now there is a girl on the way—Isabella. She's expected here, and Materro knows it. Don't you see that all the leaders are in place and that you're to be toppled over?"

"Whether I can understand it or not, I've got to see it," said Crocker. "But you, man! What brought you into this? If what you say is true, there's murder in the air. What brought you into it?"

"The odd chance," said Speedy, "plus a little kicking about, and the fact that I can read lips a bit. There's no time to talk of that. What's your plan?"

"To send to town for help," said Crocker. "I've got to get half a dozen men I can trust, and then I'll back the thugs off the ranch."

"That's one way," said Speedy. "I could ride to town for you and choose the men."

"Aye," said Crocker, "and that's the best way."

"Suppose that they find that I'm gone," said Speedy. "I couldn't be back here before some time tomorrow evening, at the earliest. Suppose that they grow suspicious after I've left and attack you and Danny."

"That's a chance that I'll have to take," said Crocker.

"Why?" argued Speedy. "There are four of 'em, all told. You and I can sneak into the kitchen and stick up the cook. When we've bundled him up helplessly, then we can go to the bunkhouse, wake up Danny, and try our luck. If the gang want fighting, we can fight till they're licked! It's the best way, Crocker. The odds will only be four against our three. But if I rode off, they're likely to grow suspicious, and bump off you and take care of Danny without waiting till I get back. We'd better arrange the showdown right now."

He could dimly see that Crocker was shaking his head slowly. There seemed to be no fear in him; there was simply a calm decision which he was making at the moment.

"There's no chance of winning that way," he said. "Danny's no good with a gun. Neither am I. I've been too busy working all my life to spend any time hunting. I can't hit the side of a barn with a rifle, and I'm no good at all with a revolver. I never pack one, as a matter of fact. And all the crowd know that Danny and I are pretty useless with guns. They'd simply concentrate on you, Speedy, if a fight began. And after they'd riddled you, they'd take up the work on Danny and me. No, a showdown is no good."

"You're right," said Speedy quietly. "If that's the case, a showdown's no good. Then there's a next best bet. You and Danny and I should slide out of the ranch, go to town, get reinforcements, and come back here to clean up Tim and his crowd."

Crocker pointed out toward the lagoon. It shimmered like silver under the moon, and beyond it was the sea, like a dull, purple mist.

"She may come tonight, Speedy!" he said. "I can't leave this place while there's a chance that she may come!"

"If she comes— But man," said Speedy, "I saw the cablegram from Materro that says she's not to reach here until between the tenth and twentieth. And the tenth is not till tomorrow."

Crocker shook his head again.

"Crocker," said Speedy, "this is life or death that I'm talking to you."

"I know it," said Crocker. "I wish that I

had words to tell you how I thank you for throwing in with me, Speedy. I haven't the words. But after thanking you, I'll have to tell you that I'd rather die—ten times over— than be away from this place if she comes. I can't go."

Speedy stared at him through the dim light, and wondered. He had seen men in love before this, but he felt that he never before had encountered such quiet and manly resolution. There was no passion in the voice of Crocker. There was simply endless resolution.

Speedy argued no more. He merely said, "Have it your own way. I'll take a horse and start back for town. If you can live through sixteen hours or twelve hours with these thugs, I'll be back with help. So long, Crocker."

"If you go," said Crocker, "the place is stripped to Danny and me. Couldn't I get hold of Danny to make the trip? He's in the bunkhouse now. I'll call him out."

"Wait," said Speedy. "They might begin to grow suspicious then. Besides, they're waiting for me to do a song and dance in the bunkhouse. They might suspect something if I don't show up for that. I'll do the song and dance, Crocker, and while I'm making noise, you find your chance to talk to Danny and to send him off. As soon as the rest turn in, he could slip off and start."

"You're right. You're always right," said Crocker. "If I'm sure of anything, it is that heaven sent you down here. I'm no good at chattering promises and thanks, but if there's blood in me, I'll show you just what I feel, before the end of me!"

They went on into the bunkhouse together. Danny was in a corner, laying down his blankets. In another corner, Chive, Chesty, and Sailor Joe were in serious consultation.

To warn Crocker, Speedy had gone farther, he felt, than he should have done in the fortune-telling. He had exposed too much of his hand. Therefore, his next desire was to dance and sing all seriousness out of the minds of these men. He came into that long, ugly room pirouetting and prancing, and throwing the cover off the guitar, he struck up a lively tune on it.

Before he had been at work at ten phrases of the piece, the frowns had vanished.

Then he stood panting in a corner and challenged Sailor Joe to show forth his wares.

"I can do a hornpipe and a jig," said Sailor Joe, "but I ain't got wings hitched to my heels, like you have, and I ain't working in the same room. Hit it up, kid, and let's see you prance."

So Speedy pranced.

He showed them how a cat walks across wet ground, while they yelled with delight; he showed them a chicken whirling in great distress when a hawk hovers over the hen and her brood; then he was the hawk itself, hovering, sweeping, sailing through the sky. And he was a lame dog trailing a leg over rough ground; he was a fat man, waltzing a German waltz; he was an old woman with her arms full of packages which continually fall.

He passed from one bit of nonsense to another, his feet never still, his guitar thrumming rapidly.

Then, as he leaned against the wall, laughing and panting, they swarmed about him, making comments.

Only Crocker was busy, talking with Danny in the farther corner of the room. The face of Danny was turned from Speedy, but he could see the head of the veteran lift, and his shoulders stiffen suddenly.

And then a husky voice sounded at the door, saying, "A fine time all you gents seem to be having."

It was Tim Lynch!

He must have walked in his boots until they cramped and tortured his feet beyond sufferance. They had been dragged off, and various parts of his clothes had been cut up to bind over his feet as gear. The result was that he was literally in tattered rags, and the blood from his chafed feet stained the floor he stood on. Ragged as he was, there was the better chance for the enormous physical strength of the man to show through. And in his face there was the agony of a tortured savage who has stood at the stake and now at last is suddenly free, and among the power of his friends.

With the first few words that he uttered, he saw and spotted Speedy. He uttered a wild cry: "The greaser!" and snatched out his gun. No matter how long the march, Tim Lynch would as soon have parted from a limb as from his Colt revolver. Swiftly he made the move, with the yell of rage still distending his throat and his lips.

Speedy, totally unprepared, his back turned at first toward the door, whirled barely in time to whip out his own gun. That of Lynch already was exploding, and the bullet tore Speedy's weapon from his hand and sent it skidding across the floor.

Speedy himself was instantly in the midst

of a swirl of the cowpunchers. They reached for him—it was like grasping at a phantom; and all the while the voice of Tim Lynch was thundering out to them orders to catch the scoundrel and hold him for one instant. A half second would be enough!

It was time to test the nerve of brave men. For Speedy, it was like a wild dance with death. For Lew Crocker, it was facing the ultimate disaster.

He knew, now, that all Speedy had told him was true. He knew that he and Danny were helpless with guns, but that it was a case of the pair of them against all the others, if he wished to intervene on behalf of Speedy.

Yet there was not a moment's hesitation in him. A Colt hung in its holster beside the bed of Danny. Instantly it was in the hand of Crocker.

"Now, Danny, or never," he said through his teeth, and the veteran snatched out a gun at the same moment. He followed forward as Crocker ran into the fray.

"Put up your gun, Lynch! Put up your gun, don't shoot, or I'll make you—" shouted Crocker.

Tim Lynch turned from beside the door with a maniacal joy in his eyes.

This was the business he had had in mind; the agony of the march on foot across the desert had sharpened him and hardened him until he was a perfect tool for murder.

"You fool, take what's coming to you!" shouted Lynch. "Chive—Joe—Chesty—this is the time. Blast them to hell!"

And he fired pointblank at Crocker.

Other guns were flashing. Speedy, his hands empty, guns on every side of his, saw Crocker pitch on his face, and Danny go down with a stagger and a slump against a bunk from which he recoiled and fell heavily on the floor. There he lay stretched on his back, his arms flung out crosswise, a horrible stain of red flowing on his head.

Speedy saw that last picture as he ran for his life. They had all swept in from the doorway during the fighting; now, while the noise of the guns still roared in his ears, Speedy cut back for that exit. He heard Tim Lynch bellowing, "Get the greaser! I'm goin' to kill him if it's the last act of my life. Damn this gun!"

He hurled on the floor a Colt which had jammed, and reached for another man's weapon.

The lintel of the doorway was splintered by two bullets as Speedy raced through it, dodging like a snipe to the right, into the open night.

All about him was the terrible silver clarity of the moonlight, and no possibility of concealment nearer than the trees along the lagoon.

Their guns would find him long before he had managed to reach to that shelter.

On the floor of the bunkhouse came the thundering of their feet as they started in pursuit.

So he fled upward, not onward. He simply leaped, caught the low projecting eaves, and swung himself with a mighty heave onto the roof. The sides of it slanted a very little. But the top of it was flat, mud covered over heavy rafters. Onto that flat portion he slithered, and lay still, panting.

The pursuit rushed out into the open night, spread, and came to a stand.

"Where did he go?" called the voice of Sailor Joe. "I wanta get at him. I wanta get at him with my hands. I've *gotta* get that throat of his under my thumbs—and then I—"

"Look out in the shed," said Tim Lynch. "Joe, you and Chive look out there."

"He didn't have time to get there," declared Chive.

"What'd he do, then? Turn into air?" demanded Lynch. "You gents all think you know too much. Go out there and look. Come on back with me, Chesty. We gotta stow the dead ones away in Crocker's room. Too bad that the pair of 'em shot each other up, that way!"

And his loud, brawling laughter broke the night.

<hr>

40

ON THE roof, Speedy lay flat on his back and watched the moon ride upward through the thin films of clouds. Again he had been beaten! It seemed as though a devil of bad luck pursued him, whenever Tim Lynch came on the scene, and now, unarmed, helpless, he had to wait and grimly consult his mind, which would offer no thoughts.

He heard the searchers return from the shed. He heard trampling feet inside the house. At last he ventured down to the ground again. If Crocker and Danny were both dead, perhaps he could purloin a fast horse and ride to bring revengers on the trail. At any rate, he must learn exactly what had happened.

He dropped to the ground, and flattened himself in the meager strip of shadow at the base of the wall, as men came out of the bunkhouse door. He ventured to crawl until he could look around the corner, and he saw three men bearing a loose body with arms that trailed toward the ground.

The head hung loose also, and Speedy recognized the face of Danny. His cheeks seemed to have sunken in against the bone. Under the brows were two pools of such a depth and blackness that the eyes could not be distinguished. It was like the face of a mummy, and the whole body of Danny seemed to be light, as though centuries had dried it.

Chesty carried the head, Sailor Joe had an arm under Danny's hips, and the cook supported the legs. They carried the body down the side of the house and around to the outside entrance of the room of Crocker. Speedy followed like a ghost. He had to crawl with redoubled caution but he managed to keep close enough.

The three who carried the body talked as they went on.

"Seems like all the weight is drained out of Danny, like all the blood out of a stuck pig," said Chesty.

"Why wasn't this job polished off a long time ago? The killing would of been just as easy a month back," said Joe.

"Where's Speedy?" the cook asked.

"Out lifting himself a fast horse," said Joe.

They came around to the back of the house, where strong lights were shining through the windows of Crocker's room. The door stood open. The yellow lantern light streamed down the steps and died on the brilliant edge of the whiteness of the moonshine. Up those steps, the three carried the helpless body of Danny.

Speedy heard the voice of Crocker exclaiming, "I might have known poor old Danny would be done in at the same time you tackled me. You've murdered him, have you?"

Speedy went to the window, and looking cautiously over the sill, he saw the whole picture of the interior. The three burden bearers had just dumped the body of Danny, so that it lay face downward. A huge red gash was scored across the head. Crocker, his hands tied behind his back, sat in blood-stained clothes on his bed. He had been shot through the right thigh; big Tim Lynch was bandaging the wound carelessly, pulling the cloth with jerks against the lacerations of the flesh. Chive completed the picture. He walked the floor with a sawed-off shotgun under his arm.

"What's the idea of the bandaging, Tim?" he demanded. "That's just a fool play. Quit the bandaging, will you? Here's Danny flopped on the floor, dead. And there's Crocker, all ready to get a couple of slugs of lead in the chest. Why don't you knock him over and then leave 'em lay—because they've just killed each other, and that's all that there is to it!"

"Maybe there's something more, though," said Tim Lynch, standing up from that roughly completed job of bandaging. He turned his half-handsome and half-brutal face toward Chive. It was plain that the two of them were the leading spirits. The others were hardly more than hired men. "What're we in this for?" asked Lynch.

"Hard cash, brother," said Chive.

"Well," said Tim Lynch, "here's Crocker in a bad pinch. A mighty bad pinch. And Crocker has money in the bank. Quite a lot of money. Maybe he'd like to write us out a check for some of that money. Would we say no to that?"

He winked at Chive, and Chive answered, "You've got sense, Tim. I didn't think of that. If Crocker's willing to talk business, I suppose that *we'd* talk business, too."

"Sure we would," said Tim Lynch.

He turned back to Crocker.

"What you say, brother?" he asked.

Crocker looked at Lynch narrowly.

"I give you a check—and what do you give me?" asked Crocker.

"Another chance," said Tim.

"What sort of chance?" asked Crocker.

"That's a thing for us to figger out," said Lynch.

"Come here," said Chive to Lynch, and drew him back to the window outside of which Speedy was waiting. The murmur of Chive barely reached those eavesdropping ears. "What's the use, Tim? What's the use in wasting time? Danny's dead, and we've gotta leave Crocker dead, too. You know that. That's what Materro wants, and he's the big paymaster."

"Never miss an extra dollar, if you have a chance to pick it up," answered Lynch. "And Crocker's willing to talk business. After we get the coin out of him, we can bump him off fast enough."

"Ah, that's the idea, eh?" said Chive.

"Sure, I'm not a fool. Don't it sound good to you?"

"Fair enough. Fair enough," said Chive.

They left the window. Speedy, venturing to look again, saw Lynch go back toward Crocker, saying, "Chive and me, we've agreed. We'll give you your chance, Crocker. But you've gotta pay high for it."

"How high?" asked Crocker.

"You've got more'n ten thousand dollars in the bank," said Lynch.

"Not half that!" answered Crocker.

"Well, call it four thousand that you've got," said Lynch.

"Call it that," agreed Crocker.

"You write out your check for that, and we'll give you a break."

"What sort of break? Turn me loose?"

"Not right away," answered Lynch. "You know that we can't do that."

"I suppose that you can't," said Crocker calmly. His face twisted a little as the pain of his wound pinched him sharply.

Suddenly the loud voice of Sailor Joe boomed, "Look out there! Look!"

Speedy slid back and around the corner of the building in haste. Had they spotted him?

Then he heard Sailor Joe roaring, "Out there on the lagoon. Look!"

Speedy looked, and he saw a two-masted

schooner, still blue and dim with distance, standing in at the mouth of the lagoon.

<hr />

41

TWO OF the men strode to a window at once, to peer at the vision of the ship. Chive and Lynch continued arguing. Chive exclaimed, "There's the main bet, right ahead of us! There's our million standing up there on the lagoon like a stack of chips on the plush of a card table! Bump off this fellow Crocker, and get at the big money, Tim!"

"Yeah?" drawled Tim. "You talk as though four thousand dollars didn't amount to anything. A day'll come, maybe, when you'll wish that you had a little stake like that four thousand. I'll tell you what, boy— it ain't decent to turn down money like that."

"Well," said Chive, "have it your own way and be damned! I don't like this business. Where's that sneaking little juggler of a Speedy?"

"Run away from the guns," answered Tim Lynch. "Likely running now as fast as a hawk. Chesty, you stay here and watch Crocker and Danny. Danny ain't goin' to give you no trouble, and I guess Crocker'll

320

stay put. The rest of us have gotta take a look down the lagoon."

The voice of Chive added, "Keep those eyes of yours open, son! You keep watchin' like a hawk."

"What's there to be scared of?" asked Chesty.

"Shadows—hawk shadows slidin' on the ground," said Chive. "Act as though there was a gun pointin' at you all the time."

Then they came swarming out from the house. All went to the corral to get horses, with the exception of the cook, who hurried around toward the kitchen. His shadow thrown far forward by the moonlight, gave Speedy his warning. He slipped to the ground and lay face down, praying that the eyes of the cook might not find him.

The kitchen door slammed, and presently the heavy tread of the cook went off behind the house toward the corral.

A horse squealed in the corral. Hoofs began to trample. Then Speedy saw the shadowy riders, one after another, sweep across the moon-whitened ground and fly off toward the lagoon.

There was a sudden commotion inside the room of Crocker, a loud shouting from Chesty, and Speedy reached the window in time to see Danny, the supposed dead man, shrunk back against the wall with his hands spread out behind him to secure support, while he stared into the two muzzles of the gun that Chesty held. Blood worked in slow rills down the face of Danny. That he was alive seemed more than a miracle.

"You will, will you?" shouted Chesty. "You'd try to trip me from behind, eh? You'll try to doublecross me, will you, you dirty sneak? Well, you're goin' to get it now. You're goin' to get hell, and I'll be the one to give it to you!"

Speedy reached the doorway, and slipped through.

"Where'll you have it?" said Chesty, his chunky body set swaying with rage and brutal desire. "Body or head? I'm goin' to be a gentleman, Danny, and give you exactly what you want."

Danny raised a hand and brushed some of the blood from his forehead. He sighed.

"Lemme think a second, will you, Chesty?" he pleaded.

"I ain't goin' to let you do nothing of the kind," said Chesty. "You come along and try to doublecross me, do you? Well, I'm goin' to give you hell, for that!"

Speedy was close behind now. He took

the edge of his palm like the iron side of an ax, and struck Chesty beneath the ear and across one of the big cords that run down the back of the neck. And Chesty spilled sidewise to a hand and knee.

The fighting instinct was still in him, but his body had been numbed by that paralyzing stroke that deadened his nerve centers. His hand could not resist as Speedy pulled the sawed-off shotgun away from him and covered him with it.

"Stand up," said Speedy.

Chesty rose. He was uncertain on his feet, and his white face was knotted with desperation. His hands worked slowly.

"You're sure having bad luck, Chesty," said the victor.

"A lot of dirty sneaks doublecrossin' a gent," gasped Chesty. "A lot of crooks—"

The irony of these remarks came home even to the dull wits of Chesty. He was silent, then turned at the command of Speedy and allowed his arms to be bound behind his back.

"Danny, how do you feel?" asked Speedy.

"Like a gent that's been in hell and hardly clear of it yet," said Danny.

"Are your knees soggy?" asked Speedy.

"No. My legs are getting stronger all the

time. They bounced a slug off my head—I guess that was all."

Danny had set free the hands of Crocker by this time, and the rancher, ripping away long strips of the sheet, was binding the bleeding head of the older man.

"I've got to stay here with Crocker and keep an eye on Chesty," said Speedy. "Danny, if you think you can do it, you're going to get the best horse on the place and ride for town. Get a dozen men together, if you can. Try to spot the deputy sheriff and have him with the lot. Tell him that there's murder in the air down here. Get your army together, and send 'em down here as fast as they can come. I don't know how many hours it'll take you to get up there, but tell 'em to kill horses all the way back. Every minute that they cut off from their traveling time is going to be saved lives down here, perhaps. Tell 'em that I'm alone, with one of the thugs and a wounded man on my hands. Now, get out and travel!"

"He can't do it," said Crocker. "The thing to do is for *you* to go, Speedy. We can dig ourselves in here, and fight for a while. And you'll get back with help."

"They'll burn you out," said Speedy calmly. "Danny, get on the way."

324

Danny said nothing at all. He gripped the hand of Crocker, and that of Speedy, and stalked from the house.

Crocker stared after him, shaking his head.

"He wobbles from side to side when he walks. What chance has he got of getting through to town?" he asked.

"One in three—or thirty; I don't know," said Speedy. "I only know that that's the only way. Now the rest of us have to get out of the house!"

42

OF COURSE Crocker could not walk. Chesty, though his hands were tied behind his back, was perfectly able to assist in the carrying of the burden. He walked ahead, while Speedy went behind, supporting the head and shoulders of the wounded man.

They passed in this way out of the house. Far before them, down the pale stretch of the beach, they saw the little flickering figures of the horsemen dip out of view into a hollow and rise again. Chesty groaned at the sight of his friends.

They went on toward the trees that filled the marsh at one side of the lagoon. Their footfalls crunched noisily upon the sand. They seemed the only bit of reality in the midst of a dream, of which the most visionary part was that apparition of blue-white sails, entering the mouth of the lagoon.

They reached the trees, a ragged forest draped everywhere with the gloomy Spanish moss. Sometimes they walked in darkness, but with spots of moonlight ahead to show them the way. Then the sleek, black face of marsh water stopped them.

They skirted the water. Beyond it, they reached a small opening in the woods, and here Speedy halted the party. With great tufts of the moss and ends of branches, he made a comfortable bed for Crocker, who relaxed on it with a groan.

Speedy watched over him for a moment, while Chesty was saying, "You gents are crazy. You're stuck here. It's goin' to take you days to get Crocker well. And Danny'll never reach town to get help. The thing you oughta do is to go out and surrender to the boys. They'll give you a good break."

"Are you feeling better?" asked Speedy of Crocker.

The latter raised himself on one elbow, and nodded. Speedy gave him a Colt revolver which he had taken from Chesty.

"Keep Chesty under the muzzle of that gun," said Speedy. "If we were practical men, we'd tap him over the head and slide him into the marsh, but that sort of a short cut to safety doesn't appeal to me. Does it to you?"

"No," said Crocker. "There's no use punishing one hound when the whole pack is at fault. Are you leaving me, Speedy?"

Speedy pointed through the trees.

"I've got to get out there," he said. "I don't know what I can manage, but I've got to try to get to the girl, Crocker."

The body of Crocker lay stretched out in the shadow, but moonlight fell upon his head, and his face puckered with wonder as he stared at Speedy.

"What sort of fellow are you?" he asked huskily. "I've never raised a hand for you, partner. And you've never seen the girl. There are four thugs who'll shoot you on sight and—heaven bless you for anything you can do!"

"Don't thank me," said Speedy. "You know how some gamblers are. When they're broke, they'll play for matches. And this is a game for something more than money. So long. Watch Chesty like a hawk. If he gets away, the game's lost."

Chesty said nothing at all. His big block of a head was turning slowly from Crocker toward Speedy, and back again. Amazement set in his eyes. He was seeing and hearing matters of which his own native common sense never had warned him before. Imagine someone who was capable of doing something for nothing!

Speedy was already withdrawing, and once out of sight of the other two, he set off at a rapid run that carried him out of the trees—skirting the foul margin of another marsh—and onto the moon-crisped whiteness of the beach.

Well before him, he saw the schooner drifting inland, with wrinkles in her sails.

He ran on the verge of the water, where the sand was hardest, until he was fairly up to the spot on the shore toward which the ship seemed to be heading. Then he cut inland. The sand was at once softer underfoot. He labored through it with a sound like swishing water about his feet.

So he came through a wilderness of small sand dunes upon sight of the ship and the four men of San Gallo.

It was a natural cover, framed in outjutting rocks, toward which the schooner had headed, and there Tim Lynch and the cook and Sailor Joe and Chive stood beside their horses, waiting. And there was a fifth horse as well—a big brute, with the moon glinting over the silk of its flanks.

The anchor was dropped by the schooner. The cable clanked noisily for a moment, then stopped its noise as the anchor struck the bottom through that shallow water. Presently a boat dropped over the side. A crew appeared in it. Oars were thrust out. Like a great insect, the skiff walked across the still surface of the lagoon.

Tim Lynch ran forward to meet it. He stood on the verge of the sea. He waded in, and caught the prow, and drew it up on land.

All of this was seen by Speedy as he lay behind a wide-armed cactus, at times lifting his head to see more clearly through the branches the maneuvering of men and oars.

Most of them were ashore now. And then he saw a hooded form, a slender thing, arise from the stern sheets of the boat.

That was the woman. That was this Isabella Materro who had ventured to love a gringo, who had escaped from her rich uncle, who had fled across the sea to find young Crocker. Because of her, two men, already, were wounded. Because of her, a stricken man was urging a horse toward the town to get help.

"Money and women—the roots of all evil." That was the phrase that continually rang in the mind of Speedy, as he lay there in the sand and watched.

A mantilla cloaked the head of the girl and shrouded her face from him, as she walked up the beach. The captain of the schooner went with her. One could tell that he was a seafaring man by his swaggering walk, by the scuffing of his feet through the sand. One could tell that he was used to command, by his other bearing. Even the moonlight showed the darkness of his face, tanned by many storms and the keen sun of the open sea.

They came closer. First, Speedy glimpsed the features of the girl. Then he could see her clearly, and he knew that it was right for men to fight and die for her. That face was like music to the soul.

Tim Lynch was beside them, taking the lead in all the talk.

"Crocker couldn't come down," he was saying. "Lew has a touch of the fever. Nothing bad. But the doctor said that he can't show himself to the night air. So he's in bed, but he's seen the ship through the window, and he's waiting. Had to pretty nigh tie him down to keep him from comin' out here!"

"A fine kind of man," said the sailor. "A fine kind of a man that wouldn't drag himself out of the grave to come to this kind of a girl that's come to him out of I dunno what kind of a hell! A fine kind of a man, ma'am," he added to the girl. "I'd do some second thinkin', if I was you! I'd do it before I leaped."

She turned to the captain and lifted her face with a faint smile, as though she would not venture to put into words all the faith and the confidence that she felt.

He saw that smile and shook his head. Speedy saw it also, but he did not smile. There was something deeper than smiles in his gleaming eyes.

She was merely pressing Tim Lynch to learn whether or not Crocker were seriously ill. English was not altogether familiar on her tongue. She spoke it clearly enough, but with a certain drawling, a slowness that made the words more musical. Lynch declared that Crocker was only to be in bed for a few days.

"I'll tell you what," insisted the captain of the schooner, "I don't like the sound of this here. It seems to me like Crocker ain't burnin' up to get his eyes on you. I'm goin' to go along and see this thing through. You don't know these folks. I won't deliver you till Mr. Crocker signs on the dotted line."

Inwardly, Speedy blessed the resolution of that big fellow.

"Come along, then," said Tim Lynch, with a calmness that he could not be feeling. He might dispose of the captain, to be sure, but there would remain the crew of the schooner and murder on a large scale confronting Lynch and his friends.

But then a sailor called in Mexican from the skiff to say that a good wind was coming off the shore. It was true. The moonlit bay was darkened by the breeze. The schooner heeled well over with it. There was a clanking and clattering of odds and ends adrift on the ship as it swayed.

The captain faltered. It was the girl herself who pressed him to go. She told him that she knew she could trust the first men she met on the American shore. There was nothing but happiness and faith in her.

The captain took hold of both her hands, finally, and said good-bye.

"D'ye understand?" he said. "You may be the queen of the land with all the money in it, but I feel as if I'm goin' off leavin' you on an island with nothin' but natives around."

Speedy heard her thanking that honest sailor, and saw the skiff push off, and go pacing away like a six-legged insect toward the schooner. Speedy himself was in an agony. For yonder in that boat, hurrying away from him, were men enough to save both the girl and Crocker, if their power was properly used.

But how could it be used?

If Speedy cried out, he would be blown to pieces by the concentrated fire of Lynch and the other three. In fact, those four armed men could master Speedy and the sailor, too, if there were a sudden showdown. The whole balance of power was in their hands, in their guns.

If only a calm would imprison that ship in the lagoon—if only some miracle could enable Speedy to send his thoughts swiftly into the mind of the skipper!

So, in shuddering suspense, Speedy saw the skiff reach the side of the schooner. Already the crew had begun to walk the anchor up from its holding ground; the captain grunted and groaned with the labor. The small boat was hoisted on board. And now the wind filled the big bellies of the sails and

sent the schooner swiftly and smoothly out
to sea.

THERE IS no bewilderment greater than that
of the clever man when he feels that he has
allowed a great opportunity to slide through
his hands, unused. And that was the feeling
of Speedy as he saw the ship and its men
pass away from the lagoon. Help had been at
hand, almost within touching distance, and
he had not been able to use it.

He ground his teeth as he lay there in the
sand behind the big cactus. He could think
now of what he should have done. He should
have stolen farther down the lagoon, and
slipped into the water unheeded, and then
he should have swum out to the schooner,
lying on his back, working his arms very
carefully so as to raise hardly a riffle. In that
way he might have gained the ship and there
he could have taken measures to warn the
crew of the crime that was about to be attempted on shore.

He could have attempted that thing, but
he had thought of it too late. Now he had to
lie there, helpless, while he saw the girl come

back with Tim Lynch from the waterside. In spite of the captain's direct warning, she seemed incapable of suspicion, and she was smiling up at Tim with a perfect trust as she walked along with him.

That smile made the resolution of Speedy a thing of steel.

More trouble was coming. Down the beach from the direction of the house, came the figure of a man, running hard, a short chunk of a fellow. He called out, and waved an arm. It was Chesty, who panted, as he came up, "Tim! Chive! Look out! The devil's loose!"

"What devil? Watcha mean? Shut up, you fool!" cried Tim Lynch, and looked over his shoulder with guilty fear toward the outline of the disappearing ship.

Chive, who was standing beside the big horse, helping Isabella Materro to mount, also turned with a start toward Chesty, who panted, "Speedy! He come back! He got Crocker out of the house. Over into the woods by the marsh—"

"Shut up, you blockhead!" shouted Tim Lynch. "Scatter out, boys. The devil take Speedy!"

The girl, as she sat in the saddle now, looked with great, startled eyes toward the men around her. Broken as the words had been, it must have been plain to her, by this time, that there was something very wrong indeed.

Chive and Tim Lynch were springing for their saddles. The cook and Sailor Joe were already mounted, when Speedy slipped from behind the cactus and dashed for the girl, his black shadow sweeping over the ground beside him.

He gained the back of that horse like a panther, and as he slid into place behind the cantle, his left arm shot past the girl and caught the reins out of her hand; his right hand held his revolver.

But all that courage and address could not have saved the life of Speedy then. The last moment of all his adventures would have come, except that the big horse, leaping wildly away as it felt the impact of that unexpected rider, crashed straight into the mustang that Chive was mounting.

The mustang went down, rolling against the legs of the big gelding on which Tim Lynch was seated. The second horse staggered, almost fell. Even so the bullet from the gun of Lynch clipped hair from the head of Speedy.

But they were through the first pinch.

The frightened horse was running like a deer over the firm sand at the water's edge, and the voice of Tim Lynch was yelling to his other men not to shoot. Even at twenty yards the danger of striking the girl would be too great, and her life, not her death, was what they wanted.

It was Lynch who was shouting that one horse could not carry two people to safety. The galloping animals poured after Speedy in a rush, and looking back, he groaned with relief to see that they were not gaining.

The girl had not screamed out; she had not struggled to escape from the saddle; it would almost have been better had she done so. But what actually happened was that fear had struck her like a club, and now she swayed helplessly to the side, a lurching weight against the arm of Speedy. He, without stirrups under him, without the support of a saddle, had to cling desperately to keep from sliding off the back of the horse.

It was only a breathing space. He knew that the instant they were driven off the hard beach and into the softness of the sand beyond, that double weight would stop the gelding abruptly. And when the pursuers overtook them—well, it would probably not be sudden death that they would grant to Speedy!

The girl came suddenly out of her faint with a cry rising from her lips. The savage voice of Speedy crackled like gunfire at her ear, saying, "Steady! They're trying to murder Crocker and kidnap you! For heaven's sake, believe me!"

She had jerked her head around and now she saw that lean and handsome face, with set jaw, with blazing eyes; and she knew that she had heard the truth.

The wind had loosened from her shoulders the black mantilla, and now the long scarf was blown behind them as Isabella Materro swayed suddenly forward in the saddle and began to ride for her life. Speedy gave her the reins. He had enough to do to keep his place now, and watch the pursuit, without trying to guide the horse, also. And she rode like a master. There was good Castillian blood in her, but there seemed to be a dash of Indian, also, from the way she rode, bending low to cut the wind.

They actually gained a little, as they reached the end of the lagoon, but Speedy knew what they must do. Headlong flight could not save them, but the trees of the marsh arose like a dingy fog above the sands, and toward it he told the girl to ride.

He gave her quick instructions.

"Head straight into the woods. Then slant to the side and stop the horse. Throw hard back on the reins to stop him. And then get off the saddle and do what I do. If I run, run with me. If I drop for the ground, drop beside me."

"I hear!" said the girl. The voice blew back over her shoulder to Speedy. "And Lew—he's been hurt?"

"He's nicked. He's not broken," said Speedy. "Now! Now!"

He beat the racing horse with the flat of his hand to drive it across the narrow stretch of open beach toward the trees. There in the cover, if only he could pick the right place— Crocker had said that he was no good with weapons! Whatever happened, the manhunt must be turned away from Crocker!

A yell of triumph, a long-drawn wolf howl of delight, came bursting out of the throats of the men of San Gallo, when they saw the prey heading in toward the cover. Then the low branches of the trees reached like hands and arms toward Speedy and the girl.

"Stop!" called Speedy, and the darkness shut over them.

The girl obeyed her instructions to the letter. She jerked hard back on the reins. The cow pony came to a halt with braced legs, hurling a big spray of sand before it. And Isabella Materro was already out of the saddle and on the ground.

Speedy, as the horse stopped, had been slung sidewise from his place. He crashed into a bush, scrambled out on hands and knees, and fired straight out from among the trees toward the beach. He could see nothing, but he could hear the yelling voices.

Those yells, and the hoofbeats, split from directly in front of him, and spread off to either side. They had not cared to push home their charge against a man in safe hiding.

Speedy got to his feet. The girl arose. She had done exactly as he commanded, and had thrown herself down beside him. Now she was on her feet, silent, waiting for orders. Shadow covered Speedy, but mottled moonlight played over her. He saw the flashing of her eyes.

The heart of Speedy leaped in him savagely. For one moment, he forgot Lew Crocker. And then the passion went out of him. For he saw that she was surrounded by fear. Fear of the yelling, shouting, shooting devils who had begun to search the woods;

fear of this strange land; fear of the black marsh water which was close to them; fear even of this man who declared that he was trying to rescue her.

He said to her, gently, "Crocker was shot through the leg. Not a bad wound. No bone broken. They wanted to keep him until they'd bled him of all his money."

She put her hands against her throat and watched his face, with agony in her own.

"They want to murder him. They have orders to do that. From Mateo Materro. But they're going"—he talked straight on, in spite of her faint stifled outcry—"they're going to double-cross Materro. He simply wants you stopped and taken back home, with Crocker put out of the way, but they want to keep you for as much ransom as they can squeeze out of Materro. They tackled Crocker tonight. The ship came in sight in time to keep them from finishing their job. I managed to get him away into the woods. He's out here now, off there to the left. His wound is bandaged up well enough. That's the story. Our job is to find him now. To try to find him before Tim Lynch and the rest come across him and stamp him out."

"We'll find him," said Isabella Materro quietly. "I know we'll find him. Heaven won't let such a man as you fail! And you haven't told me why you do these things. You haven't told me who you are."

"I'm the odd chance," said Speedy. A grin twisted his mouth. "I'm the odd chance that might win, after all. But it's just an odd chance—just the thing that happens by accident."

"The odd chance?" she repeated slowly. "I don't understand."

"Neither do I exactly," said Speedy. "But all you need to know about me is that I just happened to stumble into the picture. That's why I call myself the odd chance."

She smiled at him. He raised a hand. And out of the near distance, she heard a stealthy sound coming gradually toward them.

Speedy turned toward that noise. Over his face came an expression of animal savagery and pleasure. His body shrank closer to the ground. He began to stalk without a sound, toward that approaching whisper of sound.

The girl wavered, then gripped his arm.

"I can't stand it!" she whispered.

He turned his head slowly toward her and regarded her with unseeing eyes, for an instant, so intent was he on his work. Then, straightening with a faint sigh, he nodded to her and drew noiselessly back with her into the shadows among the trees.

44

By the noise they had heard, it was reasonably clear that they had been spotted and observed by one of the San Gallo men. More than one could hardly have moved with such secrecy, passing like a quiet breeze through the shrubbery.

It seemed what any one of several of that group would do—go keenly on to make the kill for himself, instead of trying to call in nearby friends to assist. There was Tim Lynch, for instance, with enough of resolution in his brutal nature; there was Chive, even more dangerous on any ground except that of sheer strength; Chesty, too, would prove a poisonous enemy. Only the cook and Sailor Joe were apt to be a little heavy and clumsy in the attack. It must be, thought Speedy, someone of the first three that now slipped so quietly through the woods.

Anger worked on the whole body of Speedy just like the grip of a hand.

"Go on, straight on!" he commanded. "Go quietly; feel your way along from one bit of moonlight to the next. I'm dropping behind for a moment and—"

She gripped his arm and clung to him.

"You're going back to kill him as if he were a beast," she said.

"That's what he is," said Speedy. "They're a set of murderers, and I could kill them all."

"I know you could!" said the girl. "But if there's bloodshed on account of me, my life is ruined, señor! I shall give up the world and enter a convent if I am the source of murder."

The sincerity of her emotion flowed toward him out of her whole body. And Speedy answered her, with a loud groan, "Very well. I'll go back—and simply take him off the trail. I won't do what ought to be done to him."

"Don't go back," she pleaded, whispering. "Please don't go back. Let's try to go faster. I can run—you'll see if you try me. But don't go back!"

"Hush!" said Speedy. "I've got to go. It's the only way. Walk straight on, feeling your way."

He dropped away from her, as he spoke, and watched her go slowly on through the dapplings of moonlight. Her head was bowed, her face covered by one hand, and with the other hand, she felt the way before her.

Speedy, shrinking a little back from the way they had been following, sank into a small covert of thick shrubs. Something whispered through them, almost from under his knee; a snake, no doubt, and deadly snakes they had in the marshes!

Now, with his straining ears, he heard once more an incredibly slight sound approaching. One could not imagine human feet so light that they would make so little noise among the dead twigs and leaves that covered the ground. Far more clearly he could hear the retreat of the girl.

He tensed himself in readiness, and then relaxed for he knew that nerve-hardened muscles cannot react with speed. This was not a case for gun work. He knew that, too, because he had promised the girl that there would be no blood.

Well, there was in his hands a magic that he had used many a time before, and he could use it again.

The noise drew closer. A clammy coldness passed over him, as though a wind had breathed on his back. He wanted to look behind him. Danger seemed to be pouring on him, pressing on him through the silence on all sides. Then, in a patch of deep shadow, he was aware of great, glowing eyes, close to the ground, and a moment later a stalking jaguar glided into the next patch of moonlight.

No wonder that footfall had been lighter than human. The beautiful spotted monster stalked on with head down. Speedy saw the play of the immense muscles that draped the shoulders and the forelegs. He saw the great paws laid down with tenderest care. He saw the tail swerving like a snake.

There are tales enough of man-hunting jaguars. Horror jerked Speedy to his feet with a gasp. That lightning hand of his fumbled at the gun, failing to bring it out for an instant; and in that instant the hunting beast, with a snarl, bounded out of sight—and straight down the path that the girl had followed.

Speedy himself followed, running hard, a blur of terror before his eyes. The girl screamed on a note that shot up into the brain of Speedy.

And now he saw her body lying half supported by the base of a tree trunk. One blow of the jaguar's forepaw could have torn her life out.

He leaned over her. He snatched her up in his arms and carried her into a bright patch of moonlight. There was no sign of a wound. She breathed; she lived!

His groan of relief came shuddering out of his throat as her eyes opened. Now she stood gasping, her hands clutching his arms to steady her swaying body. "Was it true—or a nightmare?" she breathed. "Did I see a monster leaping at me—and shooting by me like a great spotted shadow?"

"You saw a jaguar," said Speedy. "That was the thing that ran by you. Thank heaven that it didn't stop for the tenth part of a second. You're not hurt? The beast didn't touch you?"

"No," she said. "I'm not hurt. But there doesn't seem to be—any breath in my body!"

Yet she was breathing more easily, in a moment.

"When you're ready," said Speedy, "we ought to start moving—and start moving fast! Those fellows have heard you cry out; and they're a lot more dangerous than jaguars."

"Have I ruined everything?" she pleaded. "I can walk now. I'm all right again. I'm sorry that I screamed. There's still an echo of that screech traveling around my brain.

But I won't do it again. Trust me not to do it again!"

"I'll trust you," said Speedy. "Come on!"

He steadied her for a few moments, but then she went on as well as before, stepping cautiously but rapidly behind him, putting her feet down exactly where his had fallen.

More sounds came toward them, the noise of walking men. Speedy drew the girl back behind a tree and waited while those footfalls came stealthily on.

Then the voice of Sailor Joe said, while the men were still unseen, "It ain't this way. That yell bore kind of more to the left from here."

"Maybe," said the voice of Chesty.

They came out into the moonlight. Somewhere they had floundered into the bog and now they were drenched almost to the hips, and their clothes were clotted with mud or with slime. They paused, now, to take a breathing spell.

"A mean business," said Chesty, spitting on the ground. "There was snakes back there in that water. There was water moccasins. I seen one of 'em. It gives me the chills and fever, too, when I seen the mouth of it open up like a trap."

"Leave that be," answered Sailor Joe. "I

348

don't wanta think about it. There's enough ahead of us without thinkin' about snakes. There's Speedy—and that's snakes enough to suit me."

"I wanta get my hands on him," said Chesty. "All I wanta do is to get my hands on him. He spoiled the whole show—and what does he get out of it?"

"Not a bean, as far as I can see," said Sailor Joe. "It ain't been nothing but meanness that's brought him into the job. And may he be damned for it! Maybe he wants the girl, though?"

"Yeah, maybe it's the girl."

"She's a good looker, and she's what he likely wants," argued Sailor Joe. "But can he get her? It's Crocker that she come to see."

"Yeah, but she ain't a fool," said Chesty. "She's got a brain in her head, and a pair of eyes, too. If she was blind as a bat, she could see a difference between a big honest boob like Crocker, and the champeen wildcat of the world—Speedy."

"He's no wildcat; he's a hellcat," said Sailor Joe. "He'll walk off with the girl, all right."

"Sure he will. There ain't nobody that does something for nothing," agreed Chesty. "Let's hunt down this way."

They moved off, and were instantly lost among the shadows.

Speedy went on with the girl. He hardly dared to look at her, after what they had overheard, but he felt her eyes on him presently as they came to a moonlit stretch. And turning a little, he saw her smiling straight back into his eyes.

"People like that could never understand," she said. "But *I* understand how there can be people like you in the world, who do something for nothing."

There was no doubt in her; there was no fear in her. And once more the heart of Speedy leaped like a bright flame. He had to center his mind firmly on the need of Lew Crocker in order to banish the temptation and put it firmly away from his mind.

Now they stole through soggy ground, their feet making sucking noises as they walked. They veered away from that spot and the foul breath of the marsh. Sheering off to the left, Speedy presently knew that he was near the spot where he had left poor Crocker. He had come back in that direction as quickly as he could, but would not Tim Lynch and his men have long preceded him in reaching the place?

That was why the suspense grew heavy in

the soul of Speedy as he went on with his companion, and every moment, to right and left, vast, bearded, inhuman faces seemed to be looking out upon them from the trees. That was the effect of the drapings of Spanish moss.

Now and again, while they walked stealthily on, they heard noises of living things plumping into the slimy waters of the marsh. Nothing could have been more desolate.

"Now, very carefully," said Speedy. "We're almost where I left Crocker. He may still be there—and with Lynch and a few others around the spot, using Crocker for a bait to draw us into the trap. Go like a shadow now!"

Like two shadows they went on together, in fact, and so edged through the trees and the shrubs until they were close to the little clearing which Speedy remembered.

He walked first, here; the girl moved behind him. And so her way was blocked when he came to a sudden halt.

Carefully parting the branches before his face, he could look out into the clearing. The moon had moved in the sky, and now it covered the whole of the bed of moss that had been made for Crocker. But Crocker was no longer stretched upon it; the whole clearing was empty of sight or sound.

45

SPEEDY WALKED on into the clearing. It might be that some of the men of Tim Lynch were in waiting for this very thing to happen, but time pressed and chances had to be taken.

And no voice or gun hailed him.

He reached the bed of thick moss. The imprint of the body of the wounded man was still upon it. And from beside it, Speedy saw at once a trail where he had dragged himself away into the bush.

Speedy beckoned to the girl, then he followed that trail, losing it often, but recovering it in spots of moonlight again. And finally he heard a stirring in the bushes not far before him.

"Crocker!" he called cautiously.

The voice of Crocker answered instantly: "Speedy—thank heaven you've come back! And Isabella—what—"

She was up and past Speedy like a running deer. When he came to the place, he found Crocker braced against the trunk of a tree, and the girl on her knees beside him.

All the pain of labor and of danger passed instantly out of the mind of Speedy, for he knew that the thing he had done had been worth it all.

He turned his back, and stood for a moment staring off through the trees, making his ears deaf to the joy of that greeting, and smiling a little. But he heard the girl calling to him, and he turned to find their faces lighted more by happiness than by the moon.

"She's told me, Speedy," said Crocker. "No other man in the world would have dared to do what you've done; nobody else would have dared to try. And if I can live through the pinch, you're going to find out how I appreciate it! But what's the plan now? Are we just to stay here till help comes from town?"

"We've got to find a better place than this," said Speedy. "Lynch is no fool. Why he hasn't come here—with Chesty to guide him—I can't imagine. But after all, you don't matter so much to him. It's Isabella Materro that he wants to have in his hands. Now we'll go ahead if we can find a place where we can lie snug and fight them off even if they spot us. Can you wait here, till I try to spot a place?"

"We'll stay here," said Crocker. "Whatever you do will be the right thing, Speedy!"

The girl held up her hand.

"Listen!"

They were mute, straining their ears, and presently they heard a far-off sound of crackling, as though men were walking through the brush. But that crackling was joined, almost at once, to a dim roaring noise.

"Fire!" said the girl.

"Fire!" whispered Crocker.

The three stared at one another.

"They're trying to drive us out into the open," said Speedy gloomily. "And I don't know what we can do about it."

"We've got to go," said Crocker. "What devil put the idea in their minds? They'll burn these dead woods for twenty miles, with that fire."

"Is there any open stretch of water?" asked Speedy. "Someplace where the fire can't jump the stretch? Or are there any rocks where we'd have shelter from the fire?"

"There's a big stretch of water, a good mile from here. We'd never get to it," said Crocker. "Look! The fire's galloping like a horse!"

He pointed up above the tops of the trees, but there was no need to point, for now as the dead wood of that ancient forest and its dry clotting of sunburned moss kindled, showers of sparks flew upward, and immense volumes of smoke, and arms of red flame that made the moonlit sky seem pale. Waves of firelight began to strike through the trees and throw wavering, terrible shadows.

"We'll do something," said Speedy. "Is there no safe place in the whole marsh? Do you know the lay of the land, Crocker?"

"I know," said Crocker. "There's a freak of a hill of rocks, a quarter of a mile from here. It's generally surrounded with a narrow belt of water. If we could get to that, perhaps the rocks would keep us from being burned. But it's too slim a chance. We've got to give up, Speedy, because—"

"Take his legs," said Speedy abruptly to the girl. "I'll manage most of his weight. Try to keep step with me, and the pull of his weight won't hurt his leg so much. Are you ready to take the chance, and fight it through, or do you want to surrender yourself to those thugs out there?"

"I'll fight it through!" said the girl.

"D'you hear me, Isabella?" said poor Crocker. "It's a matter of your life, my dear! Go out to the open, both of you. I'll crawl after you—it's not far to the edge of the beach. They'll make a bargain with *you* for your life, Speedy, if they know that they're to have her—"

"They'll make no bargains with me," insisted Speedy calmly. "We're all in one boat here. And we'll fight it through together. Are you ready?" he demanded suddenly of the girl.

"Ready!" she said.

So they lifted Crocker. He still protested, but the two marched on until he had to set his teeth hard, because groans were forcing through his lips among his words of appeal to Isabella to fly for her life.

Behind them came the red wall of the fire. Huge tufts of flaming moss sailed up on the arms of the conflagration, and a wind arose, drawn inward from all sides by the strength of the upward draft of the heat.

From a clearing, they saw the hill that Crocker had mentioned, and the heart of Speedy sank at the sight of it, for it was low—very low. And though it was like a heap of broken rock, yet it was overgrown with a tangle of vines.

However, they would try it. The waves of flame might sweep over that rock and sear away their flesh, but on the other hand, they might make a wall of loose stone against the fire. It was a chance, and a lean one. But when Speedy looked back into the face of the girl, he saw her grim with resolution.

What could one wish to find in a woman more than was in her?

They hurried on. The forest fell away on either side of them. Before them lay a narrow belt of water, not many yards across, and beyond that was the hill of stones.

Speedy, stepping in, found himself up to the knees in slime. The loose mud of the bottom sucked at his feet. Every step was more and more difficult, until suddenly his forward foot sank several inches. When he tried to draw it up, he failed. A powerful suction was working on his leg. Two strong efforts merely sank his whole body to his hips.

And then he understood.

That wild heart of his which had faced so many dangers, and overcome them, now quailed. Better to face the fire itself, helplessly. Better to die in any conceivable way than by the horror that now had hold on him—for the deep quicksands of the marsh had fast hold on his feet and were drawing him down!

46

"ISABELLA, CAN you step? Are you deep in the mud?" Speedy asked, holding himself as still as possible.

"I can move my feet—but the mud is trying to hold them," said the girl, panting.

"Back up to the shore then," said Speedy. "Back up toward the dry land. Pull Crocker back with you. Crocker, turn over facedown, and walk yourself back on your hands. I'm caught in the quicksands!"

Neither of the others cried out when they heard it. They did merely as they were told. And as Crocker was moved back to a little distance, his body supported on his hands, his legs held by the girl, he lifted one arm above the water and stretched it toward Speedy.

"Throw yourself on your back and give me a hand," said Crocker.

Speedy did as he was told. The foul, slimy water covered him. He caught the hand of Crocker, and received a strong pull. But the quicksand held his feet with a terrible power. Only little by little did the sleek mud give up its grasp. The strength of the pull caused his body to sink under the surface. He closed his eyes against the foulness that poured over his face. He held his breath to strangulation, while, little by little, the fatal grasp of the quicksand relinquished its hold.

And suddenly he was free. He rose to hands and knees, gasping, sputtering out the mud and the rotten slime of the marsh.

A moment later, he was on his feet, helping Crocker back toward the dry, firm land.

They were three dripping statues of mud, three writhing, mud-blackened bodies.

Before them, the fire burned yellow and orange and deep red, as it advanced in a wall. Sometimes there were purple streaks and sometimes there were bits of intense blue. Water-soaked logs, closed in the grip of that furnace heat, exploded, casting burning gases high into the air where the sparks, the hands of fire, and above all the flaming tresses of the Spanish moss were already rising and falling.

The roaring of the fire increased, and a vast rushing sound as though of running waters in a deep canyon. The wet marsh hissed like a million snakes; the wet tree roots exploded, shaking the earth. And the fierce breath of the fire rolled more and more intensely toward the three.

There was a slightly narrower crossing toward the base of the hill that now seemed a great fortress, a place of security. Silently, carrying his greater share of the weight of Crocker, Speedy took the way to it. He placed Crocker on the ground. There were old logs, half buried in the ground, half rotting into it, dissolving with moisture and decay. He began to tear these up, hurling them out into the water.

The girl understood that idea at once, and lent her aid. She was not strong enough to manage the heavy sections, but she found fallen branches, and carried these out. They dashed the green water into foam, running back and forth, gasping for breath as the heat of the fire made all the air about them like the burning breath from an oven.

Crocker made one appeal.

"Speedy, you can't save me," he shouted. "I'm done for. Save yourselves, and heaven bless you both!"

They did not pause in their work. They did not even glance at one another, the girl and Speedy. For long ago, the understanding had been silently arrived at between them;

the three of them would win or lose to-gether.

A frightful howl came out of the edge of the woods. Then the splendid mottled body of a jaguar hurtled through the air, struck the water near the base of the hill of rocks, and disappeared under the water for an instant.

It rose again, the head and the shoulders standing clear, the tail lashing above the surface. And the great beast was still, waiting patiently, its head barely above the surface, until the waters should close over it.

"Now!" cried Speedy to the girl, and they sprang to Crocker, and lifted him.

The flames were searing the backs of their heads as they advanced into the water, slipping, staggering. It was a broken, an incomplete line of water-logged branches and tree trunks that they had dropped into the marsh, where the wood in nearly every case sank slowly to the bottom. They had to feel with their feet for the precarious bridge.

They were more than halfway across when Crocker turned suddenly into a limp weight, twice as hard to handle as he had been before. The terrible heat, the excitement, the fear, and above all the long agony which he endured from his wound, had caused him to faint, and Speedy, with dread in his heart, wondered if they were to fail, after all.

But they went floundering on until they passed the last of the wooden causeway which they had flung into the water. Into the ooze they stepped, but their feet bit through it, and found a sure support in the rocky bottom, where the roots of the hill spread out.

In a moment, they were across. They put Crocker down and turned—reeking, filthy, blackened faces—to stare at one another.

Crocker recovered, with a groan. It was hardly heard. The mere matter of his fainting was nothing now. For they had reached to the verge of their meager chance of safety.

But Speedy looked back, and across the fire-reddened face of the water, he saw merely the muzzle of the jaguar appearing above the slime. The moments were few before the ending of that fierce life.

He stepped back, therefore, fumbled through the foulness of the water, found a half-buried tree trunk, and barely managed to drag it to the surface. He was wasting moments that would be precious to the saving of three human lives, but he could not let the poor dumb beast die without one gesture toward saving it.

He went to the edge of the hill opposite

the drowning jaguar, stepped into the water to his knees, and flung the trunk as far toward the mark as he could.

The splash it raised caused the head of the beast to disappear. It was in sight again instantly. The water around it lashed into foam with the madness of its efforts to climb onto this heaven-sent new purchase for its feet. Half its body lifted suddenly clear. It bounded forward, dashed into the water again, and then floundered safely to the shore.

Speedy already had lifted the body of Crocker. With the girl he was stumbling up the slope of the hill. They rounded it. The rocky shoulders shut away most of the blast of the heat, and they found themselves in a nest of huge stones, a veritable haven that seemed to have been framed for them by nature itself.

47

THEY FELL to work with frenzied hands, heaving the smaller stones up and raising the wall about them, higher and higher. They had almost closed it at the lower side, when a wet body glided through the aperture and lay cowering on the ground. It was the jaguar again, fear-maddened, fear-subdued.

"It won't harm you!" called Speedy suddenly. For he remembered how the mountain lion flees at the side of the deer, when the forest fire is driving all life before it. And Crocker, who sat gun in hand, held the fire of his revolver.

It lay still. As the encircling wall of the fire surrounded the hill, the big brute shuddered and dropped its head between its paws and lay with tightly blinked eyes. Its tail twitched, now and again. Otherwise it lay as though dead.

Meantime, those three human lives endured the oven heat that poured through the air. Sparks fell on them. A flaming mass of Spanish moss dropped down inside their enclosure, where Speedy trampled it out as the jaguar moaned.

The roaring, the crackling, the explosions of water-logged tree trunks kept up the incredible din. And the three, wiping the slime from their faces, endured and never spoke. The girl sat beside Crocker, her arms about him, her face on his shoulder. And as the red waves of the firelight played over them, Crocker stared grimly at Speedy, and Speedy stared grimly back. Thirst raged in them.

Sweat poured from their bodies. And still they were as silent as the wild beast that had sought shelter with them.

Then by slow degrees, the torrent of the fire receded. Speedy stood up and looked over the edge of their improvised stone wall. On one side the burned-over marsh presented a thousand glowing points of light, where logs were still burning; and there were two or three hollow trunks that were burning like enormous candles, and throwing reflections out over the stagnant waters. Overhead the moon was dead in the sky; the pale gray of the morning had commenced to steal around the horizon. And on the other side, the living wall of the fire rushed on with increasing speed, fanned by the wind or its own raising. Such was the immensity of the heat that the green vines that overgrew the hill of rocks had caught fire. In some places they had entirely burned away. In other places they offered a pattern of glowing veins laid over the stones.

But the wind that followed the fire was making life more endurable. That same wind flung the flames now and again far ahead of the regular march of the conflagration. Here and there a solitary tree caught and seemed to explode upward in a torrent of sparks and shooting fires. And always, out of the air, there was a continual rain of fine ashes and little bits of charcoal, sometimes still glowing.

That was the picture that Speedy saw, and far off, along the beach, were two riders—small distant figures. And on the other side of the marsh, three more appeared.

What were the thoughts of the murderers, now they were sure that they had burned their victims? What was the savage rage in the heart of Tim Lynch, when he thought of the wasted ransom money, that fortune which he had made sure of drawing out of the wealth of Mateo Materro? And in faraway Mexico, what would Materro himself think, when he learned that his murder plot had failed, and that his heiress was safe in America with the man she loved?

The girl stood up beside him and they watched the sun rise. The air cooled. The frightful breath of the fire was far removed.

"If our man lived to ride through and get help—" said Speedy, thinking half aloud. "If help comes before Lynch and the rest know that we're here and try to rush the hill and take us—"

"They'll never try," said the girl. "Their spirits are broken. They've failed too often against you and they'll never dare to stand up to you now. Not if there were fifty of them against you!"

There was no weariness in the eye of Speedy as he looked down at her. But he merely said, "Tell me about Mateo Materro —that uncle of yours. What sort of a fellow is he?"

"Gentle to his friends, and terrible to his enemies," she said. "A tall old man, with a beautiful, stern face. He has been like a father and a mother to me. No matter what he has done, I never could stop loving him. But—he hates all Americans. To see me married to an American would be worse to him than to see me dead. Oh, ten thousand times worse. To save me from that, he would have had not one man killed, but a hundred of them, and he would have felt that his hands were clean after the killings."

"And now that you're here?" said Speedy.

"I'm the last of his blood," said the girl gently. "For a year he'll harden his heart— perhaps only for a month. And after that— well, after that it will be in all things as my husband wishes it to be."

The jaguar rose, and slunk suddenly out of the enclosure—then bolted down the slope at full speed, maddened by the ancient fear of man.

The sun climbed higher. Speedy, continually spying over the landscape, saw the distant riders draw to a focus at the ranch house and disappear inside of it.

They had given up, then, and believed their victims to be dead. And now, if poor, wounded Danny had managed to break through for help? Well, even if that were not the case, Lynch and his men had lost their battle at every point.

Crocker, exhausted by the terrible night, lay on his back, sleeping heavily.

The sun climbed toward the zenith, filling the little enclosure with heat almost like that of the fire during the night. And then, far away across the plains, a dust cloud rolled up, grew in height and clearness, and gradually dissolved into the forms of many riders. Danny had broken through, after all.

Yet still there was no sudden outpouring of men from the ranch house. They would not believe, perhaps, that the rescuing party could have come so fast. They would not leave the whiskey jug either, beyond all doubt, unless they had given themselves plenty of consolation for that night of complicated disappointments.

Nearer and nearer the cavalcade came, a score—no, thirty men, sweeping along. And at last the men in the ranch house were warned. They came pouring out, guns in their hands. They mounted, fighting. One of them fell. Some of the posse had dismounted and lay on the ground, to give accuracy to their fire. Others charged straight in. The thing was over in a moment. The surrender was complete before the sounds of the distant firing had ceased to float through the air to the watchers.

For that wedding, the entire town turned out. Everyone of importance within fifty miles found an excuse for coming in, and the church was crowded. The hour for the ceremony arrived. Still the bridegroom tapped on the floor the crutches that would help him to the altar, and shook his head!

"We can't be married without the best man. We can't be married without Speedy."

Isabella Materro shook her head, also, and made a beautiful gesture to indicate the utter impossibility of the ceremony unless Speedy were there.

It was an hour after the appointed time, before a ragged little boy managed to get into the church and at last into the room where the couple waited, carrying a note in his hand.

Crocker tore it open impatiently, and scanned the contents twice over. Then he passed it to the girl. She read:

Dear Old Man: I thought I could go through with it. But, at the last minute, my heart weakened. For one thing, there are a great many reasons why I never like to show myself as I really am to any crowd. It would be dangerous for a good many reasons, some of which you know. For another thing, if I am a witness at your marriage, my real name must go down in the book, and that name is a secret that I never can let the world know. So I can only wish you and Isabella the happiest lives, and sign myself your affectionate friend,

Speedy

The publishers hope that this
Large Print Book has brought
you pleasurable reading.
Each title is designed to make
the text as easy to see as possible.
G.K. Hall Large Print Books
are available from your library and
your local bookstore. Or, you can
receive information by mail on
upcoming and current Large Print Books
and order directly from the publishers.
Just send your name and address to:

G.K. Hall & Co.
70 Lincoln Street
Boston, Mass. 02111

or call, toll-free:

1-800-343-2806

A note on the text.
Large print edition designed by
Pauline L. Chin.
Composed in 18 pt Plantin
on a Xyvision 300/Linotron 202N
by Tara Casey
of G.K. Hall & Co.